MW01148197

LINEAR TACTICAL SERIES

# CYCLONE

*USA TODAY* BESTSELLING AUTHOR
# JANIE CROUCH

CYCLONE: LINEAR TACTICAL

# CHAPTER 1

ZAC MACKAY KEPT his body relaxed as he stared down the man standing eight feet across from him knife in hand. A guy who was undoubtedly going to rush him—arm upraised like Jason Voorhees in those slasher films—any second now.

The other guy was bigger, beefier, and about ten years younger than Zac's own thirty-one years. And he was a cocky bastard, oozing self-confidence since he was the one holding the knife.

Zac knew the guy's name but couldn't think of it right at this moment. It didn't matter. Anyone standing in front of him with the intent to harm him or the people he was protecting only had one name: *Enemy*. Zac hadn't needed his nine years in the Army to teach him that; he'd learned it on the playground in elementary school.

Zac gave Enemy a little smile, then winked.

That was all it took. Enemy flew at him, knife hand raised almost to eye level, weapon clenched in his fist, preparing to put his full strength behind the blow.

Rookie move.

The guy wanted to show off, so instead of coming straight down with the knife, he swung it crossways, looping to the left, obviously wanting to rip across Zac's chest rather than stab him.

If Zac hadn't been ready for anything—now his Special Forces training coming into play—he would've been in a shit-ton of trouble. Zac stepped to the right rather than left, angling his torso to the side. The blade came swooping across where he'd been standing half a second ago.

Any other time, Zac might have played with Enemy a little, shown him that his *destroy-everything* fighting style wasn't necessarily the best. Definitely not the smartest.

But that wasn't why Zac was here right now.

While the knife was still swinging downward, Zac took an unexpected half step closer to the man, reaching one arm under his elbow and the other above his wrist. He put just enough force on the guy's arm to stop the motion.

It wouldn't take much more pressure to snap Enemy's wrist, grab the knife from his then-numb fingers, and drive it into the softest spot of his throat.

But that would be a little overkill, given this was only a demonstration about close-quarters fighting for some college guys—including Enemy—who had paid to be here and for Zac to teach them.

Zac halted but kept his grip firm for just a couple seconds, demonstrating his control of the situation. The knife dropped to the ground. Only then did Zac release the other man.

"Okay." Zac turned and faced the group that had been watching the whole scenario. "That was at full speed, but we're going to break it down into much slower and more manageable pieces for today's workshop."

He slapped Enemy on the back. "Thanks for volunteering...What's your name again, man?"

"Brandon," the kid grunted.

"Brandon, right." He slapped Brandon on the back again. "Thanks for trying to kill me with such exuberance."

Everybody chuckled, and Zac managed a smile. Brandon had been using a practice knife with a hard rubber blade. It wouldn't have cut Zac if he'd gotten lucky with his swing, but it would've hurt like hell.

"Brandon's attack had its strengths and weaknesses, both of which we'll get to, but I want to start out with the most important aspect of close-quarters fighting." He reached down and picked up the practice knife, laying it out on his palm and extending his arm toward the group. "Anyone coming at you with a weapon with the intent to harm you is your adversary. To treat him as anything else is a mistake that can cost you the fight. Or your life."

Zac broke them off into sparring partners and went over some basic moves. It wasn't his favorite job here at Linear Tactical, but he didn't mind it, and it played to his strengths.

Zac was good with people and at teaching.

A lot of people, like poor Brandon, assumed because of Zac's surfer looks—light brown hair that had the slightest wave to it, blue eyes, easy smile—that he wasn't tough enough to teach the sort of training and services Linear provided. Things like rifle and pistol skills, self-defense, kidnapping deterrence, wilderness survival, hand-to-hand combat, and situational awareness.

And those were just the beginner level classes for civilians.

The corporate security and law enforcement training Linear provided was much more involved and dangerous— because those situations called for it.

But the people who worked at Linear were more than equipped to handle *involved and dangerous*. Zac had started the company with a group of his ex-Green Beret brothers. His best friends. They'd been trained to adapt, defend, and survive in almost every type of situation.

Zac may look like a surfer, but he moved and thought like a soldier, a damned good one. Being out of the Army for four years hadn't changed that.

A hundred more times that afternoon, Zac showed his students how to capture a knife-wielder's arm and apply the pressure needed to gain the upper hand. He explained the danger of taking the move too far—a broken wrist for the opponent—but also reaffirmed what he'd avowed earlier, anybody coming at you with a knife was your enemy. And were lucky if a broken wrist was all they got.

Committing the moves to muscle memory was an important part of the training. That's why Zac didn't mind demonstrating over and over—and having his own arm grabbed and taken to the near-breaking point many times. Even Brandon wasn't trying to kill Zac by the time they were done. Evidently, the kid did want to learn. All in all, not a bad class.

"Practice on each other," Zac told them as they finished and headed out to their cars. "But whatever you do, don't give Brandon a practice knife and tell him to attack you."

The guys laughed and made a few comments about who could take whom as they left. Zac gave a wave and ambled back toward the office.

"You can come out now, you cowards," he announced as he opened the office door. "I can't believe you forced yourself to stay inside on a gorgeous day like this."

Finn Bollinger, Zac's brother in every sense of the word

but blood, looked up from his desk. "Not nearly as much incentive to help you today as there was yesterday."

Zac grabbed a bottle of water from the fridge in the corner and plopped down on the couch in front of the office's double windows. "Yeah, I'm pretty sure I wouldn't have seen you guys yesterday either if it hadn't been for the two brunettes."

Yesterday's class had been a bridal party there for basic self-defense lessons, a gift from the groom's family to the bride and her bridesmaids.

"That's totally not true." Aiden cocked his head, peeking out from behind his computer monitor and waggling his eyebrows. "It was the redhead who had me out there."

"Ahem, not to mention," Finn leaned his hulking form back in his chair, grinning, "it wasn't *Aiden* taking a blonde out for breakfast this morning at the Frontier Diner, according to Waverly."

Zac just rolled his eyes. "Your sister needs to go back to working the dinner shift."

But he couldn't really be mad. Small-town problems. Everybody in everybody's business, especially for people like Zac and Finn, who'd grown up here in Oak Creek. It wasn't quite as bad for Aiden, who'd moved here when they'd opened Linear four years ago.

Oak Creek was larger than most towns in western Wyoming. It had everything they needed: restaurants, stores, hotels, and medical facilities. But it was still small enough that gossip reigned supreme. Zac had long since accepted it as part of his life, the annoyance and privilege of coming back to his hometown.

He parted the blinds to glance at a car he heard coming

up the driveway. "Who did something illegal? Sheriff Nelson is pulling up out front."

Finn didn't look up from his paperwork. "Anybody know the statute of limitations on indecent exposure?"

Zac stood to open the door for Sheriff Nelson before he could knock. "Come in, Sheriff. If I got a picture of the birthmark Finn has on his ass, would you arrest him for running naked through the bleachers at our high school football game all those years ago?"

"Allegedly!" Finn called out. "*Allegedly* running naked through the bleachers. Never proven. And it was a powder-puff game. That doesn't count."

Sheriff Nelson chuckled. "I think there are quite a number of ladies at this point who could positively ID Bollinger's ass."

Aiden chuckled. "Only question is if it's from them trying to kick it, or something else."

"Something else, my friend." Finn winked. "Always something else."

"What can we do for you, Sheriff, besides offer you our fugitive?" Zac asked. "Problems in town?"

Zac gestured toward a chair, but the older man refused to sit. "No, this is a courtesy call. I want to talk to you guys about an attack that happened in Fremont County and get your opinion, but first I needed to mention something to you, Zac. I wanted to let you know that Jordan Reiss has come up for parole. She'll go before the board in a couple months. Your testimony one way or the other would make a big difference in how this goes down."

Zac sat heavily in the chair he'd just offered the sheriff. How was he even supposed to feel about this? "Jesus. That kid should've been let out of prison a long time ago, Curtis, and we both know it. Six years is too damn long. Hell, she shouldn't even have gone there in the first place. She fell asleep at the damn wheel."

"And killed two people."

He dragged his hand across his face. "I know good and well who died that day."

His wife. His toddler son.

The sheriff's hand landed on his shoulder. "I wanted to make you aware of what was going on in case you wanted to take a stance either way."

Zac tried to focus on the other stuff Sheriff Nelson was saying, details about what would happen at the hearing, but the conversation seemed distant, muffled, as if he were listening through multiple panes of glass.

Becky was dead. Micah was dead. The pain of their deaths was such a part of him that most of the time he hardly noticed it. But right now, the grief seemed to creep up his spine and spread through his limbs, a near-tangible thing. He looked at Finn, his best friend since childhood.

"We'll get the details." Finn tilted his head toward the door. "Go."

Zac was moving out into the fresh air a moment later, walking toward the barn at the back of the property.

It was times like this he wished he drank. Because right now the burn of a couple shots of whiskey would be very welcome. But he didn't, not more than a beer since a night, ironically, only a couple weeks after Becky and Micah's deaths.

*That night.* He scrubbed his hand over his face again.

Mixing grief and alcohol made you do some damn stupid things. His memories of that night were mostly a blur. And the parts he *did* remember just made him wish he didn't.

Or when he was truly honest with himself, *more*. He

longed to remember *so much more* of that lost night a few days after the funeral.

He walked around the building through the woods to his apartment. He'd started living on Linear property because he'd needed a place to stay after getting out of the Army. He'd had no interest in living in town, so he'd built a studio apartment on top of the barn that had become his refuge. He'd never brought women here. He rarely brought anyone here.

Becky had been dead a long time. Six years. He missed her. Missed his redheaded, spitfire wife with her sassy mouth. She'd grabbed his heart in middle school and never let go. He didn't miss her with spikes of agony like he had in the early years, but with the quieter pain of what could've been. And sweet Micah...he'd been two years old and driving her crazy with his tantrums and tendency to put everything he found into his mouth. Zac had been deployed and missed much of it. Something he'd give anything now to change.

Zac had long accepted that wound—the loss of time and life—would never heal.

He slid the barn door open and stepped inside, some of his tension easing. No, he didn't want alcohol. *This* was what he wanted: the Harley Roadster he'd gotten when he'd been stationed in Germany. He ran his fingers over the chrome of the fuel tank.

Forget sitting at home thinking about what was never going to be. Becky wouldn't have wanted him to do that.

Of course, there were a lot of things Becky wouldn't have wanted him to do. *That night* included.

Even though it wasn't required by law, Zac slid on the helmet. Within moments the Harley rumbled beneath him, and he was taking off down the paved drive of Linear's private road. Soon he was flying down Highway 210, throttle wide open, the landscape streaming by around him.

This was what he'd needed, wide-open spaces and a fast machine he controlled with perfect precision. Too much of life was beyond his control—like their deaths. But *this* he could control.

The miles flew past. Maybe not quite as fast as they had a few years ago when he'd been stationed in Germany and ridden his bike on the Autobahn—no speed limits there— but enough to ease his mind. Help him feel centered again.

No, he couldn't hate an eighteen-year-old who'd made a shitty judgment call that had cost him his wife and child. But he damn well could hate himself for the fact that the memories of his wife's death were blended with those of *that night*.

The night he so itched to forget and remember.

He'd had six years' practice pushing Anne Nichols's face as far from his mind as possible. Six years of trying to block out the sound of her quiet sighs from his ears.

He revved the engine louder.

As always, it didn't work. So, he rode, letting the miles smooth everything from his mind. Ease the thoughts of Becky and Micah being gone forever. Fade the thoughts of Annie—sweet, quiet Annie—who was practically just as gone.

It was hours later, the sun disappearing in the distance, when Zac turned back into Oak Creek. He would stop at The Eagle's Nest, everybody's favorite bar and grill. The guys would be there by now.

Finn would fill him in on everything the sheriff had said, or they could let it all go for tonight. Plenty of time to face everything as it came.

The light turned green and Zac eased the throttle on his

bike. As he moved forward he caught the other car out of the corner of his eye. Damn it, they weren't slowing down for their red light.

It all happened like it was in slow motion. Zac hit his brakes at first but immediately realized that wasn't going to help him. He needed to move *forward*, not stop. He revved the throttle, back tire spinning just a moment before catching and propelling him toward safety.

The car was close enough for him to see the teenage driver's face wrenched in horror as he slammed on his brakes. Zac breathed a sigh of relief when the rear tire of his bike cleared the bumper flying toward him.

Crisis averted.

But hell if a dog didn't trot out into the middle of the road right at that fucking second. Zac jerked the bike the opposite direction, choosing to hit the curb rather than the dog—a German shepherd, damned pregnant one at that— the impact throwing him and the bike to the side. As he laid down his bike and slid to the ground, the heat of the road burned through his leather jacket before his head jammed into the curb on the opposite side of the street. Everything went black.

# CHAPTER 2

ANNE NICHOLS GRIFFIN never thought she'd be back in Oak Creek.

Wyoming hadn't given her much the first time around besides deadbeat, alcoholic parents who hadn't understood a thing about her. She'd been bizarre and embarrassing to them, with her nose always in a book and her pronounced stutter.

She'd only had one friend here in Oak Creek. One who Anne had ultimately betrayed in the worst way possible. So, when she'd been told six years ago to leave and never return, she'd honestly planned to follow those instructions.

Yet here she was.

Because as bad as Oak Creek might once have been, it was nothing compared to the failure her life had become for the past three years.

She was divorced, broke, and terrified of social situations to the point of paralysis. Except for being an excellent emergency room physician, she had basically zero going for her.

Anne sighed, regrouping at her office in the hospital. She needed to focus on the positive. Things were starting to look up. Although that wasn't saying much, since down wasn't even a possibility.

Counting the positives was easy. Number one: she had a new job where she wasn't known as the wife who still had to work with the husband who had dumped her for someone more attractive and charming, who worked at the same hospital.

Positive number two: she had a home and didn't have to live in a one-bedroom apartment in the crappy part of Tampa because she was so broke.

The small Oak Creek house her best friend's mother had left Anne in her will had taken care of that. Carol Peverill would never know how much she'd done for Anne, first while she had been alive, then in her passing four months ago. Anne would never have been able to afford to relocate here without Carol's generosity. Now she had a place to live rent-free and a dream job taking over for the head ER physician retiring in a few years.

And it was all thanks to generosity she didn't deserve and could never repay. Anne sighed and rubbed her forehead. Dwelling on that wouldn't help.

Positive number three: Nobody recognized her here.

They didn't give her sly or sympathetic looks. They didn't know her as anything besides Dr. Griffin, the quiet new doctor who had proven herself quite competent in the last two weeks.

So what if she'd seen at least half a dozen people she'd gone to school with who hadn't recognized her at all? Anne's last name had been different then, Nichols, not Griffin. All her classes had been advanced, some online or with individual tutors, alienating her further from her peers. And her stuttering and social anxiety had made interacting with others nearly impossible.

She'd gotten the stuttering under control for the most part, although the thought of social situations still threw her into a panic. Not to mention she just wasn't the type of person people remembered. Not even a few minutes later, much less years.

She usually wore her nondescript brown hair in a braid. Her features weren't necessarily unattractive. She had a straight nose, pale skin brushed with freckles, and brown eyes that did their job fine behind her glasses but wouldn't catch anybody's attention. She was a little taller than average and not particularly curvy.

So basically, invisible. Hell, even the name "Anne" was as nondescript as they came.

But invisible meant starting with a clean slate, so she embraced the advantage. She already knew a lot about the town, yet they weren't thinking too much about her. And she needed every advantage she could get.

She stood from behind her desk in her small office and slipped her white lab coat on over her scrubs. She preferred them so she could move freely—an important option in an emergency room—but the lab coat helped everyone remember she was a physician. Being quiet, female, and relatively young meant that sometimes people needed a subtle reminder.

She walked out of her office and down the hall to the emergency section of the hospital. Oak Creek General was one of the largest in western Wyoming, second only to Reddington City Regional, but it still wasn't even half the size of the one she'd worked at in Tampa.

But an emergency room was an emergency room. Anne loved everything about it. The cacophony of beeps, the movement, and people's voices. The constant action, something or someone always needing attention. She could feel herself straighten—*strengthen*—as she got closer, her stride lengthening. This was where she belonged.

She may have been a failure in almost every other aspect of life, but here, she kicked ass.

Anne rounded the corner and stopped short at the commotion near the rooms of the east emergency wing. She'd never seen so many nurses congregating in one area, particularly not on a Friday night after the seven PM shift change had already occurred.

Anne rushed to the nurses' station, adrenaline already beginning to pump through her system. "Holy crap, Susan." Anne grabbed the chart the older woman handed her. "Do we have a massive influx of patients? A car pile-up or something? Why wasn't I called?" She should've been paged immediately with an emergency of this magnitude.

Susan Lusher, head ER nurse, rolled her eyes. "You would think so, wouldn't you? Just a single motorcycle accident. Nothing serious. Possible concussion and definite skin abrasions, although minor. Patient is awake and responsive."

Anne's adrenaline level evened out a little as she perused the chart. Nurse Lusher was right, it didn't seem to be anything dire. Anne turned to study the gaggle of women in the far hallway. "Is there a reason why every nurse in a three-county radius seems to be hovering down there?"

"Linear Tactical," Nurse Lusher said, as if that explained everything.

Anne grimaced. So much for her hidden home-court advantage. She had no idea what the older woman was talking about. "Is that a gang?"

Susan smiled. "No. A business on the outskirts of town. They do fighting tactics and weapons training stuff. One of the most well-respected facilities of its type in the whole country. It was started by some local boys and a few of their military friends."

"Does the hospital get a lot of business from this Linear group?" It stood to reason that some sort of shooting and fighting free-for-all establishment might bring quite a few people into the ER.

Susan laughed. "I love how you say it like it's a bad word. No, the boys are pretty safe and run a tight ship."

Anne refrained from rolling her eyes. She didn't have anything against weapons per se, but she hadn't expected a training ground for them in her backyard.

"Okay, I'll take your word for it." She tucked the chart under her arm and looked toward the east wing. "But why are all the nurses there again?"

"Oh, you'll see when you get down there. Everywhere the Linear boys go, they cause quite a stirring among the female population."

Anne started down the hall. "I'm going to clear them out." She turned back to Susan, wishing it were as easy to talk to people her own age as it was the older woman. "You come save me if they form a lynch mob."

"Oh, honey, just get one of those Linear boys to sweep you up in their extremely capable arms and carry you to safety."

Anne laughed and gave Susan a thumbs-up. Anne wasn't the type of woman gorgeous guys—who evidently could have their pick of young, attractive nurses—swept off her feet.

Hell, Anne wasn't the type of woman *any* man tried to do that to. Her ex, Darren, had made sure she'd known that was true.

She gritted her teeth as she walked toward the gaggle.

She was an excellent doctor and could handle all sorts of crises. Right now, the crisis she needed to handle was getting her ER back in order. That included clearing out the fan club. She walked over to the crowd of women standing around the small, private examination room.

She cleared her throat. "O-o-okay." Her voice came out shaky and weak. Damn it.

Nobody even turned around to look at her. Anne took a breath and poked the nail of her thumb into the tips of each of her fingers in a pattern, something she'd learned to help get her stuttering under control.

Anne wasn't needed here. *Dr. Griffin* was.

"*Okay*," Anne said again in her loudest voice, which still wasn't overly loud since it came so unnaturally to her. But at least she hadn't stuttered. "If you're a day-shift nurse and your shift is officially over, I'm sure the patient appreciates your support, but it's time for you to leave."

Anne ignored the collective groan and took a step into the room. She couldn't actually see the bed and patient over the throng. "As you know, since you are off duty, you are not formally allowed in the ER. So, it's time to go. *Now*."

Anne crossed her arms over her chest and made eye contact with a number of women attempting to judge her sincerity. They'd never know how difficult it was for her to hold her ground.

Once they realized she really wasn't going to allow them to stay, they began to disperse. Slowly, but at least they were moving.

There seemed to be some sort of line to hug the patient and his friends standing next to his bed. Anne could see one of them, and *holy hell* Nurse Lusher had been right. Anne didn't recognize the guy, so he hadn't grown up here, but that didn't mean he wasn't drool-worthy. "You take care of him, Aiden," said one of the nurses as she hugged him. Anne couldn't see the other two guys through the women.

She looked back down at the chart, not actually reading anything it said.

"If you're on shift tonight," she said without looking up, "Nurse Lusher has assignments at the desk. You're needed there now." Susan wouldn't be thrilled to have them all back at one time, but she would handle it.

The other nurses shuffled out, obviously reluctant to leave in case there was an emergency that required mouth-to-mouth resuscitation.

Finally, the room cleared except for Riley Wilde, the nurse actually on duty in this section of the ER. Anne remembered Riley from high school, a friendly, happy student who'd been a few years younger, but the other woman hadn't recognized Anne.

And then there was Mia Stevenson, also an ER nurse. Riley's opposite in every way, Mia had been catty and mean in high school. And from the couple times Anne had run into Mia at the hospital, the woman hadn't changed.

She was also the person most on the verge of recognizing Anne. She'd caught the other woman studying her multiple times over the last few days, trying to place her.

It wasn't that Anne was keeping her identity a secret, she just wasn't announcing it. Her married name had made that easier. Although Anne wasn't sure anyone would've recognized her even if she'd been Dr. Nichols.

Mia waited just far enough in the hallway for Anne not to demand more space. The beautiful blonde's eyes were narrowed and her lips tight. With the room finally as emptied as it was going to get, Anne turned toward the bed and got her first clear view of her patient.

*Zac Mackay.*

All the air left her body in a rush.

His eyes were so blue they rivaled the Wyoming sky. His light brown hair had a hint of curl to it. Hard, angled cheeks saved his face from being too boyish. His nose, broken at least once, imbued his face with even more character.

That face and exposed chest were both a deep, rich tan, obviously from hours spent out in the sun with no shirt on. He was wearing jeans and reclining gingerly against the upraised section of the hospital bed.

He was still as gorgeous as he'd ever been. And her body still responded in ways she couldn't understand. Especially given his last words to her.

*Get out and don't come back.*

As his blue eyes met hers, shock, coupled with something else—Wonder maybe? Disbelief?—flitted over his features before he pulled them into a neutral mask.

Nobody else at the hospital had recognized her, but Zac Mackay definitely knew who she was. And he wasn't happy to see her.

She drew air back into her lungs, trying to figure out what she should say. Did he still hate her for what she'd done? *They'd* done? Six years was a long time, a lot of water under the bridge. Maybe he was willing to just let it go.

He finally dragged his gaze away from Anne and turned to Riley. "I'm going to need a different doctor."

Maybe not.

# CHAPTER 3

A SORT of stunned silence met Zac's remark. Everyone was looking around at everyone else, trying to figure out exactly what was going on.

Everyone except him and Annie. They couldn't seem to stop staring at each other.

They'd told him *Dr. Griffin* would be in here in a few minutes to examine him, and he'd thought absolutely nothing of it. He'd heard the doctor clearing the room over the gaggle of women who'd packed themselves into the small space.

But seeing her had been like a punch to the solar plexus.

*Annie Nichols.* Jesus, it was almost like his earlier thoughts had summoned her.

She looked almost exactly the same. Tall and willowy. Long brown hair pulled back in a braid, soft brown eyes hidden behind glasses that weren't a great shape for her face. Everything about her, from her hairstyle to her lack of makeup to her posture, was arranged to make people *not* notice her. Whether it was a conscious effort or a subconscious one, Zac still didn't know.

It looked like her plan to stay invisible had worked here in the hospital, just like it had in high school.

Except for him. He'd been aware of Annie since the day Becky had introduced them all those years ago.

Annie was a doctor, which shouldn't surprise him. Annie's major had been pre-med in college. She'd been in her first year of medical residency when Becky had died. Annie and Becky had remained friends until the end.

But she was Dr. *Griffin*, not Dr. Nichols. So, she'd obviously moved away and gotten married.

Why the hell did his gut clench at that knowledge? He'd gone back to the Army after Becky had died, hadn't been around to see what Anne had done. He'd casually inquired about her when he'd moved back to town, but most people barely remembered her, much less knew what had happened. The one person who might have, Mrs. Peverill, he hadn't dared ask.

*Mrs. P, do you know where Annie Nichols is? You know, your daughter's best friend who I fucked less than two weeks after your daughter died but conveniently remember very little of except for knowing it was unforgivable?*

Yeah, no.

So, he'd lived without knowing any details about Anne and figured he was lucky she'd moved away. Because then he didn't have to face her, knowing what they'd done.

But he had to now. And he couldn't let Anne be his doctor. Couldn't let her casually touch him and examine him as if they hadn't partaken in the most heinous of sins together.

But he probably should've found a different way of

saying it, especially since his head felt like someone was taking a jackhammer to it.

"Don't listen to him," Aiden said, pushing away from the wall, trying to ease the awkward silence. "Obviously he has even more brain damage than he did before."

"Zac," Riley put her hand on his arm, "Dr. Griffin is new, and I know she may look a little young, but I promise you, she is very well qualified. I've worked with her for two weeks now and am completely convinced of that. She'll be taking Dr. Lewis's place as head of the ER when he retires."

Zac didn't doubt Annie's ability as a physician. She'd always been the smartest person any of them knew. "It's not her age."

Riley's eyes got big. "Zac Mackay. Are you telling me it's because she's a *woman*?"

Great, now he looked like an asshole. "No, of course not."

None of these people recognized that Dr. Anne Griffin was Annie Nichols from high school? Admittedly, Anne had always kept to herself, had never spoken unless she had to.

Except with Becky. Becky had always been lively, kind, and patient enough to draw Anne out of her shell while ignoring the stutter. Becky and Mrs. P had basically forced Anne to live with them a lot of the time since her home situation had been so bad.

"Holy shit. *Annie Nichols*." Finn stood from the chair he'd been sitting in since all the nurses had left. "From high school."

Riley's eyes widened, and she spun to stare at Anne. Anne's face reddened, and she held the medical file in front of her like a shield.

"Damn it, I knew it!" Mia's voice screeched from the hallway. "I knew I recognized her from s-s-somewhere."

Everyone's eyes fell to the floor as Mia's cruel mockery of Annie's speech impediment echoed through the hallway. Riley muttered a particularly vile curse and, galvanized into movement, walked over to shut the door.

Annie gathered herself and stood straighter. "Hi, Finn. It's good to see you. You look well." Not a stutter to be heard.

Finn held his hand out for her to shake. "Thanks, Doc. Same to you. How long have you been back in town?"

"I started here at the hospital two weeks ago." Her voice was still soft, soothing.

Finn smacked Zac on his uninjured shoulder but kept his eyes on the doctor. "You have to remember Anne, right? Becky's friend. I always wondered what happened to you."

Her eyes met Zac's. He'd expected anger, disgust, embarrassment...but not what was behind those glasses of hers now: fear.

"Yes." Annie looked away and nodded. "Becky was a very good friend. She looked out for me." She clutched the medical chart tighter to her chest. "Zac isn't comfortable with me as his attending physician, so we can get someone else. It will only take a few minutes, but since your injuries don't appear to be critical, there should be no danger in waiting."

Everybody was staring at Zac like he'd kicked a small child into oncoming traffic. There was no logical reason—at least not that they knew of—why he shouldn't allow Annie to be his doctor.

Hell, there was none at all. He cleared his throat. "No,

it's fine. I just wasn't expecting to see you. Didn't even know you were back. It's fine."

It *wasn't* fine. Her touching him wasn't either, even in a professional way. His awareness of her as a woman definitely wasn't fucking fine. Especially since she was *married*.

"Anne, I can't believe you haven't told anyone who you were. Are. Whatever," Riley said, eyes wide, still studying Anne.

She shrugged. "I wasn't trying to keep it a secret. It never came up and nobody recognized me."

"Well, let me be the first to officially welcome you back to Oak Creek." Riley smiled.

"Thank you. It's good to be back."

Was it Zac's imagination or had she hesitated just a tiny bit on the word *good*?

"Would you like me to clear the room?" She took an ophthalmoscope out of the pocket of her white coat and clenched it. When he met her eyes again, they were still full of fear. Not only nervousness stemming from an awkward situation. Downright *fear*.

Why the hell would Annie Nichols be scared of him? "No, it's fine. The guys have seen me in much worse shape than this."

He watched as Annie took a breath through her nose, pulling herself together. Focusing. He'd seen it before with soldiers—pulling the professional over the personal and letting it drown out everything else.

There was no tremor in her hand as she shined a light into one eye, then the other. Her movements were brisk and professional.

"Looks like you got pretty banged up. How are you feeling?"

"Not too bad, all things considered."

"Can you tell me what happened?" She had him follow her finger with his eyes as she moved it in front of him.

"Dumbass swerved to miss a dog and couldn't keep control of his bike," Aiden said.

Zac sighed, leaning back against the bed. "Some kid ran a red light, so I had to gun it to keep from getting hit. But then, yeah, a dog decided to join the party and ran out into the street."

"Pregnant dog," Finn chimed in.

"Had to lay my bike down. Skidded down the street and hit the other curb with my head."

"Helmet?" she asked.

He nodded, then winced at the spike of pain. "Always."

"Smart. Well, the good news is your pupils are responding normally to light and motion. So, you probably don't have a concussion." Annie reached for his head. "Mind if I feel for the knot?"

"Be my guest."

They both tensed as she touched his scalp, her fingers running gently through his hair.

For just a second a memory from that night flashed in his mind. Her laying under him on the bed, breasts pressed up against his chest, her arms wrapping around his neck, running through his hair.

It was gone before he could pull the rest of the scene into his mind. His eyes locked with hers, and he knew she was remembering the same thing.

She looked away, moving further behind him as her fingers circled along the wound. Zac winced, and she stopped, stepping back.

"You've got a moderate-sized protrusion, which in your situation is actually a good thing."

"It is?" His head tilted.

She nodded and cleared her throat. "Yes, an outward protrusion means the swelling is occurring outside your skull, not inside, where it would put pressure on your brain."

"Zac's got a harder head than anyone we know. Takes more than a cement curb to crack his skull," Finn announced from the perch he'd taken at the wall.

The tiniest of smiles curved her lips. "I'm sure. Let me look at your shoulder."

Her hands were gentle as she helped him sit forward and examined his abrasions. Gentle, but professional. There were no more flashes of memory shared between them.

God, if Zac was going to torture himself with guilt over what he'd done, he wished he could at least remember that night.

"These skin abrasions are not nearly as bad as some I've seen in motorcycle accidents. Really more of a bad rug burn than anything else—first degree, nothing that will leave scars on your back. Leather jacket, I'm assuming?"

They were all he'd worn in high school. He nodded. "Some things don't change."

She released him and took a step back again. "Even minor motorcycle accidents can become major without those. I don't see any reason why you need to be admitted, but we'll order a CT scan just to be sure. Nurse Wilde will make sure the abrasions are cleaned out, and the med tech will be down to take you for the scan momentarily. I'll be back to check on you one more time before you leave."

Their gazes met, her Dr. Griffin persona slipping and fear once again clouding those deep brown eyes. That night —he cursed himself again for not being able to remember it —hung between them almost like a tangible thing.

Wariness, guilt, unease would all be appropriate feelings about that night. But she damn well shouldn't be *afraid* of him.

She took another step back, her eyes slipping from his completely, before turning to the guys. "Finn, good to see you again. Aiden, nice to meet you." Again, no stutter. She touched Riley on the shoulder. "I'll order the CT. Let me know if you need anything."

And without another word, she was gone.

# CHAPTER 4

"WOW, now that's a blast from the past," Finn said as they all stared at the door closing behind Annie. "She's still the same, doesn't say much if she doesn't have to. You hung out with her most, Zac. What do you think?"

What did he think? He still couldn't get past the fear in her eyes. He forced himself to look away from the door. "Annie was always Becky's friend. Not really mine. But you're right, she's never been one to talk much around a group of people."

Annie had practically lived at Becky's house in high school. Evidently her home life hadn't been great, and Becky and Mrs. Peverill had insisted that she stay with them as much as possible. Whenever Zac had been over, Annie had always been in the corner, nose in a book. She had rarely talked to him even though he'd been at the house all the time too. Annie had never talked to anyone, maybe because of the stuttering problem.

Or at least that was what he'd thought. It was only in their senior year he'd realized differently. He'd arrived to pick up Becky for a date, walking over to roll up the hose Mrs. Peverill had used to water her flowers earlier in the day, and heard the women through the open kitchen window, talking.

*Annie* talking. Chatting. She'd even told an off-color joke that had made both Becky and Mrs. P roar with laughter.

Zac had realized Annie wasn't always quiet, just around people or situations that made her uncomfortable. Which had included *him*.

Something had changed in him after that. He'd spent more time trying to include Annie in conversations and plans, much to Becky's delight. Not that he'd been inter-ested in Annie physically, but he'd become aware of her existence as a person.

Of course, that had led to understanding other aspects of Annie. How kind she was. How intelligent. How funny.

And yes, how attractive.

Becky had known about Zac's awareness, had even teased him about it a little. But she'd been secure enough in herself and their love not to feel threatened by that awareness.

Becky had known Zac would never betray her. They'd said vows to each other even before the ones they'd taken at the church. Till death did they part.

Zac had at least gotten that part right. He'd fucked up plenty, but at least not that. He would've never cheated on Becky.

He winced as Riley began cleaning out the worst of his road rash.

"I guess Anne is married." He tried to keep his tone neutral. "Have you met her husband?"

"She's divorced, actually. I asked her on her first day,

thinking maybe she and her husband would like to go to dinner or something."

Zac closed his eyes and grimaced again, hoping it would seem like pain from his wound had caused the reaction, not the sheer and profound relief he felt that Annie didn't belong to another man.

Because that would make zero sense. Annie being married should not make any difference to him at all.

"Okay, I'm done," Riley told him. "Frank Jenkins will be here to take you down for the scan in a few minutes."

All three men groaned at Jenkins's name.

Riley laughed. "He still trying to get you guys to take him on as a partner?"

Frank Jenkins had moved to town three years ago and had been applying at Linear Tactical for at least two. He showed up there all the time. The man liked guns, knives, and fighting. And he thought he'd make a good partner, or at least employee, at Linear.

Zac and the guys had never even considered it.

Jenkins was okay as a person, but not someone they wanted connected to the business they'd so painstakingly built. He had no restraint, no respect for weapons or fighting tactics. He just wanted to show off, throw his weight around.

That was probably true with a lot of their customers, especially civilians. But it didn't mean that's who Zac, or the guys, wanted in someone working for them—or even hanging around them.

"As soon as he heard you'd been in an accident, he took on another shift," Riley told them, gathering her supplies.

"That guy is a groupie," Finn muttered, shaking his head.

Aiden shuddered. "I thought they were supposed to be hot."

"Evidently, we're in the wrong line of work for hot groupies," Zac said.

Riley made her way toward the door. "I'll see you guys later, and I'm sure Mia will be back any minute when she's finished spreading the word about Anne. Not that many people will remember her."

Zac grimaced. He had no doubt Riley was right. In Oak Creek, gossip this good—the quiet girl with ne'er-do-well parents secretly returning and becoming one of the town's most important doctors—wouldn't take long to spread, with or without Mia's help.

There was much juicier gossip when it came to Annie and him. But thank God nobody knew about that. Hell, he didn't even know enough to gossip about it.

Frank Jenkins's entrance a few minutes later was almost a welcome distraction. His attempt to bro-hug Aiden and Finn made it even more so. The man was oblivious to his own awkwardness. Zac was actually thankful for his wounds.

Jenkins still clasped Zac on his shoulder. "So, a CT scan for you. Sorry about the accident, man."

Zac nodded and tried to smile. "Thanks."

"What do you think of Dr. Ice Queen? Mia was saying you all went to high school together."

"Dr. Griffin?" Zac kept his tone carefully neutral. "She seems like a good doctor."

Frank tried to lean casually against the wall, mimicking the way Aiden had been standing a few moments ago. "She doesn't ever talk to anyone, you know? Stuck up. I tried asking her out last week, but she shut me down. Cold as ice, man."

Or maybe she just had better taste than Frank Jenkins.

A little too late, Jenkins thought better of his words. "Hey, wait, you guys weren't friends back in the day, were you?"

Zac wanted to get this CT scan finished so he could get out of here. "Not really."

"I figured not. You would think someone who looks like her would be happy to get asked out, am I right? But she certainly shut me down."

"Someone who looks like her?" Zac raised an eyebrow. Annie had never put much effort into her looks, but she wasn't unattractive.

"Just plain, you know?" Jenkins winked. "And so severe. But I guess you don't always have to be looking at her face. She's got other things you can watch instead."

"Jesus, Jenkins." Finn shook his head.

"Now I personally don't know why you don't get back together with Mia Stevenson." Frank leaned over and nudged Zac, oblivious to the tension in the room. "She's so hot. But I guess you already know that, am I right? You're going to have to pass around some deets about that action one of these days."

Zac barely refrained from rolling his eyes. "It's bad form to kiss and tell." Not to mention he and Mia had never really been *together*, they'd only gone out a few times since he'd moved back into town, although she'd always wanted more.

Frank laughed. "I know, man, but it's *us*."

There was not an *us* that involved Jenkins. "Sorry. I know when to keep my mouth shut."

Frank nodded and winked. "Gotcha. Gotcha. Let's get you into the chair and down to the CT scan."

"Okay."

"We'll stay here in case anyone needs anything," Finn said, sitting on the bed Zac had vacated.

Those bastards just didn't want to spend any more time with Jenkins. They smiled innocently and Zac flipped them off behind Jenkins's head as the man reached for the chart on the way out the door.

The CT scan proved to be much less painful than Jenkins's constant chatter. At least he accepted Zac's head injury as an acceptable reason for nonresponse. Finally, he brought Zac back to his ER room.

"Hopefully I'll catch you guys around town this weekend," Jenkins said as he moved toward the door.

"Yeah, I'll probably be laying low," Zac said. "But I'm sure Aiden and Finn here would love to spend time with you at The Eagle's Nest."

He could feel his friends glaring at him but didn't care. Payback was a bitch.

"That would be the best ever, am I right?" Frank nodded enthusiastically. "I'll be sure to keep a look out for you. I got some friends I want to introduce you to. They've been hot to trot to take some of your classes. Plus, maybe Doc Ice will be there, and I can melt some of that." Frank began humming a porn theme and grinned at everyone as he left.

"I think we should hire Jenkins as Zac's personal assistant." Aiden shook his head as the door closed behind the other man. "Or maybe a customer service rep."

Finn rolled his eyes. "Especially for our female clients. I'm sure they'd find him charming, am I right?"

Zac didn't say anything as his friends continued cracking jokes, just leaned back against the bed on his good shoulder. Whether Annie went to The Eagle's Nest this weekend or not wasn't any of his business. Nor was what she did with Frank Jenkins or anyone else.

They'd successfully stayed away from each other for six years. It was probably for the best.

He'd never made sure she was okay after that night because, hell, he hadn't been himself. The next morning he'd gone back to where his unit had been stationed in Afghanistan and had lost himself in his missions, drowning in grief. What he could remember of that night he'd pushed from his mind completely, unable to do anything else if he wanted to keep it together.

Had anybody made sure Annie was okay?

Of course not. She'd lost her best friend and probably felt just as guilty as he had about what had happened. Hell, she'd even left town.

So, her facing him now, he could understand reluctance, even dislike. But fear? And not a surface concern, but the gut-level panic she'd shown before she'd pulled herself together? That came from something else.

Something buried in the night he couldn't remember.

Heat. Raw passion. Burning fury. That's what Zac remembered about that night, all of it visceral. And none of it sat well with him. He winced as the ache in his head spiked.

He had a feeling his headaches were only beginning.

# CHAPTER 5

ANNE RESISTED the urge to go hide in her office. No. Zac couldn't crush her now the way he once had. Or run her out of town.

Not that he'd seemed to want to.

After his initial demand for another doctor—not unexpected—he'd settled back into a sort of normalcy, treating her the way Finn and Riley had, with friendly detachment.

At least he'd recognized her. How pathetic would it have been if the man she'd lost her virginity to hadn't?

She'd wanted to run to him and away from him at the same time. To him because he was *Zac*. She'd spent her entire life fighting the urge to run to him. Away because she was never going to be able to forget that night and what had happened, how he'd broken her. In almost every way someone could be.

So yeah, one look at Zac had her brain thinking that running the other way as fast as she could was a damn fine idea. She didn't want to get broken again.

But no. She wouldn't let him. She wasn't the same person.

And he wasn't her best friend's boyfriend/fiancé/husband anymore.

Anne had been in love with Zac when he'd been each of those things for Becky. And although she'd never spoken a word of her feelings to her friend, Becky had known. One night the summer after they'd graduated, Anne spending the night *again*, Becky had let her knowledge slip.

They'd been up talking about wedding plans, even though the wedding had still been a couple years away. Becky had been so excited—had wanted everything to be perfect. Anne had been for them too.

Because, despite her feelings for Zac, she'd known he was meant for Becky. The two of them had been perfect for each other in every way. Anne would never have begrudged them their happiness.

Becky and Anne had lain down in Becky's double bed, still giggling every once in a while, or discussing some wedding detail. Both had been drifting off to sleep, Anne's eyes already closed, when Becky had whispered, "I wish I didn't love Zac so much so I could give him to you."

Anne hadn't moved. Hadn't opened her eyes. Hadn't changed her breathing pattern. But inside, her mind had been whirling. Becky *knew*.

Anne wasn't sure if Becky had thought she was asleep or had known she'd heard the whispered statement. Either way, from that point on, Anne had gone out of her way to make sure none of her feelings for Zac ever came close to the surface. Anne would've never done anything about them anyway, even if Zac had shown any sort of interest in her, which he never had. But just the knowledge that Becky had *sensed* it had been bad enough. Anne had stayed close to Becky as her friend but had eased back as much as possible from them as a couple.

Though not being around Zac had cut at her, tiny little wounds that were almost unnoticeable unless taking in the damage as a whole. Being around him, knowing he would never be hers, was hard enough.

Not being around him had been even worse.

But she'd survived it. Like she had everything.

After the wedding, Zac and Becky had moved away, and Anne had gone back to medical school. Everything had been okay. When she'd talked to Becky or visited, everything had been better, lighter. When Becky had gotten pregnant with Micah, Anne had been absolutely thrilled for her friend. A piece of her had mourned that it would never be her carrying Zac's baby, but she'd tamped it down so deep it would never make its way out.

But God, not a single day had gone by when she hadn't thought about Zac. And that night, two weeks after Becky had died, when they'd both been drinking...

After that night, she still thought about him, but now it was about how much he hated her, how he'd left her bleeding physically and emotionally, and had turned her away so brutally. Drunk or not, he'd still devastated her.

When she'd moved back, Anne had known she'd run into Zac eventually. Oak Creek wasn't large enough for them to avoid each other forever.

But she hadn't thought it would be in her second week of work.

Nor that it would be so painful or overwhelming, or that six years later the last words he'd said to her would still burn so agonizingly through her psyche.

*I can't even bear to look at you. You just betrayed the*

*only person in this town who ever wanted you here. Get out and don't come back.*

The memory almost had her running for her office again.

She'd survived that night too. And after she'd finally managed to get herself together, she'd taken Zac at his word and gotten out.

She'd even transferred out of state to finish her residency, so she wouldn't risk seeing anyone she knew. Especially Zac Mackay.

But out of options, she'd ended up back here anyway. He couldn't run her out of town now because she had nowhere else to go, no savings, no way of starting again.

She was staying. Zac would have to live with it.

Anne was standing alone at the nurses' station when she heard a voice behind her. "I don't know why you thought you could hide. It was only a matter of time before someone remembered you." Mia.

She was just as beautiful, maybe even more so, as she had been in high school—wavy blonde hair, big green eyes, full pouty lips.

Anne breathed in a silent, calming breath. "I wasn't trying to hide anything, Mia. I just didn't announce my maiden name, that's all."

Those green eyes narrowed. "I remember you. You thought you were better than everyone else. Smarter too."

Anne let out a small sigh. "I was shy. Talking to people wasn't my forte, as you well know." It still wasn't. But at least in the hospital Anne didn't have as much difficulty. Usually.

Mia's eyes narrowed. "You always followed Zac around like a puppy or something."

Other people were starting to mill around them. Anne forced herself to stay calm. She knew her own emotional triggers. Multiple eyes on her tended to induce the stuttering.

"Becky Peverill was my best friend. Becky and Zac were inseparable. So yeah, I-I-I..." She stopped. Swallowed. "I was around Zac a lot in high school." And hell, the puppy description was probably accurate.

"Well, Zac and I are together now. He's mine and you can't have him."

Anne almost laughed out loud at the absurdity of that statement. Zac had never been hers, would never be. The one night they'd gotten close, she'd ended up bloody in more ways than one.

She was saved from having to answer when Riley passed by the station at that moment, medical chart in hand. "That's totally not true and you know it, Mia. You and Zac aren't a couple. You haven't ever been a couple."

Mia glared at the younger woman. "Whatever. He's hung out more with me than any other woman in this town." She turned to glare at Anne again. "Just don't forget that."

Mia turned and headed toward Zac's room. Riley and Anne watched her go.

"I see some things never change." Anne shook her head. She wouldn't be able to look that sexy walking across a room if she had the rest of her life to practice.

Riley shrugged, handing the chart to Anne. "Yep. Welcome home. Here are Zac's CT results." She gave Anne a little nudge on the arm, then walked away.

Alone again, Anne looked down at Zac's file. Everything was fine. He would be fine. No permanent damage, no need to stay overnight or run any further tests. With anyone else, she would be happy to go back and share the good news.

With Zac, she had to brace for the emotional blow that was coming. She'd grown up with alcoholic parents who turned on a dime. She'd learned early on that a fist you were unprepared for hurt the most.

She wouldn't let her guard down with Zac. Not this time. Never again.

But Oak Creek was her home now. If she had to fight to stay, she would.

Even though she was terrible when it came to fighting, particularly for herself. She hadn't been able to do it as a child, and as an adult she was even worse. She'd never learned to protect herself. The best she'd been able to do was make herself invisible.

She wished she could go back to the last two weeks, when no one here had known who she was.

It was so much easier being invisible.

# CHAPTER 6

THE BIGGEST PROBLEM with working in the ER was the insane schedule.

Emergencies happened when they happened. And it felt like they always decided to just when Anne was trying to get off shift.

She'd ended up working another eighteen hours after Zac had left with Mia, who had smiled broadly as she'd promised to take prompt care of *any and all* Zac's needs.

Which shouldn't bother Anne. Whether he and Mia were together or not had nothing to do with her. Fortunately, the constant activity in the ER had left Anne too busy to think much about anything, including Zac. Then once things had finally calmed enough for her to head home, she'd promptly fallen asleep for thirteen hours.

But for the last two days, she'd had to force herself not to think about Zac. Not to think anything about him at all. Better for her sanity that way.

It wasn't like he'd be having motorcycle accidents all the time and showing up in her ER. Oak Creek was small as far as towns went, but big enough that she could dive headfirst behind a cart if she saw him while at the grocery store or something.

Anne rolled her eyes at herself. Yeah, she'd just avoid him. And given her schedule—it was eleven o'clock at night and she was currently wide awake, unpacking boxes in her new home—it shouldn't be a problem.

Home.

Thanks to Carol, she had a *home*, owned free and clear. With a yard where she'd be able to plant a little garden: fruits, vegetables, flowers...everything. She'd love to get a dog too—had always wanted one—but her schedule wouldn't permit it. It wouldn't be fair to leave the poor little guy on his own if she ended up working a twenty-four-hour or more shift.

But she had a *home*. Even back in high school this house had always been closer to home than the rundown, two-bedroom, government-subsidized place where her parents had lived. During their sophomore year, Becky had struck up a conversation with her—she'd found Anne inside the grocery store trying to figure out a way to stretch whatever measly amount of money she'd been able to pilfer from her parents into a week's worth of meals. Then Becky had dragged Anne to her house for dinner. From that moment on, to Anne, this place had been everything a home was meant to be.

The walls around her were no longer the pastel colors Carol and Becky had painted them in high school. They no longer held all the decorations and heavy curtains Carol had leaned toward. She'd had it painted before she died, made it a place where Anne could come in and start fresh. So, the house could be hers rather than her feeling like she was a guest.

Sadness sat heavy on her chest for a minute. Carol had died of lung cancer, although she'd never smoked, and by the time it had been caught it was already stage IV. Anne had flown in immediately from Tampa, even though she hadn't really had the money to afford it. She'd gone with Carol to the oncologist to ask the questions Carol might not have known to ask. Ultimately, with a prognosis of only six months to live and having already lost all her other family, Carol had opted against chemo.

Anne had tried to talk her out of that, but the older woman hadn't listened. And God bless her, Carol hadn't had much money, but she'd had this house. All Anne could do now was appreciate that the woman had continued to be as generous in her death as she'd been in life.

She had a home, one she planned to be in for a long time. She'd continue to pay off her massive debt, then add what she could—furniture, knickknacks—as time went on. She didn't have much money right now, but she had time. The other stuff would come.

She dragged a box across the floor. The only thing she owned right now that had any aesthetic appeal at all was her collection of books. Her furniture was mostly second-hand or cheap quality, her car only ran on good days, and she'd never been someone who enjoyed expensive jewelry.

But her few rare books were her prized possessions, not to mention a ton of non-rare that she loved. Everything from Tolkien to Jane Austen to John Green.

So, she would make the heavy bookshelf she'd gotten at a secondhand store in Tampa the centerpiece of the room. She would face the couch toward it the way other people's faced a television. Who cared if no one else understood her collection? She didn't plan to have many people over anyway. This would just be for her.

She grimaced. Moving that solid, wooden bookshelf would be a bitch. But she wasn't likely to have anyone around to help her for the foreseeable future, so she might as well get it over with.

She'd gotten it about five feet across the room, pulling from one direction and then pushing from the other, when she decided it would be easier, if a little riskier, to tilt and walk it side by side. She was moving the first corner when a pounding on her front door made her jump—and the heavy bookshelf began to topple over on her.

Anne cried out, putting all her strength under it to keep it from crushing her as it fell to the floor, but it wouldn't be enough. She wouldn't be able to stop it.

She heard the door open.

"What the hell?" came a man's muffled voice before his much more considerable strength was added to hers and the bookshelf was righted again. "Annie?"

"Zac?"

"What are you doing here?" they both asked at the same time. Then they stood in silence, waiting for the other to answer.

"How did you get in?" she asked. "I know I locked the door." It may not be necessary here in Oak Creek, but it had been in Tampa.

"I have a key. Carol gave me one when I moved back to town four years ago in case she ever locked herself out or something. I saw the lights on from the road and wanted to make sure no one was breaking into the place. What are *you* doing here?"

"I live here."

It wasn't easy to catch Zac off guard. Evidently, this news did. *"What?"*

She shrugged, stepping further away from him. "Carol

left it to me in her will. It's a big part of the reason why I moved home. Um, thanks for the help."

Zac ignored her, walking around, glancing at the walls, the boxes. The house wasn't big. Three bedrooms and an open floor plan that allowed the living room, dining area, and kitchen to open into one large space. He finally turned to study her before looking at the bookshelf again.

"Where do you want this? I can't leave here wondering if they'll find your body buried under it in a couple days."

She pointed where she'd been trying to get it and together they moved it much more easily. She grabbed a few of her most precious books and arranged them on one of the heavy wooden shelves.

"There. I feel more at home already."

"You and your books. You always had your head buried in one." He looked around again. "It didn't take you long to erase every bit of evidence that Mrs. P lived here. She told me she was leaving it to family, someone she felt could use it. I thought it would just be sold, honestly. But I never dreamed she'd leave it to you."

She flinched at his hard tone, but didn't defend herself against his accusation of erasing Carol. What difference would it make if he knew Carol had painted the walls herself before she died? "I never dreamed she'd leave it to me either. But it helped me in ways she couldn't possibly have known."

Zac looked away. "She had cancer. Didn't tell any of us until it was too late."

She nodded. "Yeah, she was already stage IV by the time she was diagnosed. I came out from Tampa a couple times to go to the oncologist with her."

His gaze snapped up and she couldn't help but take a step back. "You were in town?"

"For a couple days. In case Carol had any questions or didn't understand something her physician was talking about. It can be pretty overwhelming."

"And the funeral?"

"I was here. But again, only for a day or two." Anne had booked a room out of town both times. The thought of staying at The Mayor's Inn had been too painful. She couldn't even look at that hotel without feeling sick to her stomach.

And she'd avoided everyone—particularly Zac—as much as possible. Just in case his words about not coming back were still true. She tried to swallow the panic that threatened to overwhelm her. Maybe he still felt that way now, even though he hadn't said anything at the hospital.

"There." He pointed at her. "That look that just came into your eyes. I saw it at the hospital. It's like you're afraid of me, Annie." He took a step closer and she instinctively one back. One of his eyebrows shot up, letting her know she'd proved his point. "Do you think I'm going to *hurt* you?"

"No." Not physically. She'd never worried that he'd hurt her that way, despite having five inches and probably fifty pounds—all muscle—on her.

But he was right. She couldn't continue living in Oak Creek with them ignoring everything that had happened that night. What had been said. What had been done. Maybe she would've tried to, and to avoid Zac forever, if he hadn't ended up in her ER.

But the truth was, there weren't enough bushes in this town for her to jump into. She was going to run into Zac. A lot.

Sometimes all you could do was face the past.

She pulled a breath in. "I'm not scared of you. I mean, I

know you would never hurt me physically. For crying out loud, you wrecked your motorcycle rather than hit a dog." She'd meant for her laugh to seem breezy, but it just sounded stilted. "But yeah, I mean, we can't pretend like that night never happened. The stuff we did. Stuff you...we said."

His eyes narrowed. "That night we spent together after Becky died."

"Yeah. That night." As if they'd had another. "The bottom line is, I can't leave here, Zac. No matter what you said then, or even if you feel the same way now."

He shook his head, brows furrowing. "I don't expect you to leave. You're obviously a respected doctor, more than competent. Why would you think I wanted you to leave?"

Some of the tension she'd been carrying since his arrival in the ER began to ease. He was right. Something said in grief and anger six years ago didn't necessarily hold true all this time later. She was silly for thinking it did. "Okay, well, it's good to know you don't feel the same as you did back then."

He took a single predatory step closer, and she tensed again. "I said something that night to make you think you needed to leave?"

She stared at him, her mouth flopping open like some sort of fish. "You don't remember what you said?"

Those words would be engrained in her memory forever.

*Get out and don't come back.*

He rubbed his forehead. "That whole night is fuzzy for me."

*I can't even bear to look at you. You just betrayed the only person in this town who ever wanted you here.*

Tossing her naked into the hallway before flinging her clothes at her.

"What do you remember?" She forced the words past a throat that seemed to have dried up.

His hand moved to the back of his neck. "Honestly, not much at all. It's sort of a blur."

She retreated a step from him again. That night had been the most important night of her life. The best. The worst. It had changed the very fabric of her being.

And it was *sort of a blur* for him.

"I mean, I know we had sex, right?" Those blue eyes pinned her.

He couldn't even remember that clearly.

"Yes." Sort of.

It had all been going fine until he'd realized she was a virgin, and she'd been stupid enough to tell him she'd always loved him.

He rubbed his forehead. "And then afterward we fought?"

His hand dropped down and he watched her, studied her, evidently hoping she would shed some clarity on his fuzziness. And all she could do was try to keep the pieces of her heart from shattering into a million more right here in front of him.

He didn't remember.

That had defined her life, and he didn't remember.

She'd often wondered if he'd regretted his words. If he'd been concerned that they might have truly wounded her more than he'd meant them to. If he'd considered trying to find her and talk through what had happened, what had been said.

But he hadn't. Because *he didn't remember*.

And now he wanted her to fill in the blanks.

Like hell she would. If he couldn't remember, she wasn't going to help him.

She forced a smile onto her face. "You know what? We were drunk, Zac. That night is a little blurry for me too," she lied. "Let's agree to forget about it and move on."

His eyes narrowed. "But I said something that made you think I didn't want you in Oak Creek anymore."

*I can't even bear to look at you.*

*Get out and don't come back.*

Anne closed her eyes. For six years she'd known she should hate Zac for what he had done, what he had said, but she'd never been able to. She couldn't hate him. What he'd said had come from the unbearable pain of having just lost his family.

Still, it had destroyed her.

And he didn't remember it at all.

She tried her best to smile. "I think the statute of limitations pretty much eradicates anything either one of us said that night. Especially since you can't remember."

"I don't want you to be afraid of me."

She turned and began loading more books on the shelves. "Deal. Now that I know you're not upset that I've moved back to town, I won't have any concerns."

"Annie..."

God, she couldn't bear to hear that tone in his voice, the one that suggested he cared about her. She could forget six years ago, push down the pain that had shattered her heart when he'd left her alone, naked and bleeding—literally *and* figuratively.

But she couldn't be around him. Not as casual friends. Maybe someday, but not right now.

"It's super late. I appreciate you saving me from the

bookshelf of death, but I think I'm going to head to bed," she lied without blinking.

It at least distracted Zac from whatever he was going to say. "Yeah, I guess it is late.

"How is your head and back? Any complications?"

He studied her for a moment, then shrugged. "No. A little headache and my back is still tender. But nothing bad."

"That's good." Mia had undoubtedly helped with that. "Thanks for stopping by."

Zac walked to the door but turned back before stepping out. "Annie."

No, not tonight. She couldn't talk anymore about any of it. She moved to the door. "Thanks again for your help."

She closed it softly but firmly in his face, then made a mental note.

*Change locks immediately.*

# CHAPTER 7

"DAMN, Mackay. What bug up and died in your ass?"

Finn ducked under a roundhouse kick that would've sent the other man sprawling over the sparring mat. Zac wasn't pulling any punches, but he didn't need to with Finn. His friend could more than hold his own. The two of them had been sparring since their Army days. And wrestling since they were toddlers.

But it didn't mean Finn was wrong. Zac had been pissed for the past couple days, since he'd left Mrs. P's—damn it, *Annie's*—house.

Zac brought his arms up to protect his face as Finn moved in with a series of jabs. Duchess, that damn pregnant German shepherd, lay at the side of the ring, watching them lazily. When they hadn't been able to find her owner after the accident, they'd brought her to Linear to stay with them.

"What's the matter?" Finn's words burst out between blows. "Is Mia not taking care of you the way she should? Did she kick you out of her house? Because I know you didn't let her stay at your place while you were recovering."

Zac stepped to the side before throwing a few punches at Finn's midsection. "I didn't stay with Mia. Didn't want Mia."

Finn stepped back, holding out his hand to call for a break. Zac stopped and they both took off their protective headgear before grabbing water.

"Okay, so no Mia. Fair enough. I know you guys don't have anything permanent."

"We never really had anything at all."

Finn's eyebrow rose. "Okay. Any reason why that's such a decisive statement today?"

"She's just not what I want."

If possible, his friend's eyebrow went even higher. "That wouldn't happen to have anything to do with Becky's long-lost doctor bestie showing back up in town, would it?"

*Everything.* "Did you know Annie moved into Mrs. P's place? I know she's only been in town for two weeks, but she wiped every single bit of Mrs. P out of that house. No more of her furniture, all those crazy colored walls painted over."

Finn took a sip of water. "Actually, Aiden, Dorian, and I painted it for her about a month before she passed. She said she had family who would be living in it and she wanted to make sure that person could start fresh."

He winced. And here he'd accused Annie of erasing all presence of Mrs. P. At least this time he could remember what an asshole he'd been. "Why didn't I know about this?"

"It was while you were out in North Carolina with Shane Westman, getting the satellite office up and running. Mrs. P didn't want us to tell you how weak she was becoming. She just asked us to paint and rip out that hideous *Little Mermaid* wallpaper in the bathroom."

Zac couldn't stop his smile. "Becky loved that stupid

wallpaper when she was a kid but hated it by the time she was in high school."

"Ethan was there most of the day. He tried to talk her into putting up a nice *Star Wars* print."

Zac didn't doubt it. Finn's seven-year-old son was a *Star Wars* and Lego fanatic.

"That day, Mrs. P offered to pay me to take her furniture out after she passed. Of course, I told her I wouldn't take her money. But she paid for a rental unit for a year and had me move it there once she was gone. I know some of Becky's stuff may still be there, so if you want to look through it, let me know. Otherwise, it's all supposed to be donated to Goodwill."

Zac wiped sweat off his forehead. Of course, his mother-in-law had done all that. Caring for others had been in her blood. "Did you know Mrs. P left the house to Anne?"

Finn shook his head and took another sip of water. "Dude, I could barely remember Anne. I wouldn't have been able to pick her out of a lineup before seeing her again at the hospital. But no, I didn't. What's up with you and her? I mean, I know she and Becky were tight, but I don't remember you hanging out with her much. And you definitely never mentioned her since we moved back."

He'd hung out with Annie, of course. It was impossible not to when she was Becky's friend. She'd been Becky's polar opposite in every way: quiet to Becky's loud, pale to Becky's tan, tall and willowy to Becky's short and curvy. She'd been afraid of her own shadow, awkward in most social situations, and just generally forgettable to most people.

But not to Zac. Never to Zac.

He sat down and leaned against one of the corner posts of the sparring ring. "Annie and I slept together."

Finn nearly spewed his water. "Oh shit, when? Yesterday?"

"No. A long time ago."

Finn sat down against the opposite corner post, shaking his head. "*How* long ago?"

"Right after Becky died. The night before my leave was over, and I flew back out to resume duty. I was drunk as shit."

Finn leaned his head against the post. "You never drink."

"Not after that night. Haven't gotten drunk since. Pretty much the whole thing is a blank for me. I remember a few flashes, but nothing as a whole. I feel like shit."

"Dude, you're not the first guy who got drunk and looked for comfort after his wife died. Hell, anything you needed to do to survive that time could pretty much be excused. You'd just lost your family."

Part of Zac knew that was true. The other was utterly ashamed of what he'd done. "I've accepted that I'm an asshole for sleeping with someone else right after Becky died. The bigger problem is that evidently, I said something to Annie that night that was...unkind. She was afraid of me, Finn. At the hospital. I could see it."

"Are you sure? She's always been pretty shy."

Zac reached up to rub the tension in the back of his neck. "She pretty much said so when I saw her the other night. Said that we'd let bygones be bygones as long as I didn't still want her to leave town."

He'd been trying to piece together more since Annie had shut the door in his face. Had he really told her he didn't want her to stay in town? If so, she'd evidently taken him at his word.

He would give anything to remember that night. He remembered the heat between them, the kisses in his hotel room at The Mayor's Inn.

He remembered Annie's hair, for once loose from her braid, fanned out around her naked body on the bed, her pretty face smiling up at him. And him smiling at her in return.

And then something had happened. For the life of him, Zac didn't know what. They'd had sex—right? He wasn't even sure about that. Like they'd started...and then stopped. Why?

And then a blank. He couldn't remember anything but waking up the next day completely hungover, a knot on his head, leaning against the wall of his hotel room. No recollection of why Annie wasn't there or how things had been left between them.

Evidently, not good.

He'd barely made his transport to Colorado Springs before he'd been flown back to Afghanistan. And then he'd been so disgusted with himself, with what he'd done, that he'd forced himself not to think about that night at all. Pushed it completely from his mind.

But now he couldn't hide from the truth. "She was *scared* of me. In the hospital. Not just a general unease, but true fear."

Zac jumped up, the most unbearable thought coursing through his brain. What if Annie's fear was not because of something he'd said, but something he'd *done*?

Jesus, what if Annie hadn't really wanted to have sex with him? What if she'd changed her mind, and he hadn't understood or hadn't had himself under enough control? He would never hurt a woman that way on purpose—God, especially not Annie.

But there was so fucking much he didn't remember about that night.

Finn stood also. "Whatever you're thinking right now? The answer is no. You would never hurt a woman like that, Zac. It's not even in your DNA, for God's sake."

He wanted to believe that was true. With everything inside him, he wanted to. But he damn sure wasn't going to take his own hole-riddled memory's word for it. He was going to talk to Annie right damn now and understand exactly what had happened that night.

But then Sheriff Nelson walked in the door of the barn Linear had outfitted for all sorts of martial arts and boxing training. "Aiden told me you guys were in here beating the tar out of each other."

"Sorry, Sheriff." Finn walked over to shake the man's hand. "If you'd gotten here ten minutes sooner, you could've seen Zac crying for his mommy."

The old man didn't break into one of his normally easy-going smiles. "Well, I'm glad you're done, because I need your help."

"What's up?" Zac asked.

"Another attack. This one out in Lincoln County. A woman's car broke down, so she decided to walk into work and was dragged behind the abandoned bottling factory and raped. The Lincoln sheriff asked if you guys might be willing to do some tracking around the scene."

Damn it. Doubly not what Zac wanted to deal with right now, given where his thoughts about Annie had been. But if he and the guys could help stop a rapist, Zac's personal baggage would have to wait. "Do they think it's the same guy as last week?"

"Looks that way. I don't have any jurisdiction over there, I'm just helping Landon Rogers out in a completely unofficial capacity. But now there's been two very similar attacks in one week in counties surrounding Oak Creek. So, I can't help but take that pretty damn seriously."

"Dorian would be best for this, of course. But he's out of pocket," Finn said, then gave Zac a nod.

Dorian sometimes spent days at a time out in the woods alone. The man suffered from severe PTSD and often couldn't bear to be around other people for extended amounts of time. He was the best survival specialist they had—the man was damn near MacGyver out in nature—but when he had to get away, he had to get away.

Dorian was currently *away*.

"I'll help you, Sheriff." Zac began cleaning up the sparring ring. "I need to get out of here anyway."

"Yes, please take Gargamel here with you. Then maybe I won't have to keep kicking his ass to get him out of his mood." Finn ducked as Zac sent a sparring glove at his head.

Forty-five minutes later, Zac pulled up to the crime scene behind Sheriff Nelson. Just south of Oak Creek in neighboring Lincoln County, the scene itself already had a half dozen law enforcement personnel looking for any sort of trace evidence the rapist might've left behind. They didn't need another person in the mix further contaminating the scene.

That was okay, because ground zero wasn't why Zac was here. He needed to find out where the perp had gone after fleeing the scene or, barring that, perhaps where he'd been before the rape had occurred. As Zac had learned to do in the Army when trying to find an unknown enemy combatant, he walked in a circle, looking outward.

Where would he go if he were the rapist? Were these

spur-of-the-moment attacks? Were the women chosen because of a certain feature, like hair color, height, or how they walked? Did they know their attacker, or did he take them by surprise? Zac didn't have a lot of details, and hell, even if he did, he wasn't some FBI profiler.

The area wasn't wilderness, so there were no shoe prints or anything truly trackable. It was a cluster of buildings and warehouses on the outskirts of the small town of Hillsdale. Most were abandoned, but even the ones that weren't didn't have enough people coming in and out to help someone in trouble.

Zac continued walking around, trying to think like someone preparing for an attack. "The fact that it's the building closest to the road could suggest it was a crime of opportunity."

The sheriff nodded. "I agree. But in both cases the guy was wearing a mask."

Zac grimaced. "So, the victims might have known their attacker."

"Could be the same guy or some sort of copycat."

Zac walked a little farther to a sign that was partially overgrown by bushes. It was about twenty yards from the warehouse door and only ten feet from the street.

If Zac were planning an ambush, this was where he would do it from. He stepped in for a closer look and within a few moments had his confirmation.

"Somebody was definitely here." He pointed out branches on the shrubs. "The broken pieces are still green on the ground, so it was recent. And it looks like he got a little bored." He pointed to a tiny stack of rocks an inch or two high.

"What is that?"

"It seems as if he wasn't mentally disciplined enough not to get bored while waiting for the victim to show up."

"But he was definitely waiting?"

Zac looked around. "Yes. And it doesn't make much sense to just wait and see if some woman would randomly walk by here. I'm sure when Rogers's men take a closer look at the victim's car, they'll see whatever caused her 'breakdown' was deliberate."

Nelson let out a curse. They spent the next hour searching but couldn't find anything.

"Got time to run by the county clinic?" Sheriff Nelson asked. "Rogers is there. He might have a couple questions."

Zac once again followed the sheriff in his car, then spent the next thirty minutes at the clinic providing what insight he could to Sheriffs Rogers and Nelson, glad to see this wasn't any sort of turf war.

When the door to one of the examination rooms opened with a quiet click, and both law enforcement officers stopped talking, Zac knew the victim was in there.

"I guess they're almost finished," Nelson said. "I've got to give Dr. Griffin a ride back to Oak Creek anyway."

Zac turned to look at him. "Annie is here? Why?"

"Both doctors who work at this clinic are male, and the victim was pretty upset. I was at the hospital when I got the call from Landon, and Dr. Griffin offered to help, even though I think she'd just gotten off a thirty-six-hour shift or something."

Annie appeared in the room's doorway then, stopping to talk to who looked to be the victim's parents. The mother rushed past her after a moment, but the father seemed rooted in place, his world completely shaken. Annie stopped and spoke to him in low, deliberate tones, her voice not carrying even in the smallish room. She touched him on the arm—his distress obvious—offering whatever medical advice or comfort she could. The man hung on her words, on Annie's gentle, calming presence. His face was grim as he straightened his shoulders, nodded at her, and entered the room.

Annie wiped a hand over her face, her shoulders slumping with exhaustion before she, too, gathered her strength and moved forward toward the sheriffs, evidence bags in hand.

She faltered when she saw Zac, but then straightened once more, wariness now warring with exhaustion, eyes darting to the door like she might need to make a quick getaway.

Multiple reactions warred inside him. He needed answers for what had happened all those years ago, needed to know if he'd hurt her in ways he'd never imagined.

But more than that was the urge to help her now. To pull her into his arms and just let her rest, let her release the weight bearing down on her. To feed her and put her to bed and make sure she got uninterrupted sleep for the next ten hours or however long it took to erase that exhaustion from her eyes.

It wasn't something he was used to, and not something he would've thought he'd ever feel toward her. He wasn't sure how to make it go away.

Or even if he wanted it to.

# CHAPTER 8

ANNE LOVED HER JOB, she really did. From her first anatomy class in high school, she'd known she wanted to be a doctor.

But sometimes being one completely sucked. Like having to run a rape kit on a terrified nineteen-year-old girl who couldn't stop crying. Kimmy had kept apologizing no matter how many times Anne had assured her it was all right.

God, Anne was angry. Kimmy was just a teenager who'd walked in for her evening shift as a waitress at one of the town's restaurants, thinking she was safe in the town she'd lived most of her life. Yet, she'd been brutalized. And Anne was so pissed for having to explain to Kimmy's father that right now he had to put his own fury aside and concentrate on whatever his daughter needed.

And Anne was tired. She'd been exhausted before she'd offered to help Sheriff Nelson. Now, she was beyond weary. She needed to give this evidence to Sheriff Rogers, then she wanted nothing more than to just go home. Hopefully, there would be something in the rape kit that would be useful in the case. The rapist had at least worn a condom. Although that wasn't good in terms of evidence, it was much better for Kimmy.

Eyes burning and blurring—she really needed to get these contacts out—she turned toward the main counter of the clinic, relieved when she saw Sheriff Rogers already there. That ease ran screaming out the door when she noticed Zac a second later. She had to force the rest of her body not to do the same.

What was he doing here? Both sheriffs motioned her over, and she walked toward them, steps all but dragging, like she was being led to the guillotine.

"Thanks so much again for coming, Dr. Griffin," Rogers said.

She handed him the evidence bags. "Please, call me Anne. And although I certainly hate that I was here under these circumstances, I'm always glad to help in any way I can."

"We truly appreciate it. I'm certain having a female doctor made it easier on Kimmy."

Anne fought the urge to rub her fingers against her gritty eyes. "I don't think anything will make today easier for Kimmy."

"I suppose not. But we appreciate you coming out here anyway." Rogers gestured to Zac. "Do you know Zac Mackay? He and the rest of the Linear Tactical guys have some tracking and observation skills useful for a lot of crime scenes. He's helping us too."

She forced herself to look at him. "Yes, Zac and I know each other."

Damn those gorgeous blue eyes. They'd always pulled at her. When Becky had been alive, it had made her feel guilty. Now, it just made her feel stupid.

But they kept pulling her.

They'd agreed to distance. It was the best thing. The *smart* thing.

"You look dead on your feet," Sheriff Nelson said. "Let me get you home."

"I'd be more than happy to take you, if you can wait a few minutes while I get things wrapped up here. Maybe we could get a bite to eat first." She felt a hand touch her on the small of her back and realized it was Sheriff Rogers. Her eyes jerked away from Zac and over at the other man. She hadn't really paid attention to him when she'd arrived, too focused on getting to Kimmy. He wasn't nearly as old as Sheriff Nelson, probably only a few years older than her own thirty-one. Curly black hair just a tad too long. Friendly brown eyes. Chiseled jaw.

And was he asking her out? "Oh. Well, thank you, Sheriff..."

He smiled. "Please, call me Landon."

That smile was potent. "Landon. Okay, wow, well..."

"Actually, Annie and I already have plans for dinner, Landon," Zac cut in. Her gaze flew back to him. "She just moved back in town, and we've been wanting to catch up. We went to high school together."

Zac and Landon stared at each other for a second. What in the world was going on? And why was Zac saying they were going out to dinner?

Anne wanted to go home. She didn't have the mental fortitude to play a game she didn't understand the rules for.

After a moment, Landon gave a slight nod. "I understand." He turned from Zac and looked at her. "And we really do appreciate you coming out here. I hope next time it will be under different circumstances."

He turned and walked back toward Kimmy's room.

Sheriff Nelson popped Zac on the shoulder. "If you don't mind taking Doc Griffin back to Oak Creek, I can get some more work done." He smiled gently at her. "That okay with you, Doc? I know you and Mackay used to be pretty tight."

That was not the word she would've used, but she wasn't about to argue. "Sure, that's fine."

Zac said nothing, just held the door open and led her out, now *his* hand at the small of her back. He walked her to his truck, again opening the door for her. Silently they began the thirty-minute drive back to Oak Creek.

She knew she should say something. Just normal small talk stuff. It had always frustrated Darren that she'd never seemed able to carry a conversation with people. And right now, she was even less able to. The pitiful cries of a teenage girl filled her head, ricocheting through her mind with jagged edges, cutting her. She stared out at the stark Wyoming scenery as it flew by, forehead against the window, wishing it would sweep her away.

She relaxed some as the miles passed, her hands in her lap, realizing Zac wasn't going to force polite conversation just for the sake of filling the silence. She had no idea why he'd told Landon they were going to dinner, but now she was glad he had. There was no way she would've made it through dinner with a stranger, even one as polite as the sheriff.

"Do you want pizza or burgers?" Zac asked after a few more miles. "And before you tell me no, you've got to eat before you fall into whatever coma you're planning on going into. Otherwise you won't get the rest you need."

The hell of it was, he was right. Without food, she would sleep fitfully at best, then wake up nauseous and weak. But she couldn't afford to go out to eat.

Another two years of paying off creditors and lawyer fees, and then she could start thinking about splurging. But not yet.

"I'm good. I'll just grab something at home."

She felt his eyes on her. "Really? You're going to send me to eat somewhere alone? I didn't think you were that mean."

He didn't fool her for a second. "Yep. I'm known world over for my cruelty."

"Annie." She felt his hand on hers for a moment, a gentle squeeze before letting go. A show of friendship that cracked something inside her.

Yes, she had to eat. But moreover, she didn't want to be alone right now.

"Pizza," she finally said. "The place down on Samuels, if that's okay. That's close to where I parked."

She didn't turn from the window, afraid she'd give into the temptation to get lost in those eyes again. To touch him. To ask him—just this once—if he would hold her for a second. Maybe if she were pressed against his heart, she wouldn't hear Kimmy's cries. Her chest kept tightening.

"She's alive, you know," he said a few moments later, like he could read her thoughts. "That's the most important thing. I know that doesn't eradicate what happened to her, but she's got the chance to fight now."

He was right. Tomorrow was going to be a rough day for Kimmy, but at least she would have one. "Did you find anything that will help catch who did this?"

"Looks like he was waiting for her. That probably eliminates a stranger and so, yeah, that will help Landon a lot."

"I want them to catch this guy and put him *under* the jail."

He reached over and squeezed her hands again, letting

them go before she could figure out what to say or do. "I know you do, sweetheart. And they will."

They pulled up at New Brother's, one of the two local pizza joints in Oak Creek, just a couple blocks from the hospital. Hospital staff often chose it over the cafeteria.

She'd barely gotten her door open before Zac was at her side, opening it the rest of the way for her. She was still in her scrubs, but probably wouldn't be the only person here in them.

As they walked inside and were seated in a booth near the rear, Zac's hand stayed at her back the entire time.

"Still like pepperoni and black olives?" he asked when the waitress came to take their order.

She couldn't hide her surprise as she nodded.

"What? We ate them all the damn time in high school."

She was still smiling when she excused herself to go to the bathroom. One glance in the mirror had the smile disappearing. She looked exactly like she felt: as if she'd been run over by a dump truck that had then stopped and poured a pile of bricks over her. She redid her braid, but that was all she could do. She didn't have any makeup. She wouldn't really know what to do with it even if she did.

She slid back into the booth across from him and gratefully sipped her iced tea, which was unsweetened, never sweet like they had in Tampa. When the pizza arrived a few minutes later, she leapt for it.

She'd scarfed down nearly an entire slice—she wouldn't have any feeling in the roof of her mouth for days—before she realized he was staring at her, smiling.

"I'm sorry," she said, mouth still half full. Geez, could she be any more socially awkward? "I was hungrier than I thought."

"And you've always loved pizza. You and Becky both. I

remember how she always tried to talk her mom into coming here for dinner as much as possible. On all our dates too." He flinched and looked down at the table. "I'm sorry."

"For bringing up Becky?" Anne couldn't help it; she reached across the table to touch his hand. She kept her grip loose, friendly, fighting the urge to run her fingers along his skin. "You never have to apologize for talking about her or Micah. I know how important they were to you. I loved them too."

He gave a brief nod. "I know. She loved you as well."

She let go of his hand and slid it back to her plate. "Boggles the mind, doesn't it? That she and I could be such good friends? We were so different. I never really understood it." She took another bite of pizza.

"I did. At least from her point of view."

"You did?"

He set his slice down. "You had a focus and determination Becky always admired. You had nothing really going in your favor at home—no encouragement, no support—but you refused to let that stop you. She never had one second of doubt that you would become a doctor, and she admired you for it. You were what she could never be."

That was the most backward thing she'd ever heard. "Are you kidding? She was what *I* could never be. Beautiful, outgoing, charming."

"And never able to finish anything she started, often loud, and always opinionated." Zac laughed. "I should know, I was on the brunt end of those features quite often."

She chuckled. "God, she was loud, wasn't she? She had no idea what an *inside voice* was."

Grinning, they both went back to their pizza. Their love for Becky would always be what bound them together, not pushed them apart.

"You already look better," he said as he took another bite of his slice.

"I feel better. Thanks for making me stop. I learned quite a few years ago that working a really long shift and then crashing before I got any food in my system made for a pretty ugly next day. Today I just couldn't bring myself to care, but I would've paid for it later."

"I had some similar situations in the Army. When everything is over, sometimes it's a battle for which biological need is strongest: sleep or food. It's actually one of the things we go over in our survival training course at Linear."

She raised an eyebrow. "So, it's not all guns and knives? Blowing stuff up?" She'd looked up Linear Tactical online.

He grinned. "There's a lot of that, of course. But not everything."

"How'd you end up starting the company?"

He shrugged as she kept eating. "Mostly it was Finn, Aiden, and me. Finn found out that he had a son who was in foster care, so he got out of the Army and moved back here before I did. Aiden and I got out a couple years later, neither of us really knowing what we wanted to do in civilian life. Then we have some other partners too. Guys you haven't met...Gavin, Dorian, Wyatt."

"And Linear ended up being that? What *do* you do, exactly?"

"A lot of what we did in the Army but teaching it to others. Wilderness survival. Self-defense. Hand-to-hand combat. Concealed-weapon training. Marksmanship. Situational awareness. Basically, anything you need to know to protect yourself or others. People travel from all over the country to train with us."

She put her slice of pizza down. "Wow. I had no idea."

He shrugged. "We grew so much we had to bring in

other ex-military friends. So, five of us work full-time here, then another half dozen part- to full-time."

"You have enough work to keep that many people employed?"

"More than. We have law enforcement teams that train in our facilities—particularly our indoor weapons training center. It's considered one of the top in the country. We have a silent financial partner who helped get us off the ground, allowed us to expand much more quickly than we would've been able to otherwise. He wasn't in the Army and doesn't do any of the training, but he still comes around once in a while. Cade O'Conner."

"Wasn't he in middle school when we graduated? He had the sort of capital needed to help you start Linear Tactical?"

"Most of the world knows him now as Cade Conner, country music superstar."

She finished her last bite. "Oh. I guess I'm a little out of the loop when it comes to music. I had no idea Cade was famous."

"He would love to know that. He comes here to get away from all the craziness of his public life and just be with people who knew he was a pain. Loves to do deep-survivalist training in the woods for a few days when he can. Usually keeps his location here a secret."

"Wow. I remember him and Finn's little brother always following you guys around in school. Weren't they in, like, fourth grade when you caught them trying to ride your ATV?"

He chuckled. "Yep. Cade and Baby. Those two brats dogged our every step. Baby still works in town. He's a mechanic."

"I haven't thought about them in years."

"Baby works for us now and then. Thankfully, those guys are finally grown-up. I can still remember Baby and Cade hunting me down when I was a senior, wanting more info about sex."

She couldn't help but smile at Zac's embarrassed grin. She loved hearing about these people, this town. She'd forgotten—or had totally repressed—how much she'd loved it. She'd never been as popular as Zac or Becky, but Anne had always known these people, studied them, liked them.

And she liked being here with Zac now. Maybe staying away from him wasn't necessary. She could keep her feelings in check. She didn't need to throw herself at him.

They could just be friends. Obviously, as far as he knew, since he'd forgotten that night, that was all they'd ever been. Was all they'd ever be.

He bit into another slice. "So, there I was, these two kids looking at me like I was some sex god or something, able to provide some surefire way to get a girl naked. I don't know what they were thinking, asking me. Hell, I'd only ever been with Becky, and at that point not even for very long. Becky and I took each other's V card. Taking one person's virginity was traumatic enough. Thank God I've never had to go through that again. Would probably scar me for..."

She could feel the color leeching out of her face as he trailed off. She tried to regain her composure, knowing his words didn't mean anything. He didn't remember. He was just telling a funny story. But he was staring at her, eyes narrowed, like he could feel the memory of what had happened that night pressing against his brain.

She had to get out of here. She'd been so wrong. She couldn't be his friend. Couldn't be around him. Couldn't bear if he found out the truth now.

"I have to go."

"Sweet Annie..."

"No, don't call me that." Her voice was low. Guttural. When she dreamed of him at night, it was with the memory of him whispering her name in her ear as he kissed along her jaw: *My sweet Annie.*

He reached across the table and grabbed her hand to stop her from sliding out of the booth, concern clear in his eyes. "There's something wrong. I know I did something that night. Tell me what it is, Annie. Did I..." He swallowed hard, agony etched on his features. "Did I rape you?"

God, no matter what had happened that night, how he'd crushed her, she couldn't let him think that. She forced air into her lungs. "No. What we did that night, I wanted just as much." And evidently much more. "You would never do that, Zac."

Relief blanketed his features, but he didn't let go of her hand. "But there's something more. Something you're not telling me."

"We agreed to let this go, remember? It was a long time ago. It doesn't affect us now."

But it did. It had changed the course of her life, and as much as she didn't want it to, it was still affecting her. Everything about Zac was always going to.

"I've got to go," she said again. "I need to get some rest before my next shift. Thank you for dinner."

"I want you to tell me what happened." His voice was low, urgent. "I can't make it right if I don't know."

He couldn't make it right, either way. It was six years too late. "Some things can't ever be fixed. And there's no point in trying."

She slid her hand out from under his and walked out the door.

# CHAPTER 9

EXHAUSTION WEIGHED on Anne as she drove home. At least Zac hadn't come after her, although she'd half expected him to.

She didn't know how long it would take before she would really embrace that Zac wasn't *ever* going to, not in the way she'd wanted all her life. Yes, they'd had sex—sort of —but only once and obviously only after he'd been so drunk he was afraid he'd *raped* her for God's sake.

She would have to tell him what happened. Not the real truth—because how pathetic was that?—but a version of it.

Once she told him, assured him no force had been involved, he would move on. He'd be able to let go of this fear he had and get back to thinking of her just as Becky's quiet and rather pitiful friend, a shadow of the feisty woman he'd married, the woman who had held his interest from the time they were both twelve.

If he even thought of Anne much at all.

She pulled up under the portico at her house, wishing Carol were here to talk to. Obviously, Anne couldn't have said anything about her feelings for Zac, but Carol had always listened to her, encouraging her to date. Anne hadn't had the time or inclination in med school. Then, after what had happened with Zac, for a couple years during her residency, she hadn't even been able to bear the thought of someone touching her.

When she'd finally gotten back on the dating horse, she'd said yes to the first medical resident in her program who'd asked.

When Darren had asked her to marry him six months later, she'd said yes to that too. It had seemed like the best option at the time. At least she wouldn't be alone.

Note to self: getting married because it was the "best option" was never a good plan in the long run. She'd realized she'd made a mistake early on but had tried to make it work. That hadn't been enough once Christina had caught his eye. Honestly, it hadn't been enough long before that.

When Darren had asked for a divorce almost exactly two years after he'd first asked Anne out, she hadn't said no to that either.

She rested her head against the steering wheel. It was difficult not to think of herself as completely weak when she looked back on her choices. A fighter she was not.

Not a lover either, considering she'd only been with two men, and neither experience had turned out well. Her husband had grown tired of her after only a few months. Which was better than Zac; he'd decided she wasn't what he'd wanted after only a few *thrusts*.

So, yeah. Not a lover. Not a fighter. Just tired.

Things wouldn't seem so bleak after she got some rest. It all would be more manageable tomorrow. It always was. One thing about being an emergency room physician—it made you thankful for life, because you were so aware that it was tenuous at best.

Tomorrow.

She grabbed her bag out of the passenger side and made her way to the door connected to the portico. Balancing everything in one hand, she got the door unlocked and opened, throwing her bags on top of the washing machine in the small space that doubled as a mudroom. But when she slapped her hand against the light switch, nothing happened.

"Great."

Nothing again as she hit the one in the living room. She went back to get her phone to use as a flashlight. Where was the fuse box? Maybe in that closet near the kitchen?

Halfway there, she felt it under her tennis shoes—the squish of water. Her breath hissed out. Why was there water in the middle of her living room?

Her steps dragged as she entered the kitchen area, the water becoming more pronounced. Soon, she heard the steady flow leaking from the cabinet under the kitchen sink. She pulled it open and shined the light in.

Water poured out.

It was everywhere.

With the flashlight, she couldn't see the damage, but it had to be extensive if her feet were already squishing in it.

She found her way to the fuse box and opened it. She systematically started moving each switch one at a time, but nothing brought the lights on.

"Seriously?" she whispered. "Not even one break?"

Rubbing the muscles at the back of her neck, she leaned her head against the wall. She didn't want to close her eyes because she might just fall asleep right there standing up. She splashed over to her small kitchen table, wincing as water sloshed around the chair she pulled out, and sat down, blinking back tears.

Using the pitiful Internet she could get on her not-quite-smartphone, she looked up how to turn off the water at a house. A couple minutes later, she was up and searching for the main shutoff valve outside, Carol's wrench from the toolbox in the laundry room in hand.

If holding the wrench wasn't taking so much of her strength, she would've done a little dance when she found the valve. She breathed a sigh of relief when the house didn't blow up as she turned the water off.

The way her day had gone it would've been par for the course. She trudged back to the laundry room shivering, even though the brisk May night wasn't very cold by Wyoming standards. Maybe it was having lived in Florida for so long, where it rarely got below sixty degrees, but by the time she was back in the house, the shivers had turned to shudders. Muscles throughout her whole body began clenching, and her fingers began to tingle.

She leaned heavily against the door. Crap, she was having a panic attack. A physiological response caused by extreme anxiety mixed with exhaustion. Diagnosing it was easy, stopping it much more difficult. She slid over, gripped the washing machine, and grit her teeth, trying to get her body to obey her command to just *stop* its violent shaking.

She needed a hot shower and to go to sleep with extra blankets on her bed.

And she'd used the few she had to help wrap stuff for packing, then tossed them on the floor as she'd unwrapped items. So, they were currently acting as towels for the floodwater.

Her teeth began to chatter, and she squeezed her eyes shut against the tears that wanted to fall. If she let them out now, she wouldn't be able to stop. She was going to have a breakdown right here on her laundry room floor.

She grabbed her purse and duffel from the washing machine and went back out to her car. She didn't have a credit card since she'd cut them up to get out of debt, but Mayor Dimont knew her and would let her pay cash at the hotel. Anne had enough for tonight.

Tomorrow, she'd be able to deal with this.

She hoped.

The drive into town didn't take long. The Mayor's Inn was one of two hotels in town, the other a chain that had popped up since Anne had moved away.

Her car shuddered and popped softly—yet another thing she needed to deal with—as she pulled into one of the multiple open spots and stared up at the sign for The Mayor's Inn.

She knew Barbara Dimont and her now-deceased husband had bought the hotel before the woman had become mayor of Oak Creek. Had the hotel's name given her the idea? Townsfolk joked that the country would have a different president now if the hotel had been named The President's Inn instead.

As a teenager, Anne had worked here at the hotel, done everything from cleaning rooms to checking people in. Mayor Dimont had always allowed Anne's schedule to be flexible and been patient with her, making it the perfect job.

But now, walking into the lobby was hard. Anne hadn't been here since *that* night six years ago. Hadn't ever planned to come here again.

But she didn't have any choice, so she kept going, relieved to see her old boss sitting in her recliner behind the check-in counter, laughing at whatever television show she was watching.

"Hey, Mayor."

The television clicked off and Barbara stood. "Anne Nichols. Well, aren't you just a beautiful sight?"

Before Anne knew what was happening, the small, older woman had flipped the counter divider up and walked through, pulling Anne into her arms. "I'd heard you were back in town, of course. But seeing you with my own eyes after all these years..." Barbara reached up and cupped Anne's cheeks. "I'm so happy you're here."

"At your hotel or in Oak Creek? And it's Griffin now. I got married. And divorced."

"Both." She tapped Anne's cheeks. "And sorry about both of the other. You're looking a little tired. Everything okay? You here to visit your old boss?"

"No ma'am, although it is good to see you. There's some flooding in my house and I just need a place to stay for the night until I can find the mental gumption to deal with it tomorrow."

"Of course, sweetie. We've got plenty of rooms open."

"I don't have a credit card, Mayor." Anne could feel the chill returning. She clamped down on the need to shiver. Hopefully Mayor Dimont wouldn't ask too many questions and assume she'd left it at home.

"I know you're not going to insult me by trying to pay for a room when you're in need. Not after all the years you worked here, and everything you and I have been through together." She tucked a strand of silver hair behind her ear, eyebrow raised, her other hand on her hip.

This woman had seen Anne at the absolute lowest point in her life. It made accepting her offer easier. She nodded. "Thanks, Mayor. It's been a hard day. And money is a little tight."

Mayor Dimont patted her arm. "You and I will catch up

some other time. Right now, let's just get you a bed to fall into." She handed her a key to room 201. A real live key, rather than a card like most hotels used. It felt good in Anne's hand. Tangible. "You get yourself a nice hot shower to get rid of that chill and a good night's sleep. Ain't nothing going to hurt you here. Not this time. I promise."

Their eyes met, a river of memories flowing between them. "Thanks, Mayor."

She patted Anne's cheek again. "I'm glad you're back, Annie. This is where you belong."

As she took the key and headed down the hallway, Anne wished she could feel so sure.

# CHAPTER 10

ZAC WATCHED Annie all but run out of New Brother's. He cursed, indecision—a very unfamiliar feeling—blanketing him. He wanted to go after her, to find out what she still wasn't telling him. But she obviously didn't want him to know.

He believed her when she said he hadn't forced himself on her. Thank God. But he knew there was more. There was *so much more* to that night than she was telling him.

He needed to know.

He waited impatiently for the overworked waitress to finally bring him the check and box the leftovers, then, after paying, went to his truck. He sat there for a long minute.

He hadn't attacked Annie that night. Thank Jesus. She'd wanted it, too. He remembered that much and was thankful that part of his memory was correct. He remembered that everything had been good...right up until it had turned bad. Something he'd done had put shadows, fear, into her eyes. Not a physical attack, but...it was bad.

Discovering what that was and how to fix it—despite

her insistence it wasn't necessary—was the only thing he cared about right now.

He drove back toward Linear Tactical, the place that had brought him so much peace and purpose over the last four years, forcing himself to let it go. At least for tonight. He would talk to Annie when she wasn't so tired. The situation had been unresolved for six years. It could wait one more night.

He was all the way to his place on the opposite end of town before he spun the truck around and headed back.

No, this couldn't wait. He couldn't stand the thought of Annie going to sleep one more night carrying the knowledge that he'd done something horrible to her while he had no recollection of it. Of her carrying all the weight. Almost everyone had always treated Annie like she was invisible—her parents, the kids at school. Hell, even the people she worked with at the hospital hadn't recognized her.

He wasn't going to add himself to that list. He owed Annie an apology for something, and he wanted to make that right for her. *Tonight.* If someone else had hurt Annie, Zac would have beaten them into the ground until they apologized. She deserved to have someone as her champion, even if he was fighting himself.

It took him a long while to get to her house. She was probably already asleep. If she wasn't, he'd start by offering her the leftover pizza she loved so much. See if that would at least get him in the door. And if she was asleep, fine. He would damn well wait in the truck until morning. At the first sign she was up and about, he'd be knocking on her door.

Forget pizza, he'd get breakfast and bring it to her. Surprise her. It would be the first time he'd picked up breakfast for a woman without having spent the night in her bed, but it would be worth it.

Maybe there would be somewhere open that sold flowers. The twenty-four-hour grocery store might have some. If he was going to apologize, he might as well do it right.

As soon as she told him what he'd done. Obviously, he'd said something cruel. He'd just lost Becky, but that didn't change the need for an apology. One that Annie would never demand.

She really did need a champion. Becky and Mrs. P had realized that years ago and had done what they could for her. Becky would want Zac to do what he could, too. He'd always known that.

Disappointment swamped him when all the lights were out in her house as he pulled up. Yes, he wanted to get her breakfast and flowers, but more, to wipe away that look she got around him occasionally.

But it could wait until morning. Her needs would come first.

But as he pulled up, he realized her POS Mazda wasn't under the portico. Had she not come straight home? Had an emergency back at the hospital?

He was turning to leave when he saw the door from the portico leading into the house wasn't completely closed. He stopped and jumped out of his truck.

"Annie?" He knocked on the door, which swung open, no lights on in the house. "Annie, you're not in here, right?"

He reached over to turn on the light, frowning when nothing happened. He stepped further in.

"Annie?"

She wasn't here, but why weren't her lights working? He checked another switch. Nothing. He was already breaking and entering now; he might as well reset her fuse box, like he'd done a dozen times for Mrs. P over the years, so when Annie did finally get home it wouldn't be to a dark house.

He cursed a few seconds later as he realized the carpet was soaked in the living room and water was pooling in the kitchen. He jogged to his truck to get his industrial grade flashlight, then figured out the problem in just a few minutes. A pipe fitting under the kitchen sink had loosened and flooded the whole room. Water had somehow gotten into an electrical socket and blown power in the whole place, which happened sometimes in an old house with equally old wiring. When he saw the water had been turned off outside, he knew Annie had been there and dealt with it as best she could.

Damn it. She'd already been so tired and overwhelmed. Coming home and finding all her possessions soaked, with no way to dry them or fix this problem in the dark... If he'd been here, he could've helped her. Not much, but at least she wouldn't have had to face it alone.

The way she had faced everything else.

He scrubbed a hand over his eyes and went back out to his truck. Now that the water was stopped, nothing could be done until morning, when he could call a plumber and an electrician. He should go home. He could still bring breakfast in the morning, help her get this cleaned up.

But when he pulled out, he headed toward town—and The Mayor's Inn. Would she be there? The scene of the crime, so to speak? Hell, maybe being there would help him remember something.

Although this probably officially counted as stalking, following her from the restaurant to her house, and now maybe to the hotel.

But he still drove there. Just to see if she was there and make sure she was okay.

When he pulled up, there was her Mazda—and his confirmation that she'd found shelter for the night. He should leave. But he was parking and walking into the lobby before he could talk himself out of it.

He grimaced when he saw Mayor Dimont behind the counter. He'd known her a long time, but she didn't like him. She'd tried to use her influence with the city council to block the permits they needed to open Linear Tactical. Despite the fact that many of the guys were local, and Oak Creek had seemed to want them here, it had still been a close vote due to her opposition.

Zac had no idea why. He had no memories of her disliking him in high school. But she certainly did now. "Hi, Mayor Dimont."

Her gaze frosted over. "Mackay."

He held out a hand, palm up, in a gesture of peace. "I'm here to check on Annie. The door was open at her house, and there was some flooding. I know she's already had a bad day..."

The mayor's eyes narrowed. "So, you thought you'd pop in here and see if you could help her out in that smooth Mackay way of yours?"

He winced. "Well, I don't exactly know what that is, but yes, I was concerned about her. She and I had dinner, and she was already a little upset without finding her house resembling Atlantis."

His attempt at humor was completely lost on the mayor. "That girl is sweeter than Jesus if she lets you anywhere near her after what you did."

Zac took a step closer, gaze narrowing on the older woman. "What are you talking about?"

"That night, six years ago. I know Annie says you can't be held responsible because you were so torn up with grief over your wife and baby dying. I know that was tragic, but you'll have to excuse me if I'm just not quite as forgiving as she is."

She knew. His hands clenched into fists at his side. "But you know what happened?"

"I know enough. What you did to that girl is inexcusable, Mackay. You should be ashamed."

He wanted to rip his hair out. "Damn it, Mayor. I can't remember, but I know it's bad. Annie won't tell me. I want to fix this. To make it right. But she won't tell me."

"Sweet Annie is never one to accuse or make someone feel guilty. It's not her way. She thinks she's weak because she doesn't rant and rave like most do when someone wrongs them."

"No, she absorbs," he whispered. "Weathers. Survives. That takes more strength than all the ranting and screaming in the world. Just because she's quiet doesn't mean she's not strong."

The mayor's eyes narrowed further, her head tilting to the side. "You care about her."

He ran a hand through his hair. "I always have. Even when it wasn't okay for me to. I never acted on it—never did anything that would make me unfaithful to Becky—but I always cared."

"And you knew how Annie felt about you?"

He went completely still. "About *me*? Anne tolerated me because of her friendship with Becky—we were sort of a package deal. But that's all there ever was." *Right?* Something was itching at the corners of his mind from that night. "Anne always kept her distance from me. We were never alone together."

"Right up until you weren't married to her best friend anymore." Mayor Dimont leaned back against the counter. "Tell me what you remember."

"We sort of found each other that night at The Eagle's Nest; I'd already had too much to drink. My leave was over the next day, and I was going back to the Army. I couldn't stand to stay with Carol—too many memories in that house —so I'd gotten a room here." He closed his eyes, trying to focus his mind. "Henry at The Eagle's Nest, dumbass that he was, sold or maybe gave me the bottle of Jack. Annie and I decided to sit outside and drink it.

"We talked for hours. Hell, if I know about what. Everything. She'd finished med school and was in her first year of residency, basically working eighty hours a week. We talked about the Army, how I'd been stationed all over Europe and the Middle East. She said she'd never been out of Wyoming —how maybe one day she might like to travel, but never planned to leave here permanently."

Oh God. He remembered that clearly. How she'd never wanted to leave Oak Creek.

"But she did leave," Mayor Dimont said evenly.

Zac turned to the mayor, dread pooling in his stomach. "When?"

"She transferred to a medical program out of state immediately after Becky died." She didn't let him wallow. "Tell me what else you remember."

"She was helping me get to my room. She probably wasn't nearly as drunk as I was. I got her inside, and she was so beautiful. So willowy and tall. So serene and quiet, as always. But so *alive.* And I just wanted to taste her aliveness. That was wrong. I was using her. I kissed her."

But God, she had made the sexiest breathy noises. *That* he remembered as clear as day. He'd been drunk, and maybe she'd been too, but when he'd pulled her through the door and kissed her, it had been magic, hot, and mind-blowing.

"Once we were in the room..." He remembered easing himself away from where he'd pushed her up against the wall and ravished her mouth like his body had been waiting for years for the opportunity and now it *could*. "We talked for a while again. She wouldn't let me drink anymore. She helped me get into bed and was going to leave. Kissed me so tenderly."

*"Don't leave me, sweet Annie. I need you."*

*That smile. God, she was gorgeous. "You need sleep."*

*"I need* you. *Stay with me."*

*"Zac. I shouldn't—"*

*Even close to stupid drunk, he had honed reflexes. He grabbed her by the wrist and pulled her to him, wrapping an arm around her and tucking and rolling to his side with her half under him. He kissed her again. He had to hear that noise she made in her throat. It was so damn sexy.*

*His fingers trailed up from her hip, under her shirt to the soft, soft skin of her belly. His tongue dipped into her mouth, inviting her shy one out to play, smiling when it did, when her tongue began to duel sweetly with his.*

*His hand slipped over her breast, thumb strumming that perked nipple, and she gasped, then moaned.*

*"That's right, sweetness," he said against her mouth. "Give yourself to me."*

*He pulled back, so he could look her in the eyes. Those big chocolate eyes that had always drawn him.*

*"Yes," she whispered.*

*That was all it took. Within just a few minutes their clothes were lying on the floor, his head becoming dizzier as he kissed up and down her body.*

*She moaned again. Deep, husky, and soft. Her hands resting tentatively on his shoulders.*

That's when the problem started. Right now, standing dazed in the Mayor's lobby, he recognized it so clearly for what it was. But at the time he hadn't seen it. Too drunk. Too grieving. Too stupid. He wanted to yell at his past self to just move away from her now.

*Annie was different than Becky. Bec had always been so direct, secure, and loud. Nothing tentative about her. With every minute that passed with Annie, all he could do was count the differences between the two women. Realize that he'd only ever been with Becky and he was never going to be with her again.*

*What was he doing?*

*Annie moaned once more, her arms wrapping around his neck. "I want you, Zac. I always have."*

*What? He couldn't be hearing right. His head was spinning again. "Annie, maybe we should..." His words trailed off when one of her long, lithe legs wrapped around his hips, bringing their naked bodies closer together. Now it was him who moaned.*

*"Yes, you're right," she whispered. "We should. I never thought it would be you who..." Now her words trailed off as she tucked her face against his neck. Her fingers trailed down his waist, then beyond, digging into his hips, urging him closer.*

*So, he went. He ignored the voices in his head screaming for him to stop, and listened to his dick instead, thrusting hard into her core.*

*With her cry of pain, his world froze. Everything did. Was she a virgin?*

*"Annie? What the f—"*

*"It's okay. I'm okay. I just... I didn't..." She wiped a tear*

*from her face. "I'm glad it was you, Zac. I wanted you to be my first. I've always loved you."*

*And in that second everything changed. What was he doing? Becky had been dead less than two weeks, and he was already fucking some other woman?*

*He slid out of her and to the side. No, not some woman,* Annie.

*His wife's best friend. Even worse of a betrayal. And she was spurting words of love like they hadn't just committed the most atrocious of betrayals.*

*"Zac, I..." She reached out to him, big brown eyes staring.*

*"Don't touch me." The words ripped out of him as he flung himself off the bed, landing in a crouch like he was warding off an attacker. He couldn't stand to look at Annie in the bed. Couldn't stand the thought of her. Of himself. Of what he'd done. "You just betrayed Becky. Betrayed the only person in this town who ever wanted you here."*

*"Zac, I'm sorry. I didn't mean to—"*

*He couldn't stop staring at the blood on her thighs. "You were a virgin? Why would you do this to me?"*

*Damn, that wasn't what he meant. He just meant why would she give her virginity to him, of all people? But she was answering before he could correct himself.*

*"I just...I wanted you. I thought you wanted me too."*

*He had. Oh God, not only tonight, but for years. He shook his head. "I can't believe you'd do this to her."*

*He rubbed both hands against his eyes. No, he couldn't believe* he'd *done this to Becky.*

*He had to get out. Had to get out and not come back. No, this was his room. Annie had to go. "Just get out. Get out and don't come back."*

*"Zac..."*

*He had to get her out. He grabbed her arm and dragged*

*her out of the bed and over to the door, opening it. She was crying now. He'd made her cry. He was such an asshole. God, the room was spinning.*

*"Please," she whispered. "My clothes." He grabbed her dress off the floor and threw it at her where she stood naked out in the hallway.*

*God, she was crying. She had to go away before he brought her back in and made this worse. "I can't even look at you." If he did, he'd bring her back and make love to her over and over. And in the morning, they'd both hate themselves even more. They'd never be able to come back. He shook his head. "Don't come back. Ever."*

*Her big eyes stared at him, clutching her dress to her torso. He closed the door and stumbled back into the room, the world swaying all around him before he crashed toward the small desk, hitting his head. Blackness.*

He held his head now, could still remember the huge bruise he'd had on his temple the next morning.

"Oh Jesus, Mayor." He felt like he was going to be sick.

Mayor Dimont opened the counter and brought him through, leading him to a chair. "Sit before you fall down, Mackay."

"What I did..." There were no words. "You're right. She should never talk to me again."

"I only caught the tail end of it. Happened to be coming by the hallway and was very surprised to see a naked Annie until her dress flew out the door at her. Heard some harsh words."

What he'd said went way beyond harsh words. "She left Oak Creek because of me. What I said. What I did."

"But now she's back. And you remember what happened that night. So, I guess the real question is...what are you going to do about it, Mackay?"

# CHAPTER 11

"FINALLY GOING HOME?" Riley caught Anne in the hall as she shut her office door behind her. "How long have you been here? I've already started and ended a twelve-hour shift and you've been here the whole time."

"Yeah, they needed me, so I picked up an extra shift." Mostly because until her new contract was finalized, she got paid for any extras she picked up. And because she was too much of a coward to go home and face the damage the flooding had caused. "Some pipe broke in my house so now I have that fun to look forward to. I've been looking up fix-it-yourself videos during my free time."

She'd already showered and changed in the locker room since she didn't have any power and water at her house. She'd have to live without it for a couple days, which was totally doable— though not optimal—since it wasn't too cold. But hopefully she'd be able to clean up as much as possible and maybe figure out the problem without bringing in an expensive plumber or electrician.

"Yeah, I heard about the water damage at your house."

That had to be Mayor Dimont. Anne rolled her eyes. "I'd forgotten about small-town life. But I would've thought a broken pipe wouldn't have been worth the talk." Unless rumors were starting to fly about why Anne hadn't called for the proper people to fix it, that she didn't have the money. Ugh. She just needed to get the place livable.

Riley tilted her head and studied her. "No, a broken pipe isn't in terms of rumors."

The young nurse opened her mouth, then shut it again, so Anne just kept walking. She needed to get home while it was still light outside. She'd been working since five AM, but at least she wasn't about to have an emotional break-down like yesterday. She'd been afraid that sleeping at The Mayor's Inn would bring back all the nightmares of the past, but evidently her psyche had had enough, because after a shower, Anne had fallen into a deep sleep.

They passed Mia at the nurses' station, the other woman's eyes flinging poison-tipped, lit-on-fire daggers at Anne before turning away completely.

"Wow, what did I do now?" Anne murmured. Maybe word was also getting out that she'd had dinner with Zac last night.

"I don't think it's anything you did," Riley responded. "Ignore her. We all do."

That wouldn't be a problem. Anne had real battles; cosmetic ones weren't worth her energy.

She waved good-bye to Riley as they split in the parking lot, then said her normal prayer when starting her car. It didn't turn over with the first crank, but that wasn't anything unusual. Second crank, again nothing.

She rubbed her hands on the steering wheel. "C'mon, baby. Not this week." Preferably not any time in the next year, considering the financial and literal mess that waited for her at home. But she definitely didn't want her car to quit today.

On the third crank, she started. "Good girl. Thanks, baby." She kissed the steering wheel.

Driving home, she tried to remember everything she'd learned in the Plumbing 101 YouTube videos, as well as info on how to handle water damage. Her carpet and likely much of the floorboards underneath were probably destroyed. Replacing them was going to cost a big chunk of money. It would've been better to have done more when she'd first discovered the damage, she'd realized after her research, but she had to respect that she'd been at the end of her physical reserves.

She wasn't sure she was much better than that now, but she would get it done. When continuing was your only option, you found a way.

She knew something was very wrong when she arrived at her house and noticed two trucks and a car parked out front. What in the world?

Her front door and the side one attached to the portico were both open. She could hear men talking inside as she approached, laughing and cursing good-naturedly at one another. Her duffel bag fell to the ground as she took in the sight in front of her.

All her boxes and furniture had been moved to the side not affected by the water. Clothes, towels, and blankets that had been sopping wet last night were now hanging on the clothesline in her backyard. Boxes that had been soaked until all that was left were messy pieces were now in a pile on a tarp by her door.

There were half a dozen big, ridiculously handsome guys, all working around her house, casually throwing insults at each other as easily as they did hammers.

And they all looked to be from Linear Tactical. Some she recognized. Finn was working in her living room, some adorable boy about six or seven years old at his side swinging a hammer in imitation. Aiden and Baby, Finn's *little* brother—although he was an inch or two taller and just as wide as Finn—were also helping.

She didn't know much about repair, but they were all busy doing things that would've taken her hours alone, mostly demolition, and sorting through what could be safely dried and saved.

Two other guys she didn't know were discussing something in the kitchen, and someone else had their head stuck under the sink with plumbing parts all around him.

Over to the side, an iPod with speakers was crooning something about being drunk on an airplane. Anne was neither drunk nor on an airplane, but she certainly understood the sentiment as she stepped farther inside.

Everyone stopped talking and joking. The music cut off. One of the unknown guys in the kitchen reached over and nudged the sexy jean-covered ass hanging out from under her sink with his foot.

"Zac," he said.

Of course, the sexy ass was Zac.

"Hey, Annie." From the living room, Finn grinned and gave her a little salute, standing and sliding his hammer into his tool belt, then wiping his brow. The boy next to him followed his motions exactly.

"Um, I-I-I..." The eyes on her triggered her stutter. She swallowed and started again. "I'm not sure exactly what's happening here."

Zac finally worked the rest of his sexy body out from under the sink. "Hey, Annie," he echoed. "Let's go outside and talk. It's too loud in here."

With that remark the hammers and talking immediately resumed, making it, indeed, too loud to talk inside her house.

She was still trying to process everything that was happening—were they putting down hardwood floors in the part of her house that hadn't flooded?—when Zac stopped right in front of her. She had to lean to the side to see around him.

"What are they—?"

He touched her elbow, the contact soft, almost tentative. "Come outside with me and I'll explain, okay?"

She could only nod as she turned, his hand sliding to the center of her back as they walked out to her car. He didn't stop touching her until she sat on the edge of her hood. She didn't look at him, just kept studying the house.

"I need to apologize."

Now she dragged her eyes away from the house. "You do?"

"The guys and I promised Carol we would help with her plumbing issues about a year ago. We kept meaning to do it, but then she got sick and had more pressing needs, and plumbing didn't seem important. So, we never got to it."

"Oh."

She wanted to roll her eyes at her response. She had two degrees and six years of medical training and that was the best she could come up with?

Her thoughts scattered further as Zac leaned on the car next to her, his leg almost touching hers. "I came to give you some leftover pizza from last night. Your side door was open. When I walked in to make sure everything was all right, I noticed the flooding and loss of power. And it hit me. I allowed this to happen by not taking care of it back when Carol first asked."

"But—"

"The guys all felt the same. And since we didn't have anything going on at Linear today, they came in and helped. With the six of us, and of course little Ethan, stuff isn't taking long. In a couple days when everything dries, we'll be able to finish installing the new flooring. It's a laminate—a fake hardwood—but it looks nice, and I think you'll like it."

"Oh, but—"

"Yeah, Carol picked it out and paid for it, so I hope it's okay. It's just been sitting in storage at the office. Tearing out her floors when she was so sick would've been too disruptive."

What exactly was she supposed to do with this info? Complaining about what they'd done would just be churlish and ungrateful of her. "Oh."

Again with that? Geez. "Of course," she added quickly.

He pushed off the car to stand in front of her. "But I should've asked. I wanted to do something nice for you. Call it a welcome-home-I'm-glad-you're-here gift."

How the hell was he making six foot two and two hundred pounds of pure muscle seem so boyish and charming? His tight black T-shirt clung to his biceps and trim waist. Those blue eyes peered at her not with their normal icy efficiency, but with soft hesitation. As if he expected her to fly off the handle and yell at him for this.

Which maybe she should. Because he'd broken into her house, sort of. But...this was, without fail, the kindest thing anyone had ever done for her.

"You'll have to tell me how much I owe for the labor and supplies." Somehow, she'd pay him what she owed, even if something else had wait.

"Nothing."

She couldn't get her eyebrow up any higher. He

grinned, that little dimple in his chin deepening. "I promise, everything was already paid for. And the guys wouldn't hear of taking your money. They'd wanted to do this for Carol. And Carol would have wanted you to have the flooring she bought. The plumbing issue wasn't a big deal. I got it fixed, and we can turn your water back on soon. The pipe fitting that busted just happened to do it at the wrong time, probably right after you went to work. Then you pulled a double and went out to help Kimmy, so it had plenty of time to leak water everywhere."

Another song came on, the guys singing off-tune with Tom Petty. "And the electricity?"

"I'll admit, the thought of electrocuting myself had me keeping away from that. But I had a buddy who was able to stop by on his lunch break. He said his fix wasn't permanent —the wiring in this house is pretty old—but it should hold you for a year or two."

"That had to have cost money. I can pay you—" His arms reaching on either side of her, trapping her between his body and the car, stopped her words.

"No, Annie." All she could see were his eyes. She wanted to look away, she really did, but couldn't. His gaze trapped her. Pinned her. "You won't pay me anything. I wanted to do this. My gift."

"Why?" She didn't recognize the breathy voice coming out of her own body.

His lips touched hers in the lightest, sweetest of kisses. Once. Twice. A third time. "Because some things can't ever be fixed. But you damn well try anyway."

# CHAPTER 12

ON THE WAY to a crime scene was not how Zac wanted to spend time with Annie, but he would take it.

They'd actually seen each other a lot over the past month since he'd brought the gang in to fix water damage in her house. Everything he'd said that day had been the truth. The team had told Carol they'd be happy to put down the floor for her. And it had been sitting in the storage section of the barn for months. Hell, it was even true that it was a welcome-back-to-town gift.

So, he hadn't lied, but he hadn't told her the whole truth either—that he remembered now what had happened between them that night. That he would do whatever he could to help make the rest of her transition here as easy as possible. Like he'd said when he'd kissed her, some things couldn't be fixed, but that didn't mean you didn't try.

And he definitely hadn't told her that he'd run a basic search on her. Hell, he wasn't proud of it, but he refused to make any more missteps when it came to Annie and what she might need. And because of the work they did at Linear, they ran them—they weren't quite a background check, but all public info available about a person—often.

She'd been divorced for two years and had declared Chapter 11 bankruptcy fourteen months ago. Unless she had developed some sort of shopping addiction while she had been married, it looked like she'd been left with a lot of debt. Some of it was from when her parents had died, a lot from the divorce. None had been lessened by her decision to move out of state in the middle of her medical residency, a decision that had been directly linked to what had happened between them that night.

*Just get out. Get out and don't come back.*

Jesus. He hadn't meant out of the state, just out of the room before they made a huge—*huger*—mistake. But how could she have known that? He couldn't blame her for the way she'd taken it. He couldn't blame her for anything about that night.

Her public record showed that she'd ponied up with her creditors and had tried to make individual deals that would keep everyone happy and her from declaring complete bankruptcy. Zac had nothing but respect for that.

Nothing but respect for everything about Annie. Now all he could do was show her.

She'd had basically no money when she'd moved here. Every spare penny was going to creditors. So, he was thankful he'd been able to make the repairs at her house without it costing her anything.

He'd spent the past month doing as much as he could, anything to help her out without making it seem too obvious. And he'd roped everyone into the plan.

He'd checked with Riley to find out Annie's hospital schedule, then gone back to her house with Aiden and Finn three days later to install the floors and repair the drywall.

The day after that, they'd painted and moved all her furniture to its final destination. She'd protested, but they'd quickly explained they were doing it for the good of the town, to make sure the emergency room doctor didn't get injured. She'd reluctantly agreed and instructed them where to put each piece.

At Zac's request, Dorian had gone over a couple days later and asked if he could cut firewood, explaining the repetitive motion helped his PTSD. Annie hadn't refused, of course.

On Riley's day off, when Annie had been working an eighteen-hour shift, she had asked to borrow Annie's POS car, and Annie had quickly agreed. Riley had taken it over to Baby at the garage, who had fixed the worst of the offenders. At least now Annie wouldn't get stranded in the parking lot in the middle of the night because her car wouldn't start.

Hell, he'd even sent Finn over to repair the porch and screen door, bringing his secret weapon: Ethan. Nobody could resist Ethan with his tiny tool belt. He just wanted to hang out with his dad and hammer things. Annie hadn't been an exception.

Even though all of them had refused payment of any sort, willing to help a neighbor, they had teased Zac unmercifully over his actions and schemes.

And he couldn't care less.

History couldn't be altered. His little helpful team of fixer-uppers wasn't going to change the past. Everything Zac was orchestrating now couldn't possibly make up for what he'd done and said that night, but it was the only way he knew how to try.

So, what he did was out of guilt, to a degree. Because how could he not feel any for being the bastard who'd taken her virginity, and then in the next breath thrown her out on her ass?

But it was more than that. Taking care of Annie, even if it was through third parties, felt *right* to him. It had less to do with guilt and everything to do with wanting to be near her. To earn back the *possibility* of being near her.

He didn't want her beholden to him. He just wanted to hold her to him.

He rolled his eyes at the thought. Jeez, next he would be spouting sonnets. The guys weren't far off when they called him whipped.

But it was still how he felt.

Annie obviously had other thoughts, and none of them had to do with getting closer to Zac. She was always polite to him, friendly, like she was with everyone else. She'd baked cookies and pies for him and the guys to thank them and brought them over to the Linear office. And Zac had run into her around town a few times. But she was careful not to get too close, not to let them be alone. There hadn't been more soft kisses.

But he'd caught her staring at him a couple times when she hadn't known he could see her, passion flaring in her eyes. She wasn't immune to him. Wary—which he couldn't blame her for—but not immune.

So, yeah. If riding with her to and from a crime scene was the only way to spend time with her, Zac would take it.

But another goddamn rape. In Lincoln County again, but in the larger town of Kingston, rather than last month's in rural Hillsdale. Kingston wasn't as big as Reddington City or Oak Creek, but it was still a good-sized town with a population of over twenty thousand.

"I know Rogers appreciates you coming out and

providing your assistance," he said to her as she sat in the passenger seat.

It wasn't lost on him that Landon had specifically requested Annie. No doubt because she was an excellent physician and already had familiarity with the case. But that definitely wasn't the whole of it. And when Sheriff Nelson had mentioned it, Zac had made sure to be the one giving her the ride.

"I'm glad to help. But I wish it weren't needed. What will you be doing?"

"The same I did last time. Look around. See if there was anything that was missed."

"Would you mind if I came with you?"

Again, not the way he'd been hoping to spend time with her, but he would take what he could get. "Please do."

Zac waited in the clinic lobby as Annie went in to see the victim and talk to the nurse and female deputy from Lincoln County. He was still waiting there about thirty minutes later when Landon Rogers jogged through the door.

The men stared each other down. Not unfriendly, but not friendly either.

"Wasn't expecting to see you here today, Mackay. Your man, Dorian Lindstrom, is already seeing what can be tracked at the scene. Nelson sent him straight there."

Zac shook the man's outstretched hand. "Yes, and he is the very best when it comes to tracking. If there's any physical trail to be followed, Dorian will find it."

Landon nodded. "The attack occurred early this morning, just before sunrise. Veronica works at the veterinarian's office. Everyone there takes a turn coming in early and letting out the animals that stay overnight. It was Veronica's turn. She parked behind the building and was grabbed right before she went inside and dragged behind a storage shed they have out there."

"So, no malfunction of the car this time?"

"No. And no relation between the two victims—outside of living in this county—that we can find, although that certainly hasn't been exhausted yet. We're also expanding our search to other counties and even down into Colorado. This may be much bigger than we think."

"I wouldn't be surprised. Do you think the perp was watching her like he did last time?"

"I'm hoping your man will be able to give me more insight." Landon looked toward the door where Anne and the victim were. "I'll be honest, I didn't expect you to show up with Dr. Griffin."

"I thought I might have a little insight too, since I saw the last scene. Not trying to step on your toes. I want to help catch this bastard."

Landon tilted his head and raised an eyebrow. "Which Lincoln County appreciates. And, I'll assume, using my well-honed detective skills, you're also here to keep me from talking Anne into having dinner with me."

Zac barely managed not to grit his teeth. "Anne is free to date whoever she wants, of course." The thought of it brought the vilest of curses to his lips, but he didn't voice them. Damn it, Annie *was* free to. If she wanted someone with whom she had no history, Landon Rogers was an excellent choice.

But if there was any way Zac could talk her out of it, he was going to try.

"Okay, we're finished in there." Annie walked up to the two men, her stance between them an echo of what had happened a month ago. "The team did an excellent job with the rape kit. There's nothing I would've done differently, although, sadly, I don't think it's going to provide much help. Veronica wasn't able to claw him at all, so there wasn't much under her nails. The rapist used a condom again. Great for Veronica, not for DNA collection."

"Any similarities or differences you noticed that might provide any illumination into the case?" Landon asked.

Her lips were pinched, but she didn't look quite as emotionally battered as last month. "Veronica's physical wounds aren't as pronounced as Kimmy's. Definitely not as much craniofacial damage."

"So, he didn't hit her as much," Zac said.

"Exactly. I don't know why. Maybe someone or something spooked him, and he took off, or something about Kimmy made him desire to hurt her, but Veronica didn't elicit that same response. I have no idea. And don't get me wrong, it's still atrocious. But at least she won't have quite as much physical healing to do."

Landon reached over and touched her arm. "Thanks again for coming in, Dr. Griffin."

Annie's friendly smile to the other man was a punch in Zac's gut. "Anything I can do to help. Honestly. And please call me Anne. I'm going with Zac now to look at the crime scene before I go back to work. Maybe based on Veronica's injuries I can provide further understanding."

Zac swallowed a smile, her words effectively rejecting any advances Landon might make before he could even try. The sheriff's eyes met his briefly, and Zac knew the other man was feeling the same way.

"We'll keep you posted if there's anything worth reporting," Zac said.

"You do that. Thanks again for coming out." He touched his hat and smiled at Annie, who just blushed and looked down. How would Landon look with a couple teeth missing?

If Zac were a better man, he would give her space and let her decide what she wanted. *Who* she wanted. He'd give Landon a chance to take her out and show her that she had options if she wanted them, wouldn't put any sort of pressure on her to choose him over Landon.

As he put his hand on her back—a thrill zinging through him when she swayed closer rather than farther away—he had to face facts. He wasn't a better man.

# CHAPTER 13

THIS RAPE SCENE had a lot of similarities with the first. There were a number of places the perp could have sat and watched, waiting for Veronica to arrive, if he'd known she was coming. Also, the shed at the back of the office parking lot had provided cover, like the abandoned warehouse had last month.

But it was also different. Less isolated, so much more gutsy on the rapist's part.

"What are you thinking?" Annie asked him as they walked farther from the shed, which was still roped off, although the crime scene processing team had already left.

"Trying to put myself in this guy's shoes. Figure out where I would've waited."

She nodded. "Any place particularly stand out?"

He looked around again. "There are a number of places he could've waited, if that's what happened. There's always the possibility it wasn't the same guy, but I think it was."

"This area seems so busy. Like there would've been no

way Veronica could just be snatched out of the parking lot without anyone noticing."

He nodded, looking around more. "But it's lunchtime now, much busier. At five o'clock this morning, it would've been a lot quieter." He took her hand gently. "Want to walk through it with me? It will help us both understand the attacker a little better."

"O-okay."

They walked over to Veronica's car, careful not to touch it.

"She parked here, probably this same spot every day, or at least when she had the early shift. This is some of what the guys and I teach—and a big part of what we learned in our Special Forces training: situational and tactical awareness."

"I'm not sure I know what that means exactly."

"Just being aware of the potential threats around you. I do it automatically now, but we try to teach people how to develop situational awareness for themselves."

"Like what? Tell me what you see."

Zac closed his eyes and pictured the scene in his mind. "There are two cars parked in the front of the building, both empty. We're being watched from at least two different places. One to the east" —he held his arm out to the right— "but I would assume that's Dorian making his way back here after tracking the perp as far as he could. The other set of eyes is farther off to the south. To be honest, I'm not sure if that's a threat or not. After what happened here this morning, word has gotten out. People are curious. So, it's probably someone trying to figure out why we're here if we're not cops." He turned a little more. "The safety lamp over the door was broken recently."

He opened his eyes to find her staring him with wonder.

"Oh my gosh, that was amazing. How did you know someone is watching?"

"Sunlight reflected off what was probably binoculars farther up the block. Or it could be a rifle scope." Not uncommon in Wyoming.

"And the safety lamp? How did you know that was broken?"

He took her hand again and led her closer to the door. "Glass on the ground. Veronica parked out of habit, then took a few steps." They bent down, and he showed her a slightly deeper footprint in the gravel. "She stopped right here, probably realizing the light hadn't kicked on the way it normally did. And FYI, when we follow patterns like Veronica probably did, we make the bad guy's job easier."

They scooted over another couple feet and crouched near the ground. "She hurried, maybe a little freaked out, then stopped again here, perhaps when she heard glass crunch under her feet." The next step was decidedly more pronounced in the gravel. "See how deep that is? She was holding all her weight on one foot, probably to try to look at the other and see if there was glass on her shoe."

"She didn't want to track it in and hurt the animals."

He couldn't help his smile. She'd always been so damn smart. "I wouldn't be surprised."

Annie studied the ground. "And he grabbed her here."

She was right. "Yes, how do you know?"

"No more steps. He waited until she was distracted, off-balance, and grabbed or hit her."

"Yes, that's probably it exactly. Let me know if you decide you want a job at Linear."

They both stood. "I don't know what happened after that."

He pointed at the shed. "Crime scene tells us. I would

imagine that he stunned her with a crack to the jaw, then probably carried her to the shed since there are no marks of any kind."

"He had to be strong. Veronica's like me. Neither of us could ever be considered petite or helpless."

"Anyone can be stunned with the right initial blow. And take you. You're, what, five foot nine? But it wouldn't take much for me to subdue you. Especially if no one else was around. You really should come around to Linear. I could teach you a few moves that would help you out if you got in trouble."

Her smile was soft. "I'd like that. Thank you."

"It would be my pleasure." He turned a little to the side. "You can come out, Dorian. We're done walking through the scene."

Dorian moved his large frame silently around the shed. "I didn't want to interrupt." He tilted his head at her. "Ma'am."

"Hi. I had no idea you were there," she whispered.

Most people couldn't believe how quietly Dorian moved, considering his hulking size.

"You know you have eyes on you in the south about half a mile?" he asked softly. "Whoever it is has been watching since I got here."

"I spotted the glare a few minutes ago. Probably somebody curious as to what's going on. This sort of thing shakes up a small town."

Dorian grunted an affirmative, still looking in the direction of the eyes. "Whoever it is, they're using a scope."

Shit. "More than likely some overly concerned dad. Everybody's going to sleep with their rifles tonight." But he still didn't want Annie out here in the open. "You able to track anything?"

Dorian pointed to the building across the parking lot. "He was up there. I found another rock pile like you described from the other scene. He was waiting. Would've seen her pull up and had plenty of time to take out the light then and still make it her when she'd parked."

Annie was still looking around. Zac touched her back. "You ready to go? I know you need to get back to work."

She nodded.

"I'm going to walk south a mile or so and look around," Dorian said. If anyone could find who was watching through the scope, it would be him. Without another word, he was gone.

Annie filled the ride back to the hospital with questions, about the Army and what specific training they'd given him that allowed him to be aware of stuff most people never thought about their entire lives. He told her about missions in Afghanistan where situational awareness had always made the difference between life and death.

He didn't tell her how sometimes even the keenest instincts didn't keep you safe. About how a bullet had grazed him in the head in the Afghani mountains, and if it hadn't been for some of his Army brothers carrying him out, he wouldn't be here right now.

She wanted to know about the company and the types of classes they offered. What was the most popular? Who came for the different types? How did people keep their training fresh once they'd come to Linear?

God, he loved how her mind worked, how fast she processed information but still listened intently to everything he said.

"By practicing it as much as possible in their everyday life," he told her after answering all the others. "It doesn't do any good to take the training if they don't apply it."

She shook her head, taking it all in. "I'm never parking in the same spot ever again."

He caught himself one second before telling her that having a car that now operated properly would do a lot more for her safety than switching parking spots.

That would've raised a lot of questions.

"What's your favorite thing to teach?" Her question saved him.

"Actually, I enjoy a lot of different things. We all have our own specialties, but we're also pretty well-rounded. For example, I'm never going to be as good as Dorian at tracking or wilderness survival, but I still know a lot more about it than most people. I can do it and teach it. Same for him with hand-to-hand combat training. Dorian—God bless all six foot five of him—can teach it, but honestly, he intimidates the crap out of people."

She laughed softly, a beautiful sound. "I can see why."

"Plus, Dorian doesn't really like being that close to people. So, he doesn't do a lot of that sort of training, although he can. But to answer your question, I'm probably best at that and close-quarters fighting."

"Not only due to your training, but because you have accelerated reflexes and ridiculous spatial awareness." She said it factually, then grinned. "Does it frustrate you to have to slow down to teach it to mere mortals?"

He smiled back. "It used to, because obviously I'd rather have mortals fan me and feed me grapes."

There it was again—her soft laughter. God, he loved the sound of that.

"But the first time a guy came back a few weeks after taking my class and told me how what he'd learned had saved his life when two guys jumped him in a bar fight?

That's when I realized being able to teach others what I do is more important than just knowing it myself."

They arrived at the hospital, and he drove through the parking lot, hoping there wouldn't be a spot, not wanting her to leave yet. "Listen, why don't you come by Linear sometime? We can go over self-defense basics." And then he could talk her into going to dinner with him.

She gave him a friendly nod. "That's a good idea. I'll look up the schedule online and see when the next beginner's class is."

And of course, here was a spot right near the front. He couldn't pass it without it being obvious, so he pulled in. "Actually, I meant I'd like to personally teach you some close-quarters moves." Crap, that sounded way dirtier than he'd meant it.

Although, hell, he'd take the dirty version too.

Her smile turned a little awkward. "No, that's okay. I wouldn't want to take up your time, Zac. I'm sure Linear has a class I'll be able to make. Thank you for the ride."

He reached over and grabbed her hand before she could move toward the door handle. "Annie, I'd like to teach you some self-defense moves because yes, it's good for you to know them. But more than that, I would like to spend time with you."

She gave him a crooked smile. "We just spent the whole morning together, and a bunch of time together over the last month."

With anyone else, he would think she was being coy. Playing some sort of game to try to further snare his attention. Not that Annie could any more than she already had.

But she wasn't playing or teasing. She'd never been that way.

Most women wanted to play games, liked the give and

take of gentle flirtation when a relationship was beginning. But Annie and that giant computer-like brain of hers were always going to work best with absolutes rather than nuances.

"Annie, I enjoyed spending time with you today, although I wish it wasn't under these circumstances. And I've enjoyed when we've been able to hang out the last few weeks, even though we've had a bunch of people around. But what I'm saying is I would like to take you out on a date."

Her eyes flew to his, her mouth opening in a little O like a goldfish in water. "I-I-I have to go to work."

She was out the door, and unless he planned on using some of his combat moves, he wasn't going to be able to stop her. He watched her jog across the street to the building, wincing as she almost stepped in front of a moving vehicle.

He should let her go. She didn't want someone chasing after her.

He gripped the steering wheel and closed his eyes. No. That was the problem. She was used to people leaving her alone. That's what had happened her whole life.

He got out of the car and jogged toward the hospital doors, wincing again as he, too, was almost hit by a car.

If she shut him down cold and told him to fuck off—in a polite Annie way, of course—that she would never consider going out with him after what he'd done, it was no more than he deserved.

But damn it, he would at least try.

He could see her down the main hallway. "Annie!"

Okay, that got her attention, and everyone else's. But she stopped and turned. He jogged the rest of the way to her, getting as close as he could without moving into her personal space.

"Um, hi." She was looking everywhere except at him.

"You didn't answer my question."

Those brown eyes darted up at him before looking away again. "I don't think you actually asked me one."

The corner of his mouth pulled up. She was too smart for her own good. "Then allow me to change my syntax. Will you go out on a date with me, Annie?"

There were people watching. In a town the size of Oak Creek, there always would be, ready to spread the word.

He didn't care.

"Zac..."

"It's not a hard question, Dr. Griffin. A simple yes or no will suffice."

"You don't really want to go out with me."

Now, he very deliberately took a step into her personal space and lowered his volume so only she could hear. "You can tell me to go to hell if you want to. I wouldn't blame you for that. But you do not get to tell me that I don't want to go out with you. Do you know why?" He put a finger under her chin and tilted her face up.

Now those big brown eyes were locked on his. "Why?" she whispered.

"Because there's nothing I want more. Say yes, Annie." His face was just inches from hers.

"Why?" she whispered again.

There were so many reasons why. Because he wanted to redeem himself. Because he wanted to show her how sorry he was for what had happened six years ago. Because he wanted to remind her that Oak Creek was really her home, and it was a wonderful place. Because he didn't want her to stay at home on a night off with all her books if she wanted to go out.

But really there was only one that mattered.

"I want us to know each other. The 'now' versions. Not our high school selves or the each-others from six years ago. Those people are gone, and who's left are the you and me from *now*. This Zac"—he touched his chest— "wants to know this Annie." He touched her cheek.

"But..."

His lips touched hers. He wanted to back her against the wall and kiss her until neither of them could think straight, but now wasn't the time. Another soft kiss. "Say yes, Annie."

"Yes."

# CHAPTER 14

ANNE COULD FEEL Zac's fingers against her cheek long after he smiled and said he'd call her later to work out the details.

And why was it so hot in the hospital? Normally they kept the temperature much cooler to make sure patients and employees were comfortable.

"It's the regular temperature in here," Riley said, grinning.

Had Anne said that out loud?

"Zac's just got you all hot and bothered," she continued.

Anne spun on her heels and headed back toward her office. Had Zac truly asked her out? Had she really said yes?

"Yes, he did," Riley responded, catching up with Anne. "And yes, you did."

Seriously, Anne had to start keeping her internal monologue *internal*.

"I saw it, and a bunch of other nurses did too. That was nigh-near swoon-worthy, watching him rush in after you like that."

Oh, good Lord. "Look, it's a casual thing, okay? Not a real date. Zac doesn't really like me in that way."

Riley took one look at her face and burst out laughing. No, guffawing. So loud everyone around them was staring. Anne grabbed her arm and hauled the younger woman into her office, closing the door behind her.

"I'm sorry." Riley held her stomach, trying to get her giggles under control. Anne moved behind her desk and stood there with her arms crossed. "It's just, you're so smart, Anne. How can you think Zac doesn't like you?"

"Let's say there's enough bad history between us for me to doubt this offer is seriously romantically inclined."

A vision of him flinging her dress at her naked form standing in the hallway filled her mind. But then those tender kisses from a few minutes ago battled it.

Riley finally stopped laughing. "Look, I was a kid when Becky died, still in high school. I was sad because, hell, all of us were. But I didn't really know her. Honestly, I didn't know Zac either, until the last couple years."

She didn't have time for this. "Riley, I enjoy your company, but I need to report for my shift."

"Zac likes you."

She sighed. "Zac's a friendly guy. He likes everyone."

Riley shook her head. "No, he *likes* likes you."

"While I appreciate the sentiment" —and would love for it to be true— "I can say with pretty good authority that Zac doesn't."

"Look, I don't know what happened between you guys in the past, but I've never seen Zac try this hard to get a woman's attention while at the same time remaining completely behind the scenes. It boggles the mind."

"I have absolutely no idea what you're talking about."

"He fixed your floors."

"Yes, and I truly appreciate that."

"He brought the guys in to finish moving all your furniture, so you didn't hurt yourself."

"Yes, that's true too. And I—"

Riley raised an eyebrow and tilted her head, her pixie haircut framing her small face perfectly. "Anything else good happen in the past few weeks? I don't know, your washer and dryer working better than they used to? Your fireplace flue all cleaned out? Enough firewood in case we have some super cold nights? Your car running better?"

Anne slowly sank into her office chair. "Oh my gosh."

"Zac. Either directly or because he called in a favor or batted his pretty blue eyes at his buddies. None of the guys minded stepping up to help, but Zac initiated it. It's been Zac who has been thinking about you nonstop for the past month."

Was that even possible? "But..."

"Zac's a pretty stand-up guy, but I would still get my locks changed if I were you."

They already had been. Finn and little Ethan had shown up a couple days ago, new lock in hand. Finn had winked and said he wouldn't want Zac to have a key to his place either. She'd been too caught up in his son's utter cuteness to even pay attention to the details.

Like how would Finn have even known about Zac having the key if Zac hadn't told him?

"This could still be him just being friendly."

Riley smiled. "I hang out with the Linear guys all the time. Not the guns and fighting, but the adventure stuff they do on that property sometimes: repelling, rock climbing, hang gliding, you name it. The guys forget I'm there. And let me tell you, they have harassed the shit out of Zac for all the stuff he's been doing for you."

"Oh." That wasn't good. She didn't want him fighting with his friends.

"At first he ignored them. Hell, it takes more than name-calling to get Cyclone frazzled."

*"Cyclone?"*

"That was his call sign in the Army. Evidently because Zac can be surrounded by a cyclone and not lose his head during a mission. So yeah, he ignored them. Until Finn finally asked why he was really helping you so much."

"Was it because of Becky?" she whispered. It was the only thing that made sense.

"Zac just said he'd finally seen you. That he'd known you most of your life, but now he could *see* you." Riley shrugged. "I'll admit, I didn't know what the hell he was talking about, and was getting ready to repel down the side of a cliff, so I didn't care too much. But watching him today with you, I finally get it. He only had eyes for you in that hallway. We all could've been running around naked or on fire, and he still would've only been interested in you."

Her chest hurt. She'd recognized a few days ago how much easier her life had been lately. The car...running. The house...a relaxing place to come home to, where she could rest and unwind rather than spending all her time off fixing, changing, and unpacking. All her bills had been easier to pay because she hadn't had to come up with more money to fix things.

A lot of her stress had been lifted. Evidently, she had Zac to thank for that. Like Riley said, all the guys probably would've been willing if she had asked. But she never would have.

Zac had seen the needs—seen her—and just stepped in and done what needed to be done.

"Look, don't you dare tell him I let the cat out of the

bag, or I'm going to be banned from the fun stuff, okay? And we're supposed to go paragliding next month in Colorado, so that would suck. But that man cares for you, Anne."

She nodded and waved her hand toward the door. "Okay, I promise not to tell on you. Now get out so I can go to work."

Work was what she needed, what she understood.

Zac Mackay? Not so much.

Anne buckled down the next few days and refused to even think about her upcoming date Friday night. It was the only way she'd survive with her sanity intact.

By Friday morning, it didn't matter, it was shot.

She'd been able to focus on her job in med school when she hadn't had enough to eat or sleep. She'd been able to when Darren had dumped her and told her she wasn't the type of woman a doctor with his future would want on his arm.

One would think she could focus through a six-hour shift. A date wasn't life changing. She'd known Zac for decades. There was really no excuse for misfiling a chart three different times in the past two hours.

Riley had the day off but was coming over to Anne's house at six, two hours from now, to help her get ready for her date at seven. She was bringing Wavy Bollinger—Finn's sister, who worked at the Frontier Diner.

They were going to help Anne with her hair and "do a little" with her makeup. Riley was even bringing over a couple of her own outfits, although what good would that do? Riley was at least four inches shorter. Any skirt she brought would be obscene on Anne.

She'd also texted and asked for Anne's shoe size a few hours ago. Somehow that didn't reassure her at all. Riley was way too excited about project "Doll Anne Up and Send Her Out to the Wolves."

Or just *Wolf*.

Why had she ever said yes to this? Not only going out with Zac, but to The Eagle's Nest? It was Friday night. Everyone would be there.

She tried to type a patient's data into her hospital iPad, then set it down at the nurses' station and rubbed her pounding temples. "Susan, why doesn't this work?"

The older nurse looked over at the device, then pressed a button. "Because you're trying to file it on archive. Again."

Anne blew out a breath. "You think I'm an idiot. I *am* an idiot."

Susan's smile was kind as she patted Anne's arm. "I think you're not the first woman to get a little flustered at one of those Linear Tactical fellows taking them out."

Did everybody in the whole hospital know?

If she could think of a reason to call off the date, she would. This couldn't possibly go well. Was it wrong to pray for a bus accident? Not with any serious injuries, of course, just sprained ankles and contusions—enough to keep her here for the next six or eight hours.

At five o'clock, she handed the ER reins over to Dr. Lewis. "Are you sure you don't want me to stay? It's no problem." Anne couldn't be blamed if there were a medical necessity, could she? Zac would understand. Riley, maybe not so much.

"No, no." Dr. Lewis shook his head, smiling. "Nurse Wilde mentioned you have plans and that unless there was an emergency not to let you stay. So, you go have fun since you have tonight and most of tomorrow off. Enjoy your young-person stuff."

Damn Riley. This is why Anne didn't have friends. They always stabbed you in the back and made you go out with the guy you've been in love with your whole life.

She walked down the hallway to her office to grab her purse and keys. Mia Stevenson was waiting outside her door.

If Anne could've left without getting into her office, she would have. Mia had been trying to corner Anne all week. This conversation wasn't going to be pretty.

Straightening her shoulders, Anne put on her best head-of-the-emergency-department doctor face. "Nurse Stevenson, were you waiting for me? Some sort of hospital business that needs to be dealt with?"

Mia's eyes narrowed. Obviously, she had expected to have the upper hand in this conversation from the start, but Anne had sidetracked her by keeping things businesslike.

"No. This has nothing to do with the hospital, *Anne.*"

"I see. Well, I'm about to leave, so now isn't a good time."

"I know you're going out with Zac tonight."

Anne put the key in her office door and unlocked it, walking in. "I'm sure many people have plans for the weekend."

"I've already heard about you throwing yourself at him in the hall the other day."

Anne turned and looked at Mia. People were beginning to glance their way—which may be exactly what Mia wanted: a scene. Anne wasn't going to give it to her. She opened the door to her office and let the woman enter, shutting it to a crack.

"Mia, you and I don't really know each other. We're not

friends. I'm not sure how what I do or who I do it with is any of your business."

"You've been gone from Oak Creek a long time."

Nobody was more aware of that than Anne. "Yes, I have."

"Things have changed since you've been gone."

It didn't really seem like things had changed that much. Mia was still the gorgeous girl at school who pretty much held court whenever she wanted. Anne was doing something Mia didn't like, so she'd been hauled before the throne.

Anne walked to her desk and got her purse out of the bottom drawer. She wasn't going to fight with Mia—one, because she had no idea how to fight interpersonal battles that had no rules, and two, because even if she did, there was no way she would win against someone like Mia, who lived for them.

"I would certainly hope we've all changed since high school."

Mia blew one perfect curl off her forehead with a breath. "Look, I'm not trying to come in here and be all *Mean Girls*, okay?"

"Okay," she said slowly. Dealing with a reasonable Mia wasn't going to be as easy as ignoring Prom Queen Bitch Mia.

"Zac's not with me. I get it. We only went out a few times and he never made any promises, so I can't fault him for that."

"Okay," Anne said again, waiting for the sucker punch.

"Everybody likes Zac, and rightfully so. He's the town golden boy, made even more so by the tragedy of Becky and the baby's death."

"Micah. His name was Micah."

Mia rolled her eyes. "Of course, you know that even after all these years. I'm not sure if it's because you're super smart or you're in love with him. Or both."

She knew because Becky and Micah had both been people important to her and Zac. "What's your point, Mia?"

"I just want you to be careful." She held out a hand, palm up. "I know that sounds ridiculous, because, well, it's me, and I'm a bitch. But like you said, we've all changed since high school, since Becky's death. I don't know that Zac is emotionally capable of committing to anyone anymore. Maybe that died with Becky."

Mia smoothed back a little of her perfect blonde hair. "Zac dates but keeps a part of himself distant. He's notorious for it."

Anne took a step forward. She really didn't want to hear this. "Thanks for the warning."

"I'm not trying to upset you. Just, I thought someone should let you know, okay? So, you're not going into the situation blind. You're new and shiny, so he wants to play. But don't let your heart get involved."

Anne grit her teeth. "Again, thanks for the advice."

She shook her head. "Now I've made you mad. I wasn't trying to. I just don't want to see you get hurt, see you in another situation where everyone is talking behind your back like in Florida."

Point made, Mia turned and left.

Anne took off her glasses and rubbed her eyes. Mia had been checking up on her at the hospital in Tampa. It wouldn't have been difficult for her to get details from Anne's previous place of employment. Everybody knew the drama of the two Dr. Griffins. One moving forward and the other left behind.

Maybe it really was a friendly warning, or thinly

disguised jealousy. But Mia wanted her to know that she was out of her league with Zac. Anne was going to ignore her.

After all, she'd been telling herself the exact same thing since the beginning.

# CHAPTER 15

ZAC SAT at a booth at The Eagle's Nest, a beer he hadn't taken more than two sips of growing warm on the table. He glanced at the door for the tenth time in as many minutes.

"Not like you to be nervous before a date." Finn was sitting across from him, grinning like a moron, drinking his own beer. "Of course, not like you to meet a woman for a date rather than pick her up. Didn't you get your motor-cycle for the express purpose of impressing women?"

"Meeting here wasn't my choice." He respected it, but he was also half afraid Annie wasn't going to show up. If he had known Finn was going to sit with him and give him a hard time, he wouldn't have arrived thirty minutes early.

"I'm assuming you got all that stuff worked out about what you told me before, or Annie wouldn't be agreeing to a date with you."

His eyes moved from the door to his friend. "Yeah, ends up I was definitely a colossal bastard, but I didn't attack her that night."

He told Finn what he'd remembered, didn't hold back

the ugly details of it even though the thought of it still made him a little sick.

"Dayum." Finn shook his head, took a big gulp of beer. "You're going to need to find more stuff for us to do around Annie's house."

"Pretty sure I could build her a mansion from the ground up and it wouldn't make up for what I did. Crazy thing is, I know if Becky was here, she'd kick my ass, not for sleeping with Annie, but for the way I treated her after." Not only the stupid stuff he'd forgotten, but for not staying in touch with her. Not checking on her. He'd lost his wife, but Annie had lost her best friend. He'd had friends, family, and his brothers in the Army to get him through. Annie hadn't had anyone, especially once she'd left.

"So, what is this? Some sort of pity date? Trying to make up for past sins?"

There was nothing he could do that would ever make up for that night. And pity? "Hell, no. I haven't been able to get her out of my mind from the minute she walked into that hospital room. If anything, she's taking pity on me by agreeing. I just want to be with her, you know?"

Any way he could. Physically, yes. Oh God, yes, he hoped he could eventually get her to give him another chance. But if not, it was like he'd told her at the hospital. He wanted the *now* Zac to get to know the *now* Annie.

Finn nodded solemnly. "I get it, man. Love is a battlefield."

Zac couldn't stop his grin. "Did you just throw Pat Benatar at me, jackass? Are we gonna have a dance-off now?"

Finn laughed. "You know I would totally beat you in one. I have moves you've never even dreamed of."

"You wish. I—"

He nearly swallowed his tongue. Annie had just walked through the door.

"Holy shit," Finn whispered. "This really wasn't a pity date. Good luck, brother." Finn left the booth, but Zac couldn't tear his eyes away from Annie.

He realized immediately he'd made multiple tactical errors. For someone known for assessing a situation and immediately recognizing the strengths and weaknesses of manifold routes forward, it was an unusual feeling. He shouldn't have chosen here for their date.

Word had already gotten around that they were going out. People were looking at Annie and she was panicking. He should've picked somewhere quieter, more intimate.

And people—*men*—were eyeing her, finally realizing what he had known all along: she was fucking *gorgeous*. She downplayed her beauty all the time because she didn't know how to deal with the attention it drew. But she wasn't hiding it tonight.

Gorgeous.

He immediately stood and made his way to her. One, because she looked like she was going to run out the door at any second. Two, because if he waited another ten seconds, one of these other guys was going to beat him to her.

"Hi," he murmured, reaching down to kiss her on the cheek. "You look fantastic."

Black tank under a jean jacket, black denim miniskirt that showed off her long legs before they ended in red cowboy boots.

Zac was going to be dreaming about those for a long time.

She grimaced. "I became Wavy and Riley's science project."

"Thank God for science," he murmured, taking her arm and leading her toward the table.

"One would think I wouldn't be able to fit into one of Riley's skirts, given that she's four inches shorter than me."

He glanced down at her legs again, resisting the urge to wipe under his chin in case he was drooling. "One would indeed think that."

They sat down at the booth. Her back ramrod straight. "Everybody is s-s-staring at us."

He took her hands on the table and rubbed his thumb across her knuckles. "You know how small towns are: gossip for a second about something before moving on. It's Friday, so soon everyone will be drinking and line dancing, not paying any attention to us."

She nodded, taking a breath. "O-o-okay." She grit her teeth, her frustration with herself obvious.

He didn't let go of her hands. "I shouldn't have brought you here. I thought it would be good to go somewhere famil-iar, but I didn't take your anxiety into account. I know you don't like to be the center of attention."

She closed her eyes and took a deep breath in through her nose then out through her mouth. She repeated the process. Her hands slid out from under his and he let her go, recognizing the need for whatever ritual she was doing to calm herself. She touched her thumbs to each of her four fingers, then repeated the motion.

When her eyes opened she looked better. This was obviously a tactic she'd used before. "I actually don't like crowds where I'm expected to mingle and make small talk or, heaven forbid, public speaking. Here, as long as the band is playing loud, and everyone is ignoring me, I-I'll be fine."

Her hands touched his again. He turned one over and ran his finger gently across her palm and up her wrist, smiling when she shivered slightly. "Not everyone will be ignoring you."

He had a feeling no one would. As much as he loved the sight of her legs in that skirt and those boots, and how big her brown eyes looked with no glasses blocking half her face, not to mention her hair falling around her shoulders and beyond...he sort of wished he could have her back in her scrubs and glasses.

The waitress came over, and they ordered food and talked as best they could over the din. Zac had been here countless times to hang out with the guys. And for dates sometimes. He'd never realized how crowded it was. Or how noisy.

Probably because he'd never really been trying to make meaningful conversation with anyone.

Their burgers and fries arrived. He enjoyed watching Annie attack her food with such gusto.

She caught him staring, finished chewing, and put a hand in front of her mouth, eyes worried. "Am I eating too fast? I always do."

"No, not at all. I'm sure working at the hospital all day builds up your appetite."

She looked relieved that he understood. "Yes. Some days there's no time to stop for meals. You just eat a bite or two as you can."

"Yeah, that happened a lot when I was in the Army."

"I thought they gave you guys three square meals a day." She was relaxing. He would talk to her about anything she wanted for as long as she wanted if it meant her smiles were focused on him.

"A lot of times they did, at boot camp in particular, and during regular training afterward. But later...once I was a Green Beret, sitting down to enjoy cooked food was a luxury. For most of our missions, MREs were the order of the day."

"Meals Ready to Eat," she said. "We did a study on their nutritional value when I was in med school. Nutritionally, they're excellent."

"Did you taste one?"

He wanted to lean across and kiss the scrunched-up face she made. "Yes, and they were god-awful. I suppose the nutrition doesn't count if you can't keep them down."

"Believe me, in most cases we didn't mind." On some missions they would've given anything to have MREs available.

She studied him but didn't press for details. Zac appreciated it. It hadn't take long after Linear became successful for the guys and him to realize that some women—and hell, guys like Frank—were soldier groupies. Zac's and all the team's Special Forces background was listed on the company website. Some people wanted to hear about the violence and danger they'd lived through. Hell, some women wanted it in their bed.

Zac had a few stories he would tell, pretty tame ones overall, mostly just to satisfy the curiosity of whoever was asking. The rest he would take to his grave.

The most popular question he got from men and women who knew he had been a Green Beret: Had he ever killed anyone?

Zac's answer: yes. Then a change of subject.

He'd killed. Multiple times in multiple ways. And it had cost him a piece of his soul every time. It had cost all the guys a great deal to serve their country, in ways they hadn't even understood sometimes until they'd returned home. But that was the sort of thing you didn't talk about with civilians.

Annie raised her glass of beer. "To the times we couldn't sit down for a meal because people were depending on us to do other things, and do them right, even when they were hard."

It was as if she'd dug into his mind and pulled out what he'd wanted to say. He lifted his glass and clinked it against hers. "And to those still suffering."

He thought of Dorian and how the man continued to wake up screaming—when he could get any sleep at all—from things that had happened to him in Afghanistan. And he thought of the poor rape victims Annie had helped and treated.

An ER physician was similar to a Special Forces soldier in a lot of ways. But today she deserved time off from that. They both did.

Today Annie was just a smoking hot woman he was on a date with. And he planned to enjoy her.

She must have recognized the predatory look behind his smile because she put the last bite of her burger down. "What?"

"Nothing. Just glad to be here with you. But next time I'm going to take you out to a restaurant where we don't need to shout to hear each other."

"Next time?"

"Oh, yes, ma'am. There will very definitely be a next time."

The band was picking up in volume, and people were starting to dance. The waitress came back and took their plates away and brought Annie another beer, but Zac switched to soda.

Annie's eyebrow raised as she gestured to his glass with her chin. "Afraid to let your guard down?"

It was time to tell her. Past time. "I don't really drink anymore. One beer, that's it. No exceptions."

She nodded. "As a physician, I completely applaud that. Although the benefits of a single glass of red wine have been proven to—"

He cut her off. "It's been my rule for six years. Since that night with you in the hotel, Annie. Since I woke up the next morning, after hitting my head on the corner of the desk when I passed out, and realized there was an entire night of my life missing."

"Zac..." The tension was back in her face, in her voice, but he had to press on.

"But I knew, even without remembering, I had done something horrible. I promised myself I would never be that out of control again. A few weeks ago, when I went to The Mayor's Inn looking for you after the flood in your house, I found the mayor, and she laid into me."

Her lips pinched together. "She shouldn't have done that."

"Oh, she should've, and way before last month too."

"I don't know what she told you, but—"

He reached over and placed his hand over her wringing ones on the table. "She didn't have to. I stepped into that hallway and remembered. What I did, said. It was unfor-givable."

She shook her head. "You were drunk. Becky and Micah had just died."

"You're too kind for your own good, Annie Nichols Griffin."

Her hands tensed even more under his. "Is that why you're out with me? Why you've done all those nice things over the last month?"

He didn't even care how she'd figured it out. "There's

nothing I could tinker with, fix, paint, or build that is ever going to change that night. I wouldn't insult either of us by even trying in that way. But I want to make your life easier. You take care of a lot of people—"

"That's my job."

"—but you rarely, if ever, let someone take care of you. I'd like to be that person. And it has nothing to do with pity or guilt. It has everything to do with the fact that you're an amazing, beautiful woman, whether you're in your short skirt and red boots—about to blow my damn mind, by the way—or your scrubs. Both are beautiful, sexy."

"Zac..."

"The *now* me getting a chance to know the *now* you. That's all I'm asking for."

"Okay." She paused then slowly broke into a smile. *"Cyclone."*

He couldn't hold back his groan. "Oh, hell no. I cannot believe that has gotten back to you." It was becoming too loud to talk, so Zac stood and sat back down on her side of the booth, sliding her over with his legs.

He was crowding her space and didn't care one damn bit. She seemed a little surprised but didn't move away.

"I still feel like everyone is watching us," she whispered after looking around and taking a sip of her beer.

They were drawing more attention than other people here. "Everybody is looking at the hot girl. The guys are wondering if they have any sort of chance with her."

"Admittedly, I look a little better than I normally do at the hospital. But I don't think anyone would mistake me for a *hot girl.*"

Zac put his elbow on the table and leaned on it, facing her, blocking her from the view of the rest of the bar. He grinned. "I love how you say that. As if they're dirty words or something."

"No. There's nothing wrong with being attractive. I just —" She shrugged.

"You just what?"

She gestured toward herself. "This is not who I really am."

He reached over and poked her on the nose. "Feels pretty real to me. Unless you used your huge brain to build a life-sized robot you're controlling from home." He slid an arm around her shoulder and pulled her closer. "I like this look: red boots, skirt, and mussed hair. But you know what? I like the look of Dr. Griffin in her scrubs just as much."

She turned to face him, hair falling over her shoulder. "I don't think—"

He closed the few inches between their faces and kissed her. Just for the briefest of seconds. And he promised himself this was the last of the brief touches. Their next kiss would be neither brief nor innocent. "How about no thinking tonight? Just feeling." He slid toward the edge of the booth, catching her hand. "And dancing."

# CHAPTER 16

HER BRA WAS ITCHY, her skirt too short, and it felt like everyone in the entire town was staring while they danced. Anne ignored it all—the staring was actually easier to ignore than the lacy red bra Wavy and Riley had sworn was necessary.

She couldn't ignore she was dancing in Zac's arms. She'd never thought that would happen.

They'd moved a little awkwardly at first, swaying to the Dobie Gray's "Drift Away." Rigid, unsure exactly how they fit together. They were boxy, stiff, trying to keep an appropriate distance from each other.

But then Zac had laughed ruefully, wrapped his arm around her waist, and yanked her hard to him. Her hands latched onto his shoulders to balance herself, then stayed there. That close, there was no room for stiffness, no awkwardness.

"Better," he murmured against her temple, keeping her against him.

It was better. It was so much more than that. The song

changed, still staying slow, about being drunk on love, and Zac kept their bodies moving. This was more than a dance. She knew it, and he did too.

This was a fresh start.

His lips moved against her temple again, the fingers of one hand trailing up and down her back. Anne wasn't going to try to process what it all meant, where it was all going, all the things about herself she couldn't protect when it came to Zac.

Like he'd said, tonight she wasn't going to think. She was just going to feel. If she had to pick up pieces later, then she would—and hope she had a big enough broom.

As the song ended she looked up into his eyes, unsure of what to say. If anything needed to be said at all.

"It's time for line dancing!" someone shouted over the microphone. "You fellas need to get your asses off the floor, so the gals can start it off right."

Anne laughed and shook her head. She was just starting to move off the floor with the men when Wavy and Riley— the terror twins—each took an arm and dragged her back.

Zac's whole face broke into a grin. "Have fun."

They showed her the basic steps to the Cowgirl Twist and soon they were all laughing as they moved around the room.

"I'm not even going to ask if you're having fun," Riley said between turns. "Your grin says it all."

"She wasn't grinning when Zac had her plastered up against his body," Wavy shouted. "Which was super sexy, because obviously that man wants you, and everybody here knows it. But also, kind of gross because Zac is basically my brother."

"I *am* having a good time." Anne spun and started another set of steps, messed up, then jumped back in. The turn brought her around to face the bar where Zac sat with Finn and Aiden. She messed up again, then flashed Zac a grin, shrugging.

He held up his soda in a little toast, winked at her, and smiled.

Oh, good Lord. He was hard enough to resist when he wasn't turning on the charm. Now that red lace bra felt *really* itchy. Her whole body did. And she knew just what she needed to scratch it.

"You know," Wavy said as they spun once more and Anne could no longer see Zac without making it obvious. "The Eagle's Nest is open and has dancing every weekend. It's not just something they set up for Zac to take dates. The three of us need to hit the town more often."

"Hell yeah, we do!" Riley let out a whoop that got all the other women on the floor going too.

Anne needed friends, she realized. She'd always been too caught up in her goals: pre-med, med school, residency, surviving the humiliation of working with a husband who had left her for another woman.

Line dancing with girlfriends had never really been an option. Girlfriends hadn't either. Surviving had been her sole focus.

But now she was home. She had a good job, was digging her way out of her financial hole, and was making friends. She only had herself to blame if she didn't enjoy them.

Even if they made her wear short skirts and itchy bras.

The song ended, and Anne reached out and pulled Riley and Wavy to her in a hug. "You're right. You guys were about it all. Thank you."

Riley giggled. "You're so gonna get some Zac love tonight!"

She didn't know if that was true or not. Didn't even

know if she wanted it to be. No matter what happened tonight, it couldn't be worse than the last time she'd left a bar with Zac.

"But listen, Annie," Wavy said, eyes serious. "You be careful with your heart, okay? Zac is a good guy, and I love him like a brother, but he's never been one to get serious with a woman. I don't want you to get hurt."

She nodded, not surprised Wavy was echoing Mia's earlier warning. A fresh start didn't necessarily mean a relationship, just that they were moving forward.

The men joined the ladies as more line dancing resumed. She was surprised to see Zac, Finn, and Aiden out on the floor. She shouldn't have been surprised that Zac had moves though. He taught her new dances, both laughing when she sometimes ended up going the opposite direction as everyone else. After another hour she was getting the hang of it and having fun just trying, being relaxed with Zac. Feeling, not thinking.

Zac excused himself to go to the restroom. Anne was looking for a table or seat somewhere—their booth now occupied—when Riley and Wavy once again scooped her back out onto the floor for another ladies-only dance.

Frank Jenkins wolf-whistled at her as the dance took her closer to where he and his friends were standing against a wall, shots in hand. Of course, he'd waited until Zac was nowhere in the room to do it. Two of his buddies laughed. The third smacked Frank on the back of his head, mouthing "sorry" to Anne.

It was good to know Frank had at least one decent friend, although now Frank was pushing at him with one hand, gesturing to his half-spilled shot with the other.

The song ended, and Anne was determined to sit down and give her legs a rest. Besides, she couldn't ignore how crowded the whole place was getting. That was never going to be her forte, but she didn't want to make a scene.

She found a seat at the end of the bar and did the breathing exercises a teacher had shown her during her psychiatry rotation in med school. She touched her thumbnail to each of her fingers, focusing on the tiny dot of pain rather than the room around her. She let the oxygen and physical sensation center her.

The music changed again, slowing down, the lights dimming. The dance floor thinned out, but that made the bar even more crowded. Crap. She'd need to get out of here soon. There was only so much her system could take. Zac wouldn't know how to find her and—

"One last dance?" he asked, his big body blocking the rest of the bar.

She nodded, relieved, and took his hand, letting him lead her out to the floor, panic ebbing as they left the crowd behind. His arms wrapped around her and the rest of her discomfort melted away.

"I guess I'm not up for a full night of dancing," she said against his shoulder. "Everyone else is just getting started, and I'm already tracking the door."

He chuckled, arms sliding around her more securely. "For a bar in a small town in the middle of Wyoming, The Eagle's Nest can get pretty crazy on the weekends. Like I said, next time somewhere quieter."

Next time. "That would be nice."

His head lowered, his lips hovering an inch above hers, their bodies hardly moving now. She could barely breathe with the need to kiss him.

"I want to take this as slow as you need," he murmured, tucking a strand of her hair behind her ear. "Don't want to rush you into anything."

She went up on her toes, so her lips touched his. "What if I want to?"

He closed his eyes and when they opened again, they were bleak. "What happened before..."

She lifted her hand from where it rested on his neck and put her finger on his lips. "What happened before wasn't all bad."

He kissed her finger. "I hope you'll give me a chance to show you the *all good*."

Oh God. "*Yes*. Tonight."

He kissed her. It was nothing like the feather-soft kisses earlier this week or at her car last month. This was possessive. Hot. Needy.

And completely inappropriate for a dance floor.

"Shit," he said as he broke away, looking as dazed as she felt. "I'm taking you home, right now."

Riley and Wavy made kissy faces and gave her a thumbs-up as he led her to the bar to pay the bill, arm wrapped securely around her. More people were watching. Hell, probably everybody was. Frank was now talking to Mia. Both sneered at her, but when Zac came back and helped her put on her jacket, she couldn't bring herself to care what they or anybody in this whole damn town thought of her.

"Let's get out of here," Zac whispered, heat burning deep in those blue eyes. He tucked her under his arm and headed toward the door.

Anne didn't think of resisting. There was no else she'd rather be with.

# CHAPTER 17

ZAC DROVE ANNIE'S CAR, since he only had one helmet for his bike. He had honestly never dreamed she'd let him this close to her again, much less tonight. It was all he could do not to fall to his knees and thank every known power in the universe.

He was damned well going to do everything right with her this time.

He kept both hands on the wheel for the fifteen-minute trip to his place. Because if he didn't, he wasn't sure they were going to make it. He couldn't remember ever feeling this all-encompassing need for a woman. Even with Becky, it had been different. She'd always been part of his life. They'd eased into the sexual part naturally. And the women he'd had since her had always been temporary. Fun. Never like this, with a burning, aching need.

Everyone at The Eagle's Nest would be talking. Zac's actions—his obvious possessiveness of Annie—were out of the ordinary for him. PDA, a dramatic exit...all fuel for the gossip fire, and actions he'd never given into. He didn't want people in his business. But about this, he hadn't given the gossip mill a second thought. Let them talk. He wasn't going to hide how he felt about Annie.

When they pulled up to his house, she turned to him. "Zac—"

He reached over and kissed her, deeply, filling it with promise. His tongue thrust into her mouth in an imitation of the act that would come later.

They both groaned.

He broke the kiss and jumped out of the car and around to her door, opening it for her. He grabbed her hand and pulled her up the stairs to his front door.

It was as far as he could get without kissing her again.

His hands cupped her face. As he bent his head toward hers, he inhaled her scent, something like lavender. Nothing too clingy—subtle, soft. Something you would miss if you weren't paying attention. Just like the woman herself.

His entire body tightened. Hardened.

Her hands found his waist, untucked his shirt, and scraped her nails on the tender flesh. Zac groaned and pushed her against the door with his body. Every inch of them was touching.

She gasped, and he took full advantage of her open mouth. His tongue swept inside, the faint taste of the cinnamon whiskey she'd sipped firing every nerve in his body.

"Damn it, woman, I'm not even going to make it inside the house if we don't stop."

He could feel her smile. His tongue dipped between the seam of her lips again. He slipped one hand down and fought to get the key in the door without looking. After a few moments, he let a frustrated groan escape his lips.

She slid her head back and smiled, reaching down to

take the key from him. She turned in his arms to put it in the lock.

Which left the whole back of her body pressed to his. He didn't even try to suppress his groan when Annie bent a little at the waist to gain better access to the lock. Instead, he grabbed her hips and pulled her back hard against him.

This time they both groaned.

She got the key in, and they stumbled through the door as it opened. Zac kicked it shut and kept their momentum going forward until her body was fully up against his hallway wall, her back still to him. He peeled her denim jacket down her arms, then threw it on the banister.

He ran his hands up her back, across the shoulders, caressing the skin her tank top left bare, and down her arms with a featherlight touch until he reached her wrists. Then, he pulled her hands out and placed them on the wall above her head.

"Leave them right there," he murmured against her neck. He slid his nose and lips along her jaw and hairline until he arrived at her ear. "I just want you to stand here and feel. There's so many things I'm going to do to you, sweet Annie. We won't be done tonight until we're both too tired to move. And your voice is hoarse from screaming my name."

Her gasp was the most beautiful thing he'd ever heard. He ran his fingers back down her arms and up again to her shoulders. He slid them down her side, oh so lightly as to not tickle her, then spread out his fingers to grasp her hips.

She gasped once more as he pulled her ass against his hardness. She had no idea how much he'd wanted her this month. Hell, Zac hadn't even known he could want a woman this much.

He bent his knees slightly and allowed his fingers to run along the outside of her thighs, to where the skirt ended, trailing down her bare skin.

"You walked into the bar tonight, and I immediately wanted to march you back out."

"Why?" Her voice was husky.

"Because they all figured out tonight what I already knew." He ran his fingers along the backs of her knees, then up the insides of her thighs.

Her breath hitched. "And what was that?"

"That you're someone everyone should be noticing. Every guy at The Eagle's Nest tonight was kicking themselves for not asking you out first. A hot doctor wearing red cowboy boots? Hell, they're kicking themselves for not asking in high school and tying you to them years ago."

He slid his fingers back up her hips, then dipped them under her tank top, trailing them up her stomach.

"I'm selfish, Annie. I want to be the only one who notices you. And I damn sure want to be the only one you notice." He whispered the words in her ear before bringing his lips down to the place where her neck met her shoulder and biting gently.

At the same time, his hands reached up to cup her breasts through her bra. Her nipples tightened into hard nubs beneath his palms as his lips continued their assault.

"You're so damn sexy," he whispered. "I've dreamed of this."

And he had. Even when he couldn't remember that night—hadn't allowed himself to think of her at all—he'd dreamed of having her in his arms like this.

He pulled on one taut nipple before soothing it with his palm. His other hand was splayed across her smooth stomach, and he used it to press her back against his hips again. Her breath labored in and out.

He couldn't go another second without kissing her. He spun her around, pressing her to the wall with the length of his body. His lips crashed onto hers, and her arms slid around him, pulling him closer.

Damn it, this wasn't what he wanted. He owed her more. Better. He had planned to make this first time last for hours, but now he just wanted to devour her. Where was all that famous Cyclone self-control? He'd stayed on task in the Special Forces, even when bullets rained and explosions thundered close around him.

But this woman's kiss blew his focus straight to hell.

"God, Annie." His voice was so gritty he hardly recognized it. "I don't even know if I can make it to the bed."

Her hands slid down over his jeans and grabbed his ass, pulling him closer. "Then don't."

Zac barely keeping it together was the sexiest thing ever. "Take me right here."

She meant every word. Yes, she wanted slow. Wanted tender. Wanted all night in a bed. And that would happen. But right now, she just wanted him. Period. Wall. Floor. Stairs. Wherever. He took a breath, pulling some measure of control over himself. But he was still sweating, and she loved it.

He knelt in front of her to take her boots off. "In case I haven't mentioned it enough, I love these."

She was glad she was leaning against the wall as he began kissing her knees and thighs as he got rid of her footwear. He kicked his own shoes off as he stood back up.

Emboldened by the heat in his eyes, she grabbed his shirt and pulled it over his head, then grabbed her own tank and did the same. She then shimmied out of her skirt.

The way his breath hissed through his teeth at the sight of her in the matching red bra and thong made her want to rush back in time and give Riley and Wavy a kiss.

"Dear God." His eyes roamed from top to bottom.

She smiled. "You like?"

She recognized the moment his control snapped. Finesse gone, his strong arms circled under her hips and buttocks and lifted her in the air, so her breasts were right in line with his mouth. He plundered one sensitive nipple and then the other through her bra.

God, it wasn't itchy anymore.

Her legs wrapped around his hips, his weight pinning her against the wall as he reached up with one hand and opened the clasp.

His mouth found her bare breast, and she couldn't hold back a moan. His hand tortured the other nipple. She wrapped her fingers in his hair and kept his mouth—and teeth, with their sharp little bites—plastered to her. Her hips ground against his of their own accord.

She moaned in distress when he set her down, but then she realized he was taking off his jeans. Through a daze, she heard him ripping open a condom and sliding it on.

He knelt in front of her again, his breath hot at the juncture of her thighs through the red underwear.

"Sexy," he growled, like he was incapable of making a more coherent sentence. She felt the pressure of his mouth on her core through the thin material. Oh, holy Moses.

His fingers wrapped around the backs of her upper thighs, fingers sliding under the lace, keeping her exactly where he wanted her: pressed against his lips. Sweat broke out on her forehead. She needed more. More than just that sturdy pressure on the outside.

He was driving her crazy. And he knew it.

He drew back and looked up at her as he peeled the red lace down her legs, then stood, pressing his completely naked body against hers.

His lips teased hers softly for a second before he moved to her neck and sucked hard right as he slid his fingers into her. Deep.

Anne gasped, losing her breath as sensations bombarded her. His fingers moved in and out, his thumb pressing with expert finesse over her sensitive clit.

The pressure built inside her.

"Zac..." she keened as his fingers worked their magic.

"Yes, baby. This time, so much yes," Zac murmured against her throat before nipping at it again. "Don't hold back."

A second later Anne exploded, waves of pleasure falling over her as she moaned his name. He eased his fingers out and hooked one of her legs around his hip, slowly working his way inside her.

"This time, so much more," he said, forehead against hers. He reached down and pulled her other leg around his hips, both moaning now as he filled her completely.

She was trapped between Zac and the wall, arms around his shoulder, legs circling his waist. She'd never felt more alive or feminine, held there by only his strength.

His hips never stopped moving, and she didn't want them to. She was building her way back up, the pressure inside becoming unbearable. Her fingernails dug into his shoulders. Almost distantly she heard the thumping against the wall as he pounded into her at a furious pace.

His thumb moved against her core, finding that bundle of nerves again. The world exploded, and she screamed his name. He yelled, too, as they flew over the edge together.

# CHAPTER 18

ANNE DIDN'T HAVE much experience with morning-afters and none with one-night stands. The last time she'd had one, they hadn't even made it to morning.

Not that she was afraid Zac was going to throw her out now. He wasn't. Last night had been the antithesis of the first time around.

She winced silently as she reached down to grab her clothes in front of Zac's front door. Certain places on her body ached, places that hadn't been used in so long they'd almost been forgotten. She couldn't even look at the wall without blushing, heat flooding her whole body.

She should have absolutely zero desire for sex right now. After the wall, the shower, before finally making it to the bed—and then the bed *again* a couple hours ago, although that time it had been his very clever mouth that had driven her crazy—there was no way her body could take another round with Zac.

Her heart couldn't either.

So, even knowing he wasn't going to start screaming at

her and throw her out, she couldn't stick around for awkward conversation. And when he'd mentioned them going to breakfast at the Frontier before he'd drifted to sleep next to her, she'd known she had to get out.

Call her a coward, but she just couldn't do it. Not until she got her emotional fortitude rebuilt. So, she should be ready to face him in another six years or so.

Pulling on the matching red lingerie and wiggling into her skirt—never again—she barely swallowed a shriek as something fuzzy brushed against the back of her legs. A very pregnant dog wagged her tail and slowly sat down.

"Hey, you," Anne whispered, scratching the top of her head. "It's all your fault I'm in this mess, you know. If you hadn't made Zac wreck, I probably could've avoided him for another couple years."

How was she supposed to keep her heart safe from a man who'd brought home the dog that had almost killed him?

She petted the dog again and then threw on her shirt and jacket and dashed out the door. The only thing worse than the awkward morning-after would be getting caught obviously trying to *avoid* it.

She relaxed a little when she made it to her car and down the private road that wound through the Linear property. Her stomach was growling. She'd grab a to-go plate at the Frontier—God knew she'd burned enough calories in the last twelve hours to deserve it. It was just after dawn on a Saturday morning. No one would be around to question her about Zac, but she pulled on a pair of scrub pants she kept in her car for emergencies, so she wouldn't have to walk in wearing last night's skirt. She pulled the scrub shirt over her tank top, but there was nothing she could do about the boots. She'd keep a low profile; nobody would even notice her.

She realized her mistake the moment she stepped foot inside.

"There's the slut I love!" Wavy called out as soon as Anne walked in. The woman was impossibly bright and cheerful to be working this early, considering the shot drinking and line dancing she'd partaken in just a few hours before.

"Jeez, Wavy." Heat was creeping all the way up her neck and face. Fortunately, there weren't many customers: an old couple in the corner booth who didn't look like they could hear much of anything anyway, and a drunk guy at a table who had fallen asleep, coffee cup in hand.

"Get over here, girl." Wavy waved her closer. "Where's Zac? You guys did go home together, right? Is he coming in?"

At least she wasn't shouting it. "Yes, we did. And no, he's not. I left him in his bed this morning." She wasn't sure if that made her a coward or the smartest person on the planet. Or maybe both.

"Trey!" Wavy kept her wide eyes on Anne as she called back to the cook. "I'm taking fifteen. And Doc Griffin wants the full breakfast platter."

The big dark-skinned man didn't even look up from the newspaper. "'Kay."

"To go," Anne said.

"You wish." Wavy shoved a cup of coffee in Anne's hand and dragged her to a booth. "Okay, wait, so you left him in *his* bed?"

"Yeah."

"And he was asleep. So, he doesn't know you're gone." She threw back her head and laughed. "Oh man, I would give my next paycheck to be there when he wakes up and sees you beat him at his own game."

Anne poured some sugar into her coffee. "I doubt there would be much exciting to see. I'm sure he'll be relieved."

Wavy gave her a soft smile. "You don't get it, and that's okay. You will eventually."

"Get what?"

"How much that man cares about you."

"Wave, it was just one night." One mind-blowing, hoarse-from-screaming-his-name night, but still only one.

"Did he *say* it was?"

"Well, no. But it's not like we have a relationship." She took a sip of her coffee.

"Every relationship starts with a first night, you know. Do you want it to be just a one-night stand? Is that why you left?"

Did she want a relationship with Zac? On the one hand, it was all she'd ever wanted. On the other...her heart couldn't take another beating. Her previous encounter with Zac had left her emotionally wounded. And then, just as those had stitched and healed, Darren had ripped them wide open again.

She couldn't take any more right now. She didn't know if she could survive someone deciding *again* she wasn't worth it. She'd always done best when she'd remained invisible.

"I just want to do what you guys said. Protect myself."

Wavy grabbed her hand. "That's smart. And I don't blame you. But let's get to the juicy stuff—I assume it was good or you would've snuck out much earlier this morning."

Oh, hell. She studied her coffee. "Um, yeah, it was nice."

"*Nice*?" Wavy laughed again. "Oh, if Zac was here he would totally die—"

"Order up, and people coming in, Wavy," Trey called from the open kitchen area.

"Okay, hold that blushing thought." Wavy stood. "We'll talk more later."

Two separate groups came in, one a set of college-aged students who sat down by the sleeping guy. Anne grimaced as she saw the others walking through the door: Frank Jenkins and his friends from last night.

They obviously hadn't gone home after The Eagle's Nest. Since the bar had closed at 2 AM, she didn't know what they'd been doing—but it looked like they'd taken the drinking out to the woods. One had a small branch stuck to the shoulder of his shirt. All of them were dirty and quite drunk.

Wavy brought Anne her food and refilled her coffee. "I've got to take care of customers, sweetie. We'll talk later." She made her way over to the college kids.

Frank and his friends took a table near the window, in clear view of Anne's table. She began shoveling food in her mouth. There was no way this was going to end well. She just wanted to get out of here.

She wasn't even a few bites in before Frank saw her. He said something to his buddies to make them laugh before standing up and walking over to her.

"Saw you leave with Mackay last night, *Doctor*." He sneered her title, then laughed as if he'd come up with a clever insult. He ran his fingers through his greasy hair.

"I'm here to eat, Frank." She could feel the eyes of his friends on her. "J-just looking for quiet." Damn it. She began her breathing exercises.

"I guess you weren't even worth taking out to breakfast."

He plopped down in the booth across from her. "Such a shame. I would've. Maybe now that you're defrosted, we can go out some time."

There was no way in hell. "Not going to happen, Frank." She could hear his friends guffaw at the rejection. He glared at them over her shoulder.

"You looked hot last night. You're back to your scrubs now, but then..." He licked his lips.

Anne put her fork down, her appetite completely gone. She took a deep breath, so she could force her words out with as few stutters as possible. "No. I'm trying to eat, F-Frank. You need—"

"Jenkins, you're making an ass out of yourself. Leave the doctor alone."

Frank's friend, the same one who had tried to curb the catcalling last night, grabbed Frank by the shoulder and hauled him out of the booth.

"Shawn, c'mon, man!"

Shawn shoved Frank in the direction of their table. "Leave the lady alone. She doesn't want to talk to you."

"I get it. I get it." Frank held his hands up in mock surrender and took a couple unsteady steps back toward her. "You're only interested in the Linear guys, not regular dudes like me. But we're going there for a class in a couple days so Shawn can see what all the fuss is about." He put an arm around Shawn's shoulder and tapped him on the chest. Shawn looked much less drunk and far less amused than Frank. "And the Linear guys are talking about bringing me on as a partner. So be careful of telling me no so quickly, Doctor. You might regret it."

Shawn rolled his eyes and pushed Frank once again toward their table. She was glad when he kept going this time. "Sorry to have bothered you, Dr. Griffin. I'll keep a tighter leash on Jenkins if I can."

"Thanks for your assistance," she whispered. Everyone in the restaurant was looking now. Shawn nodded and left.

"Jenkins is such an asshole," Wavy said a couple minutes later when she was able to stop by. More people were coming in. "Sorry I couldn't waylay him."

"Don't worry about it. Everyone ignores Frank."

"Why don't you go home and get some sleep?"

Anne grabbed her wallet. "Yeah, I might just do that. Thanks for breakfast."

Wavy pushed her hand away. "Keep it. You hardly got half of it finished anyway." She reached down and hugged her. "It'll all work out, Annie. You'll see."

She'd once shared the younger woman's confidence in a happily ever after. But she just didn't anymore. "Thanks, Wavy."

Wavy linked arms with her and walked her to the door. True to his word, Shawn kept Frank under control.

But as soon as she got out to her car, Anne knew she wouldn't be able to go home and sleep. She was too wound up. Since she was so close to the hospital, she just turned and walked in that direction.

At least there she knew who she was, where she fit. There she didn't have to do breathing exercises to keep her stuttering under control. She was Dr. Griffin, the person who had the answers. The person who could make a judgment in the middle of a crisis and save lives. In control. Focused.

So much the opposite of who she was as Anne.

She slipped into the back door and immediately headed to her office. After grabbing a new set of scrubs and a spare pair of tennis shoes, she headed to the women's locker room.

Twenty minutes later, she was showered, hair braided and out of her way, her glasses on. Ready.

Dr. Lewis was a little surprised to see her back so soon before her shift but certainly didn't mind heading home early after being up all night.

The work for the next few hours was steady, requiring Anne's focus. Twenty-one stitches for a little boy who had decided to do the bike trick he'd seen his older brother doing the day before, kidney stones that had a grown man crying like a toddler, and even the birth of a baby who'd decided to leap into the world a month early while his mom and dad were out for a leisurely hike.

By lunch things had settled down, patient-wise. The regular nurses' shift had changed. New ones came on and were chatting with each other, as usual. It didn't take long for Anne to realize that *she* was what everyone was talking about.

She tried to go about work as usual, ignoring it all.

"Yeah, I heard it was amazing how good she looked last night. Nobody could believe she actually had a body under those scrubs and a non-hideous face under those glasses."

Anne was completing a patient's file on her iPad at the corner of the nurses' station, out of sight. The two nurses, whose voices she didn't recognize, obviously didn't know she was there.

"Zac Mackay, that's quite a catch," the other nurse said. "But, I mean, I hear he didn't even take her out for breakfast this morning. So obviously he doesn't plan on pursuing it, at least according to Mia."

"Look, I have no problem with her," the second nurse continued. "I think she's a great doctor. And anyone who makes fun of someone else's speech impediment is just an asshole."

"An extremely jealous asshole." The other nurse laughed. "Zac has told Mia numerous times he isn't interested. She needs to move on. Next time she talks trash about Dr. Griffin, I'm going to call her on it. It's not right."

Anne smiled, her heart lifting. She still didn't know which two nurses were talking, but they obviously respected her and wanted a good working environment. Those were the sorts of people they needed here. She started in their direction to tell them so.

"Same," the other nurse said. "I won't let Mia get away with it either. But let's be honest, it doesn't matter how great of a doctor she is, there's no way Zac is going to stay with someone like Dr. Griffin very long. Some things just aren't meant to be."

"Oh yeah, totally. I wouldn't be surprised if they're already done. He scratched that itch and that's that. Not that he'll be mean. He'll find a way to let her down easy."

Anne swallowed and turned the other way.

# CHAPTER 19

ZAC WAS *PISSED*. Had been that way since he'd woken up and found Annie wasn't in bed with him. Not only not there, but completely gone.

Duchess—who seriously was going to birth that litter any second now—just calmly gazed at Zac as he looked out the front door to see if Annie's car was gone, muttering every obscenity he knew when he discovered it was.

He waited all morning for a word from her, a text or voicemail telling him she'd been called into the hospital for some emergency. That he could understand, even if he wasn't thrilled with how she'd handled it.

Nothing. Not a single word from her.

It wasn't pride that bothered him.

Okay, it was, but it was more than *just* that. He'd wanted her here. He'd wanted to wake up next to her and make easy love to her in the sunlight, watch those big brown eyes go all unfocused, that giant brain completely shutting down so all she could do was feel and hang on.

And after that, he'd wanted to have coffee with her, see

what her morning routine was like. Was she grumpy until the caffeine kicked in, or did she hit the floor with all cylinders running? Did she like to read, watch TV, or catch up on emails while she sipped that first cup, or just look out the window?

He'd wanted to take her to breakfast—or make it here or, hell, eat two-day-old leftovers, he didn't care—so they could talk. About everything and nothing. Last night had been their first night together.

This morning should've been their first morning together.

But Annie had run.

He shouldn't be surprised. He knew that. Everything about last night had probably overwhelmed her. But he was still going to read her the riot act.

By lunchtime, he realized she really wasn't going to call. He'd tried her phone a couple times, but she wasn't picking up. When he remembered that he'd left his Harley at The Eagle's Nest, he cursed again. One of the guys would have to give him a ride into town so he could get his bike back.

He walked into the office twenty minutes later. Finn was talking at his desk phone. Ethan was scowling at a book in his hand.

"Hey, Uncle Zac."

Zac's heart clenched, as it sometimes did, looking at Ethan. Micah would've been buddies with the little boy if he had lived, Zac had no doubt about it.

He plopped down on the couch next to the boy, ruffling his hair rather than pulling him in for a hug like he wanted. "Hey, bud. What book you got there?"

"Dad says I've got to meet with another specialist today." Ethan let out a sigh, this apparently a fate worse than death. "I always have to bring a book when I meet one."

Ethan was falling further and further behind at school. He'd come so far since Finn had gotten custody of him five years ago, but now it was becoming an issue as he was finishing second grade. The last thing Ethan needed was for his self-esteem to take a beating. He'd been through enough in his short life.

The book was something about a tree house with magic. "Looks pretty interesting."

He shrugged. "Yeah. But it's *Saturday*." Everybody obviously knew they were not meant for reading.

Finn hung up. "That was Frank Jenkins and his crew. They're confirmed for an overall basics course for Monday. After that, they'll decide what else they're interested in."

"Great. A little more Frank is just what we need around here. Is it officially too early for me to call 'not it'?"

Finn stood. "I think the official phrase is 'Nose goes' and I've already called it."

"So that's settled. We'll make Aiden teach the class."

Finn chuckled. "He'll love that."

"Are you guys going into town?"

Finn came over and ruffled Ethan's hair. The kid beamed up at his dad, his face so full of love it was almost hard to look at. "Yeah, we're going to the Frontier to meet with a private tutor Ethan's the education department suggested."

"You don't have to go to the school or an office?"

"Nope. She wanted to meet somewhere E felt comfortable. So, we already like her better, don't we, sport?"

Ethan grinned—a look so similar to his dad's it was scary. "Aunt Wavy and Trey's pie makes me comfortable."

Zac laughed. "Me too, buddy. Can I catch a ride into town with you guys?"

"Yeah. But I don't know how long we'll be."

"That's okay. I'll get some lunch, then grab my bike. It's still at The Eagle's Nest."

Finn looked like he was bursting at the seams to ask questions but couldn't because of the presence of an impressionable seven-year-old.

But as soon as they arrived at the Frontier, and Ethan asked if he could go sit at the bar and talk to Trey while the man cooked, Finn pounced.

"All right, Zac. Spill. How did you get home last night if your bike's still in town?"

They slid into a booth. Zac sighed. "I actually took Annie to my place. We drove her car."

Finn's mouth dropped open. "Your place? You never take women there."

Zac shrugged. "I wanted her there."

"Please tell me you did not kick her out in the middle of the night."

He rolled his eyes. "No, for Christ's sake. I did not." Admittedly, he had never been one for actually *sleeping* with a woman. He'd never wanted that sort of intimacy. He had with Annie. He'd loved pulling her in next to him, her long legs entwining with his.

He'd loved waking her up in the hour just before dawn by kissing his way down her shoulders, taking a long time on her breasts—feeling her breathing pick up even though she was still asleep. By the time he'd worked his way down her belly and eased his lips up and down her thighs, she'd woken up, those big brown eyes staring at him as he'd draped one of those shapely legs over his shoulder and proceeded to make sure she was *fully* awake.

"She have an emergency or something?" Finn asked. "Occupational hazard with an ER doc, I guess."

Wavy chose that second to sit down in the booth next to her brother, sliding two glasses of water toward each of them. "You talking about Anne? She came by here this morning. Evidently she left Casanova sleeping and took off."

Finn spewed the water he'd just taken a sip of. "Oh my God, she *Coyote-Uglied* you?" He turned to Wavy. "That's when you wake up next to someone so horrible that you would rather chew your arm off than face—"

"I know what it means. And yes, that's exactly what happened."

Zac resisted the urge to tell them both what they could do to themselves. "She came in here? What did she say?"

Wavy began to giggle. "She told me she went home with you and that it was *nice*."

The word Zac muttered under his breath was not meant for polite company. "Nice?"

"You know Anne. She's not one to elaborate." Her laughter died down. "She's trying to protect herself, Zac. And I'll admit, both Riley and I warned her that she should."

"Why the hell would you tell her that?"

"You date, but you're closed off. You never seem to be interested in any woman seriously. Anne doesn't play casual; you know that."

He sighed. "Maybe I'm not either." Hell, nothing about Annie had ever been casual for him.

"She's in waters she doesn't know how to navigate." Wavy stood back up when Trey yelled that an order was ready. "She doesn't know exactly how she feels about you, and she especially doesn't know how to deal with all the attention that's being flung her way. Like Frank Jenkins asking her out."

"What? This morning?"

"Yep." She backed toward the kitchen window. "He was drunk, and she, of course, said no. But now she's going to be getting that attention from all sorts of guys."

He watched Wavy grab a few plates and put one in front of Ethan, who was still chatting with the cook, and take the others across the diner. She was right, Annie would be getting a lot of attention.

He thought they'd established a connection last night. He sure as hell had. She'd felt it too. He knew she had. What they'd done last night had been so much more than physical—although that part had been mind-blowing.

Zac stood. "I'm going to talk to Annie."

Finn cocked an eyebrow. "To tell her that last night was *nice* for you too?"

"Annie works best when she knows all the parameters. That's how her brain functions." She may not choose him once she had all the facts, and that was her choice. But he would still make sure she *had* them, including the most important one: he wanted her. Not just for one night. Not just casually. But as something much more serious. "She works in exacts, not—"

His eyes tracked to the woman walking through the door, dressed in jeans and a blazer, long blonde hair framing her small face. This was not good. He sat back down. "Oh shit."

"What?" Finn turned around. "Oh shit."

Charlotte Devereux.

Zac shook his head. "I never thought she'd be back here again. I thought we were all beneath her."

Finn swallowed hard, eyes narrowing. "Yeah, me especially." He stood as she walked closer.

"Your Royal Highness." Finn bowed with an exaggerated flourish. "On behalf of the peons and plebeians of Oak Creek, we welcome Your Honor into our humble abode."

Surprise flashed through Charlotte's blue eyes before they narrowed, her shoulders straightening and neck stiffening, making her look more like the regal figure Finn had accused her of being.

"Plebeians." Zac would swear she was looking down her nose at Finn, although she was nearly a full foot shorter. "Wouldn't have expected you to know that word, Bollinger."

"Why are you here, Charlie?"

Her eyes narrowed at the nickname. "I didn't realize it was a sin or illegal for me to enter a public restaurant in Oak Creek."

Finn shook his head, arms crossed over his chest. "It's not, just in bad judgment."

Charlotte blew out a breath. "Look, Finn, I'm not here to see you, okay? I'm here to meet a family to help their son with some tutoring."

"*You're* the learning specialist Mrs. Johnson suggested for Ethan?"

"Yes, I'm here to meet with a child named Ethan. The agency doesn't give me a last name until after the parents have approved me as a tutor. Do you know him and his family?"

"Ethan is right behind you at the bar. And he's *my* son."

"You have a *son*?"

"Sure do, sweetheart. And you think you're getting near him? That would be a *hell no* with a side of *no chance*. I don't know what your game is or who you paid to make Mrs.

Johnson think you're a specialist at anything, but you need to leave. Now."

Something flashed across Charlotte's face— Desperation? Fear? Weariness?— but it was gone before Zac could figure out what. Not that he really cared. In this battle, he was firmly on Team Finn.

"I see." If possible, her chin lifted even higher, the wealthy-girl facade wrapped around her like a well-fitting cloak. "Good-bye, then."

She was out the door a moment later.

Finn sunk back down into the booth.

"You okay, man?" Zac asked.

Finn shrugged, then took a sip of his water. "What the hell just happened?"

"Charlotte Devereux happened."

"Why would she work for a tutoring company? That makes zero sense."

"Do you think she's moved back to Oak Creek?"

Finn shook his head and shrugged. "I don't give a damn."

"Dude, you give so many they're practically visible from space."

"I'll have to call Mrs. Johnson and tell her it didn't work out. See if there's someone else. Why would Charlotte pretend to be an education specialist?" Finn stood and called out to Ethan. "E, no meeting any teachers today. You're off the hook."

The boy hooted and gave Trey a high five as he walked by the kitchen window. Finn just looked pensive.

Zac stood. "You okay? I still want to go talk to Annie."

Finn shook his head, his normal easy-going smile nowhere to be found. "Women are too complicated, brother. Get out while you can. It's too damn hard."

Zac put a hand on his friend's shoulder. "Nothing worth doing is ever easy."

He didn't wait for Finn to respond, just tousled Ethan's hair and waved to Trey and Waverly as he walked out the door and straight to the hospital.

He didn't have a plan, didn't know what he was going to say to her. But he wouldn't let her exit this morning grow into some big wall between them.

Zac was becoming more familiar with the hospital than he'd ever expected. But he had no idea where he'd find Annie now and doubted he'd be allowed to walk around unaccompanied for long.

He was heading down the hall to the nurses' station when he heard some women talking around a corner. He stopped when he heard his name.

"—doesn't matter how great of a doctor she is, there's no way Zac is going to stay with someone like Dr. Griffin very long. Some things aren't meant to be."

"Oh yeah, totally. I wouldn't be surprised if they're already done. He scratched that itch and that's that. Not that he'll be mean. He'll find a way to let her down easy."

Small town. He loved Oak Creek, but for God's sake, the rumor mill here was vicious. And he knew there was only one way to stop it.

He stepped around the corner. "Actually, I don't have any plans to let Annie down easy. I don't have any to let her down at all. She, on the other hand, may decide she has other, better, options, but I plan to be around until she comes to her senses."

Both women—he'd seen them before but couldn't think of their names—laughed nervously. "Hey, Zac," one said.

The other shrugged. "Yeah, we were just speculating. Didn't mean any harm."

He smiled. "Wanted to make sure I set the record straight. Do you happen to know where Dr. Griffin is?"

"I'm right here." Annie stepped around the opposite corner.

The two nurses flushed in mortification to be caught by both people they'd been gossiping about. Within seconds they made excuses and left.

"Busy?" he asked Annie.

"No. I came in to work because I was...wound up. But I was about to head home."

He leaned against the wall. "So, there was no emergency that called you here? No triple appendectomy that made you leave in such a hurry this morning that you couldn't wake me up and say good-bye?"

She flushed deeper than the gossiping nurses had. "I thought it would be better that way. That it was how one-night stands worked. I didn't want things to be awkward."

"It's going to be quite a bit awkward if I have to throw you over my shoulder and carry you out of here."

"Is that what you want?" she asked softly.

"Well, what I really want is for you to come with me, sleep the rest of the afternoon—because I don't like those circles under your eyes even if you have them because of all the sexy times going on last night—then let me make you dinner before showing you *more* sexy times."

He heard a female sigh around the corner and knew this conversation would be blasted all over the place within the hour.

He didn't care.

He stepped closer and cupped her cheeks. "What's between us is definitely not a one-night stand, okay? Now kiss me and promise me no more running away."

"I promise." She went up on tiptoe and pressed her lips

to his before backing away. "And there's no such thing as a triple appen—"

His arms wrapped around her and yanked her back to him. He slid his hand into the hair at the nape of her neck and held her still, so he could plunder her mouth. After a few seconds, she sighed as she gave herself over to it.

That was the only sigh that mattered.

# CHAPTER 20

OVER THE NEXT FEW DAYS, Anne developed a much better understanding of what it must be like to suffer from multiple personality disorder. There was Dr. Griffin, the emergency room physician who could handle any crisis coolly and calmly, who spoke with authority, moved with brisk efficiency, and commanded respect.

And then there was Annie, who had flown in the back door to the hospital and into her office this morning, ninety seconds from being late, hair damp and hanging down her back, and one shoe untied all because she hadn't been able to get Zac out of her bed.

Admittedly, it hadn't been completely his fault. She'd had to leave her car parked at the Frontier Diner because she'd rushed in to grab breakfast pastries and coffee, and when she'd come back out, it hadn't started. She'd then had to walk as fast as she could without spilling her coffee through the drizzle to get here.

Which meant it wasn't all his fault. Just a big chunk.

She caught sight of herself in the mirror in the corner of her office and had to stop and laugh.

She was a mess. Zac, with the help of the rain and a cantankerous car, had made her a mess.

She began to braid her hair, so it wouldn't be in her way, but she couldn't ignore the healthy flush of her cheeks and the smile she couldn't quite tamp down.

Zac Mackay might make her a mess, but it was a beautiful, happy one.

This Annie, she may not know what to do with exactly. This Annie got a little uncomfortable with all the rumors floating around about her relationship, spoke more softly and still with an occasional stutter when she was uncomfortable. But she couldn't deny—didn't want to—that this woman was part of her personality too.

She finished her braid and bent down to tie her shoe, wincing at the aches from muscles that had gotten more of a workout in the last week than they had her whole life. Zac had been at her house, or she at his place, whenever they could carve out time.

He'd come over at eleven at night if that's when she got off—cue eyebrow wag and giggle about *getting off*. And she'd spent yesterday at Linear Tactical, since she hadn't had to work, watching from the swing on the front porch of the office as Zac taught a class for a couple hours until Aiden arrived. She didn't even mind that the class had involved Frank, Shawn, and their posse. Watching Zac go through some fighting moves and weapons tactics sans shirt had gotten her so hot and bothered that she wouldn't have minded if he'd been teaching the Muppets.

Once Aiden had taken over the class, Zac had made his way to her, leaning against the railing. "Want to get some lunch?"

She'd stood and walked straight into the V his long legs made, wrapped her hand around his head, and fisted his hair, pulling his mouth an inch from her own. "No. I don't want lunch right now."

Her lips had covered his and she'd devoured him, reveling in the feeling of his large hands grabbing her hips and yanking her closer. Of his breathing coming faster. Because of her.

After a couple minutes, the catcalls from the guys had finally made it through the sensual fog of her mind. She'd opened her eyes, still plastered to him. Zac had chuckled against her lips, wrapped his arms under her hips, and carried her, her legs around his waist, to his apartment over the barn. He'd flipped the guys off as they'd gone by and barely gotten them up the stairs and to that same wall inside his door before he'd plastered her there and taken her.

No doubt the story of them together as Zac carried her across the compound was going to spread to everyone, since Frank had seen it. It was probably already all over the hospital.

Leaving her office, she walked briskly to the nurses' station. If Susan had heard about any of the shenanigans, it didn't show. But then Anne saw Sheriff Nelson standing at the edge of the station, looking at his phone. Her heart dropped. Not again.

"Oh no, Sheriff." She set down the chart she'd picked up and walked over to him. "Was another woman raped?"

"No, no. No more that have been reported."

She let out a sigh of relief. "Oh, thank God."

The older man nodded. "And Rogers and I have spread the word to a wider area to make sure other counties know we could have a serial rapist on our hands. Nothing will be taken as an isolated event. Of course, if the perp moves on to different states entirely, then future attacks may never be connected to the ones here."

They both knew this guy wasn't going to stop. Not after getting away with it two, possibly more, times. Like the sheriff said, it was just a matter of when and if the cases would be linked.

"Please, let me know if I can help in any way." And she would, to help Kimmy and Veronica. Even if it meant getting up on the stand at a trial and stuttering in front of everyone, she would do it. "Is there something else we can help you with?"

"Um, no." He looked sheepishly over at Nurse Lusher. "I'm waiting to take Susan to eat on her break."

"Oh!" The surprised squeak popped out of her before Anne could stop it. She looked at Susan to find the normally unflappable woman fidgeting. "Yes, of course. I'll get caught up on all the charts without you, Susan. Please, go ahead."

A few minutes later the two walked, a little too closely to be just friends, down the hall toward the cafeteria. As Anne headed toward a patient's room, she heard two nurses.

"I'm only saying, I think it's sweet. The biracial thing doesn't bother me at all. And love doesn't care how old they are."

Another woman answered. "I just don't know how long it will last. The sheriff has been married twice before, you know."

It looked like the gossipmongers had moved on to someone else.

～

The day was steady, as she liked them. It kept her focused

and made the hours fly by. She got a text from Zac around dinnertime saying he wasn't going to make it to the hospital to eat with her like he'd hoped, some sort of electrical problem at Linear. She texted back.

*I should be done by 9 PM. I'll just come to your place.*

*Perfect. I plan to have you naked five minutes later.*

She rolled her eyes even as her body tingled at the thought.

By eight o'clock, things had slowed down enough that she decided to leave. It was still drizzling as she walked out the front door toward the hospital lot and cursed under her breath when she remembered she'd parked at the Frontier this morning. Hopefully her car would start this time. It looked like she was back to praying to the patron saint of automobiles. At least she had someone who could come and get her now if she got stranded.

That was a nice feeling.

Wishing she had an umbrella, she began jogging around the hospital toward the diner. She could cut down Main Street or take the shorter back path through the small park she'd walked through this morning.

Rain. Shorter was better.

But as she stepped toward the park, it seemed darker than usual. Was that the rain? Was she being overly suspicious because of the sheriff's presence at the hospital earlier? She strained her eyes, searching for the path she thought a lamp normally lit. She hadn't really paid attention before, but hadn't there been a couple lights along this path? And now they weren't on.

Situational awareness.

Was she being paranoid? Maybe. But if someone had shot out the lights like they had at the vet's office, Anne wasn't taking a chance. She turned and walked down the street instead. It was Sunday, the clothes shops, hair salons, and hardware store that lined the road were all closed, but at least the streetlights weren't out.

She kept her head down, shivering, darting from the overhang of one building to another. It didn't take long before she wished she'd gone through the park. She would've already been at her car by now.

Having excellent situation awareness wasn't going to help at all if she died from pneumonia or hypotherm—

There was no warning at all, no movement or sound to alert her. A hand clamped over her mouth, and an arm wrapped around the front of her body, trapping both her arms against her chest. She froze, her brain trying to process exactly what was happening. She waited a split second, hoping this was a joke, Zac or someone messing with her.

But it wasn't.

The man—bigger than her, stronger than her, and very definitely not Zac—began hauling her with bruising force down the alley that ran between the nail salon and the coffee shop, away from the main street.

Anne's brain finally caught up with the situation, and she fought, twisting and kicking. She screamed, but only muffled sounds escaped from behind the man's hand. No one was out in this rain, nor would anyone inside be able to hear her.

She tried to use her height to her advantage—Anne was no dainty, petite woman. She threw her weight to the side, knocking both her and her attacker into the concrete wall of the alley. Her legs scraped painfully against it, but he didn't let go. He just dragged her farther along.

Fear flooded through her, thick and slimy. This was the rapist. He'd waited for her like he had for Kimmy and Veronica.

Anne fought harder.

Working one arm free, she twisted, trying to claw his face, but found some sort of ski mask beneath her fingertips. Her nails couldn't do any damage, so she tried to hit him instead. She barely got in one ill-aimed punch before he slammed her head into the wall. White dots floated in front of her vision, agony spiking through her skull where her forehead had hit.

Everything blurred. She needed to fight. He was dragging her toward the end of the alley, and each step took her farther from safety and closer to where he wanted her. She tried to yank away again as he took her behind a large garbage container.

He pulled her closer, hand still over her mouth, his breath hot, fast, and sickening in her ear, as he forced her down on her stomach in the gravel and mud. She couldn't manage to get her arm free to protect her face from the rocks ripping into the skin at her temple. She twisted to try to move his suffocating hand from her mouth, but it wouldn't give. His heavy weight on her back forced her flat onto the ground.

He reached for her scrubs, pushing the elastic waistband lower, exposing her. Wildly, she twisted, trying to bring her legs back to strike him, to do any damage she could. He hit her again, slamming her head against the ground.

Anne fought to hold on to consciousness, focusing on the sound of his breath in her ear. It kept her conscious, but she began to gag.

Her scrubs tore under the man's hand, and her terror multiplied. She ripped at the hand over her mouth again, forcing one of his fingers close enough so she could bite it. He howled before slamming her head into the concrete once again, this time finding a place with a puddle and holding her face in it.

Anne choked as she breathed in the dirty water. She tried to lift her face, but he jammed it down.

God, was she going to die in two inches of water? That was all it took.

His hand yanked down her scrubs, the cold rain hitting her back and buttocks before he covered her with his body again.

"I always catch what I hunt," he said in a raspy voice full of triumph.

Utter loathing gave her a final burst of strength. She flung herself as hard as she could to the side, catching him off guard in the midst of his gloating. She brought her elbow up and drove it into his head, causing him to loosen his grip.

It gave her the moment she needed. A scream blasted out of her puddle-flooded lungs. She grabbed a small rock and began banging it against the metal trash container. The sound echoed through the night.

It was enough.

A shout from far off caused her attacker to jump away. One of his black combat boots flew at her midsection, the force of it slamming her backward before she felt anything. Then the pain exploded. She rolled to her side, not even able to cry out as he kicked her again in her femur.

Then he was gone. Anne struggled to pull air into her lungs, lying face-first on the ground.

She heard other noises around her, saw feet. Panic set in again. She had to get out of here. She tried to turn herself, so she could face the exit of the alley. But that small movement took every bit of strength she had.

Through the haze of pain, she realized the shoes were different. White tennis shoes. Not black boots. It didn't matter because Anne couldn't find the strength to move anyway, no matter who it was. She lay still, just trying to draw in enough air to survive. The shoes ran away.

A few moments later, the white shoes returned. She heard more yelling, but it seemed distant, like she was watching the whole scene from far away. The shoes' owner bent down.

A big black man with a chef's apron. Trey. From the Frontier. She knew him.

"Oh God, Dr. Griffin. *Doc*. It's going to be okay. He's gone now. No one's going to hurt you. Hold on, help is coming."

She'd never heard Trey talk so much.

She just lay there on her side with her cheek on the ground, looking at him. She should say something, but she couldn't. She still couldn't get air fully into her lungs—some distant part of her diagnosed it as a bruised or cracked rib. She couldn't even muster the energy to cover herself. All she could do was shiver.

Trey took off his apron and laid it over Anne's waist and hips. At first, she thought it was because he was trying to keep her warm, but then realized he was trying to cover where the attacker had ripped her scrubs. Shudders racked her body, and she struggled not to vomit.

Trey yelled to someone at the end of the alley, and soon there were more people around. Anne just closed her eyes. She was so cold now she couldn't feel anything anyway.

"Call 911," Trey said.

"We're only two blocks from the hospital. We could carry her there in less time ourselves." Another man. Frantic. Worried.

"I'm not sure about her injuries," Trey said. "If we should move her."

Someone else ran up. A woman. "Oh my God. What happened?" Wavy. "Is that Annie?"

"Wavy, you talk to her," Trey said. "She knows you."

"Is she conscious?"

"I think so. She was a minute ago."

She couldn't force herself to open her eyes. The men kept talking, one agreeing to run to the hospital to get help. Someone moved near her.

"Anne, sweetie, can you open your eyes?"

Wavy's voice was so soft, concerned, Anne forced herself to do what the woman asked.

She found Wavy's face a few inches from her own. The other woman's cheek was also on the ground, lying on her side, mirroring Anne. Like two girls gossiping at a sleepover.

Anne closed her eyes again. She'd never had many sleepovers.

"Can you hear me?" Wavy asked. Her fingers gently touched Anne's cheeks. "Can you open your eyes again?"

"Yes." The word came out as a croak, but she did what Wavy asked.

Wavy smiled. "Good, sweetie. It's cold out here. We need to get you to the hospital."

A few moments later a dry blanket floated over both Anne and Wavy. The warmth felt wonderful, although she knew it wouldn't take long for it to get wet in the rain.

She had to get up. She didn't want Wavy to get hypothermia from being in this weather. Everything hurt so much.

Anne struggled through the pain and haze to find the physician part of herself, to evaluate herself objectively. She knew what Wavy was most worried about.

"He d-d-didn't—" Anne couldn't say the word. "Trey scared him off before..."

Wavy's eyes closed briefly. "Thank God. But you've got other injuries, honey. You still need to go to the hospital."

"He kicked me." Anne tried to take a deep breath but gasped at the sharp pain. "I think one of my ribs might be fractured."

More people surrounded them now, and the blanket was getting wetter.

"I want to go inside." Her voice was tinny. Weak. She didn't like it. She tried again to categorize her injuries but couldn't think about it right now. Everything hurt so bad. "I want Zac."

Wavy nodded. "I know you do, sweetie. He'll be here soon."

"I need everyone to clear this area," a man shouted. "If you're not Trey, Wavy, or a medical professional, you need to remove yourself right now."

"I think I have to go," she told Wavy, worriedly. Everything was spinning. Did she have a fever? The flu? No, of course not. She had a concussion. "The yelling man didn't mention my name."

Wavy's brow furrowed and she reached a hand out toward Anne again. "That's Sheriff Nelson. He's here to help. And I think it's okay for you to stay too. *You* are a medical professional."

"That's true. I'm so tired, Wavy. And my head hurts. Everything hurts. Will you stay with me, so I can take a nap?" She inched her fingers toward Wavy's outstretched hand until they touched.

"Absolutely. I'll be right here."

Anne closed her eyes and let the blessed darkness take over.

# CHAPTER 21

"WHAT DID YOU GUYS DO, throw a firecracker in here or something?"

Zac and Aiden were sitting in the dark of their 20,000-square-foot training facility, holding flashlights for Louis Bellman, the same electrician Zac had called to fix Anne's electrical problems after the flooding.

"Yeah, it looked like a mess to me, too," Zac said. "That's why we decided to call you."

The training facility—by far the most valuable part of the property—was massive. It was used for all sorts of training and had its own electrical room. Louis had been studying the damage ever since he'd arrived a couple hours ago, when they'd found the power completely dead in the building.

They'd thought it might be a city issue, that the power was just out in their grid, until they'd gone into the electrical room. Some sort of complete meltdown had happened in one section.

"You guys have any sort of sabotage problems, pranks,

anything like that lately?" Louis asked, looking through the wires that had melted together.

"No." Zac looked over at Aiden who shrugged. "Why?"

"Because if I had to take a guess, I think someone did this on purpose. It *might* be some sort of faulty wiring causing a meltdown. But with a building this new, and as good as you take care of it, it's not likely."

Fuck. It was going to be a long night if they were talking sabotage.

"What would someone gain from blowing the power to our training facility?" Aiden asked. "I mean, it's a pain in the ass, and probably a sizable expense, but we've got insurance."

"Rival company, maybe?" Louis continued to study the melted wiring.

"It's possible." Zac shook his head. "But it's not like we're unfriendly with each other. No turf wars or crap like that."

"We don't even have anyone on the schedule for using the building this week, do we?" Aiden shifted to give Louis more light. "So, if someone was trying to sabotage us, they picked the least painful week to do it."

"Maybe it really was a freak thing. It happens." Louis turned to them. "I'll have to rebuild part of this panel, but it should only take a day or two at most. Looks like all the damage was isolated here. Nothing else has been—"

Finn came running into the electrical room at a full sprint. Zac and Aiden both spun, ready for battle, looking for whatever enemy needed fighting.

"What?" Zac barked.

"It's Anne." Finn's eyes were anguished. "Someone attacked her in town as she was walking to her car."

Aiden cursed, Zac barely registering the sound.

"I've got this," Louis said. "You guys go."

Within seconds they were running for the parking lot. Zac wanted to drive but Aiden shook his head.

"I'll drive."

Zac wanted to argue that he could drive, to feel like he was in control of *some* fucking thing, but he didn't. It would just waste time.

Annie.

He jumped in the passenger side of Aiden's Jeep, and Finn climbed in the back. He felt slightly better when Aiden tore out of the driveway faster than even Zac would have taken it.

Zac took a deep breath and focused. "Tell me what you know."

"Wavy called me," Finn said. "Somebody jumped Anne as she was walking to her car from the hospital. It was parked at the Frontier. Bastard pulled her down into that alley by the nail salon."

Zac's knuckles grew white from the grip he had on the dashboard. Annie was alive, that was the most important thing. All the other questions he pushed out of his mind. She was *alive*.

"Trey went to take some trash out. He heard a scream and something banging on a dumpster and ran over there. Scared the guy off."

Zac wiped a hand across his face as Aiden pushed the gas down harder. If someone hadn't been taking out the damn trash...

Finn put a hand on his shoulder. "Wavy told me Anne said she wasn't raped, man. That Trey scared the guy off in time."

Zac held on to that. Wanted it to be true with every

fiber of his being. He had to get to Annie and talk to her himself. "Okay."

"But she's hurt. Bastard kicked her and slammed her head against the ground or a wall. She's unconscious and doesn't look very good. Wavy's damn near hysterical."

Zac had known Finn's sister all her life. It took a lot to make Waverly Bollinger lose it.

"Okay," he said again.

"I'm just telling you this, so you can be prepared."

"I know, Finn. Thank you."

Finn didn't want him rushing in there and letting all his fury loose in front of Annie. That was the last thing she needed. Zac would keep the rage flowing through him under control. For her. To be whatever Annie needed.

Even if she didn't want to see him at all—which, given everything, was a distinct possibility. He'd just sit out in the waiting room.

"Is anybody with her?"

"Wavy's still there. And Riley Wilde. Sheriff has already been on scene and in the hospital. They moved her directly into a room, she's not in the ICU or anything. So that's good."

"I'll get Dorian out there ASAP," Aiden said quietly, not taking his eyes off the road. "The rain makes things tougher, but you know he'll do his damnedest."

Why hadn't she parked in the hospital lot? Why would her car have been at the Frontier?

The ten minutes into town were the longest of Zac's life. Aiden let them off at the front of the emergency room. Wavy met them at the entrance. She was still in her Frontier uniform, the side of her face dirty, her auburn hair completely out of its normal, neat ponytail. Finn pulled his sister in for a hug.

"How is she?" Zac asked, fighting every urge to blow by them and sprint to Annie's room, the need to rush to her side itching through his skin.

Wavy walked to Zac and put both hands on his biceps, forcing him to focus on her. "She's asleep right now. Medicated. That's good. It will probably be a few hours before she even begins to stir."

Zac nodded, focusing, calming himself.

"She wasn't raped, Zac. She said that from the beginning, and the assault kit test confirmed that. It was definitely his intent, but he wasn't able to do it."

"Thank God." He sagged, realizing he hadn't believed it when he'd heard it the first time. He still needed to see her.

They began walking slowly toward the elevator.

"She wasn't raped," Wavy continued, "but it's still pretty bad. He hit her and ground her face into the pavement. Kicked her in the abdomen and bruised two of her ribs pretty severely."

Both he and Finn muttered vile expletives. Both knew what it was like to have broken and bruised ribs. The panicked feeling that you couldn't get enough breath. The pain that nothing really seemed to ease.

The elevator door opened, and soon they were outside Annie's door. Zac touched Wavy's arm.

"Maybe I shouldn't go in there. Maybe she doesn't want to see any men right now." God, the thought ripped him to shreds. But his wants weren't important.

"No, come in. She wants you. When she was lying out there in that alley, she specifically asked for you. She'll want you here."

He closed his eyes, tamping down his fury and helplessness. "Then I'll be here."

"I'm going to find Sheriff Nelson," Finn said, slipping

his arm around Wavy again. "I definitely don't need to be in there, and I can do more good helping him. I'll keep you posted."

Zac nodded, leaving them and slipping quietly into Annie's hospital room. He gave a brief wave to Riley, who was sitting next to the bed, then allowed his gaze to fall on Annie.

Zac had seen things as a Green Beret—death, destruction, agony on both an individual and countrywide level. Sometimes he'd been sent in to stop it, to fight it, and set wrongs to rights. Sometimes—not as often, but the far more difficult times—he'd been forced to stand to the side as a country destroyed itself and its own people. To only step in if asked by a local or national government or given a specific order by his own.

He and the team knew the agony of watching others suffer, and not being able to do anything about it. They had seen things that even now, years later, woke them in a cold sweat.

But none of that even came close to the despondency Zac felt when he saw Annie's still form lying in the hospital bed. He moved to her side, touching her arm near her elbow, which seemed to be one of the few places not injured.

The side of her face was scraped from where the asshole had ground her into the pavement. One eye was swollen, her cheek bruised—she'd been hit with a fist, at least once.

The area around her mouth was the slightest shade of blue, and bruising was already forming over her lower jaw. Zac's own jaw tightened. Her attacker had covered it with his hand.

Her arms were covered with red marks that would turn

to bruises soon. Some were generic from hitting a wall or the ground. But others were very specifically shaped like a man's fingers. Her left bicep, her right wrist. Bandages now covered the palms of her hands, no doubt from abrasions there too.

"She's going to be okay," Riley told him softly from where she sat on the other side of Anne's bed. "She's strong."

Zac nodded. He knew that was true, but hell if she looked strong lying there.

"She wasn't raped. Thank God."

His lips flattened. "Wavy told me. She still looks pretty bad."

"He slammed her head against a hard surface, the ground or the wall or both, we're not sure. Minor concussion, a big source of her pain. As well as her ribs."

"Bastard kicked her."

She nodded. "But she screamed, banged a rock against the dumpster, and caught Trey's attention when he went out to empty some trash. Her attacker kicked her before running off."

"Why is her mouth blue? Hypothermia?" It was May, warm enough that no one was wearing any jackets. But in the rain after the sun had set, Wyoming could be quite cold.

Riley's eyes narrowed, lips pursing. "He held her face in a puddle. She almost drowned."

A vein throbbed in his neck. The desire to go after the person who'd done this warred with the need to stay by her side, to protect her.

He could trust that Aiden and Dorian would be gathering whatever intel was available from the scene outside. That bastard had just attacked one of their own. They'd find anything the cops missed.

He eased into the chair on the other side of Annie.

"Was she awake when they got her here?"

"In and out." Riley leaned back in her chair. She was still dressed in her scrubs. "I was getting off work when someone came running into the ER yelling for a doctor, saying that Trey had found someone hurt down the street. Ironically, we all looked for Anne first. She almost always works late."

Zac nodded.

"Dude who came in wasn't sure exactly what had happened. But once we found out it wasn't a life or death situation—the victim was breathing, there hadn't been a car accident or anything—a couple EMTs grabbed a gurney and headed out." Riley ran a hand over her eyes. "If I had known it was Anne... Hell, if I had known it was any woman who had been attacked, I would've gone with them."

"I know. Anne will too."

Riley shrugged. "At least Wavy was with her. She and Trey were afraid Anne might have had a back or neck injury, so they very wisely got the EMTs. Thankfully, nothing with her spine was affected, and they brought her right in."

Riley brought both hands up to her face. Obviously, Annie's state when she arrived hadn't been pretty. "It was the same guy who raped those other women, wasn't it?"

Zac shrugged. "Maybe. Probably." Aiden and Dorian would make sure he knew more soon.

He just continued staring at Annie. Running his fingers along her arm, over the bruises on her wrist and the back of her hand. He didn't know if she could feel or process it in any way yet, but when she began to wake up, he wanted to know she was safe.

"Dr. Lewis was great," Riley continued. "He immediately got Anne into one of the private rooms and expressly forbad anyone from entering except me and Susan, the head nurse. She's older and has an excellent relationship with Anne. Nobody else was allowed in. You know how everyone gets around here with gossip."

He couldn't take his eyes off Annie's face, the bruising, the blue that signaled how close she'd come to dying. "I know she would appreciate that. She has no idea how much people respect her around here. How much people care."

"Zac." The word came out a breathy whisper. Annie. He hopped out of his chair, moving closer to her face.

"I'm here, sweetheart. It's okay."

She didn't say anything else.

"She's done that a couple times. Wavy said she was asking for you in the alley as well, before she lost consciousness."

He eased into his chair again. "When will she wake up?"

"They've already started easing back the barbiturates, so it won't be very long."

He would be right here when she did.

# CHAPTER 22

ANNE CAME BACK to consciousness slowly, for a few seconds at a time. She couldn't remember exactly what had happened, her mind couldn't focus on anything that specific, but she knew it was bad. She became aware of pain, terrible and throbbing through her whole body, and wanted immediately to go back to the darkness. To stay there forever.

But then she heard Zac's voice, could feel his fingers trailing a pattern on her arm.

She tried to say his name—maybe even succeeded—but fell into the darkness again. It was warm. Safe. Like a huge, cozy blanket that kept her wrapped inside and everything else at a distance. When she held on to it, she couldn't feel the pain and didn't have to remember.

But she couldn't stay in the dark forever.

She rested, gathered her strength, and listened. She let the friendly, even voices of people who wouldn't hurt her wash over her.

Eventually, she couldn't deny that it was time to unwrap herself from her blanket.

The pain came. In her ribs. Her face. Her hands. But she didn't try to hide from it this time. The memories clawed at her mind too, but she kept those pushed back. One thing at a time. Right now, the physical pain was all she could handle.

"Ouch."

She wasn't aware she'd said the word out loud until the friendly voices moved closer, talking to her. Asking questions.

She opened her eyes.

The hospital. The familiar sights and smells swirled around her. And with all the pain in her body, being in one made sense.

Zac's blue eyes, and Riley's brown, hovered nearby, both faces lit with concern.

"Hey, sweetheart," Zac crooned. She liked his voice.

She tried to sit up toward him but sucked a breath through her teeth as her whole body lit up in agony. She closed her eyes again.

"Don't try to move." The voice this time was Riley's. "You have a bruised rib."

Anne nodded her head, which also hurt a little, but it wasn't agonizing like her midsection. "Okay."

"Dr. Lewis will be here in a minute to adjust your medication."

"Am I in the emergency ward?" She couldn't hear all the sounds that usually went along with her normal workplace.

"No, you were admitted and taken upstairs to a regular room. You're definitely going to need to stay a couple days, Anne."

"Okay," she whispered.

The memories were pressing in closer, demanding her attention. Why was she hurt? An accident? She didn't want to think about them. She wasn't ready to let them in. Instead, she went back into the darkness.

The next time it eased back, it was like a rubber band had snapped, thrusting her out into the light, pain, and cold with no way of going back.

And all the memories came with it, whether she was ready for them or not.

Sobbing, she tried to find her way back into the darkness. Her eyes were closed, and she couldn't see anything, but the peaceful darkness that had blanketed her was gone.

She heard an unfamiliar voice and flinched. She felt warm air near her and remembered the hot, bitter breath of the man who'd attacked her.

She remembered all of it.

Her eyes flew open. Her body jerked.

It wasn't her attacker near her, it was Zac and Riley. The unfamiliar voice belonged to a doctor she'd seen around the hospital multiple times. But it couldn't stop her panic.

Her arm flew out in front of her even as the pain made her gasp. "No. No. I— I—"

"Anne, it's okay," Riley said. "You're safe now. Nobody's going to hurt you."

The unknown doctor stepped back. Zac did too. She wanted to reach for him, wanted him closer, but she couldn't get the words out. She just focused on breathing.

"Someone attacked me in the alley," she finally got out.

Riley nodded. "That's right. But you fought him off."

Anne let all the memories flood through her. Terror when she'd first been grabbed and had realized his intent.

Recognition that it was the same man who had raped Kimmy and Veronica. Pain when he'd hit her and slammed her against the pavement.

Oh God, the cold and rain on her back as he ripped her scrubs and pulled them away from her, pushing her stomach into the ground, the knowledge she wasn't going to be able to stop him.

"Annie." It was Riley, right up in her face. "Look at me, Annie. You fought him off. You bought yourself enough time to get help. You screamed and banged on the dumpster."

She looked at Riley, then closed her eyes again, trying to get her breathing under control, trying to work past the most terrifying parts of what had happened to the rest.

He *hadn't* raped her.

"He didn't— He didn't—"

Riley smiled. "That's right. He *didn't*. Focus on that part."

She breathed as deeply as her agonized ribs would allow as she forced her mind to remember the rest. "Trey a-and Wavy."

"I'll come back later," the doctor said. Riley nodded at him.

"I'll go too." Zac's blue eyes were agonized as he kept his distance from the bed.

"No, please stay," she whispered. She stretched her fingers toward him. It seemed all she was capable of.

But it was enough. "Sure." He sat down next to her, his fingers on her arm again, tracing circles. "But Annie, I understand if you want me to leave, okay? I won't be offended."

She nodded and closed her eyes. She was safe. No one could hurt her here.

Over the next few hours multiple doctors stopped by, a few, like Dr. Lewis, in an official capacity, and others to extend their well wishes. Although Anne appreciated the gesture, it taught her a lot about how overwhelming a hospital visit could be to a patient. So many faces, even well-intentioned ones, could be difficult.

At some point Zac's hand had stopped tracing circles on her arm, and his fingers had linked with hers, taking tender care not to hurt the wounds on her palms.

He stayed that way for hours as she answered questions, and nurses poked and prodded her. He stayed next to her holding her hand when Sheriff Nelson came by to ask a few questions of his own.

His face grew stony as she told the sheriff what had happened, including as many details as she remembered.

"He was wearing a mask, so I didn't see his face. The only thing he said was, 'I always catch what I hunt.'" She would hear those words in her nightmares for years to come. She gripped Zac's hand harder. "It was the same guy, wasn't it?"

The sheriff nodded solemnly. "We're still determining that, but yes, we need to take it into consideration. I'm so sorry, Anne."

"It wasn't as bad as it could've been. He didn't rape me. And honestly, I thought I was going to drown in two inches of water."

Sheriff Nelson glanced at Zac before returning his eyes to her. "That's something we're looking at closely. If it is the same guy, is he escalating or was he just not aware of how close you came to dying?"

Zac's fingers tightened on hers.

The sheriff excused himself, promising they would talk later. "Okay," she whispered.

After that, the visitors ceased, and things quieted down. As in all hospitals, the nurses would be in and out all night, but no more doctors would check on her until the morning. She ought to send both Zac and Riley home. They had to be exhausted.

She was safe here at the hospital. She was surrounded by people, lights, and security.

But fear closed around her throat at the thought of being alone.

She hid it as best she could. She'd taken care of herself for a long time now. She could handle this too. "You guys should go home and get some rest." She gave them her best smile, although the state of swelling on her face made it awkward. "These pain meds are going to kick in soon, and I'll be completely out."

She gripped the sheet, fighting the urge to ask them to stay. It was unreasonable to want them to. Unfair to ask. She'd just have to suck it up.

She attempted a better smile this time.

"I'm staying," Zac said, looking at her, studying her with those piercing blue eyes.

"You don't have to. You've already been here last night and then all day today. I know you have—"

He leaned closer, so his face was only a few inches from hers. "I'm staying."

Then his eyes turned tentative, as if he wasn't sure he should be this close to her.

"Kiss me," she whispered.

His lips were the gentlest of butterfly wings on hers. Soft. Warm. Comforting. Safe.

Yesterday she would've said his kisses made her feel anything but safe. But not this one.

This one made her feel cherished.

"Thank you," she whispered. He winked at her and she could feel herself blush.

"Okay, kiddo," Riley stood. "I'll let Zac stay and come back tomorrow to relieve him or just hang out with you two." She kissed Anne's cheek. "You're so strong. Don't forget that."

"I'll see you tomorrow," Anne whispered and watched her friend leave. The medicine from the IV was beginning to pull her under again, taking away all the pain, making her sleepy.

Zac pulled his chair a little closer to her bed. "I'll be here all night. You don't have to worry about anyone coming up on you unaware."

Her eyes flew open. "How did you know?"

"You spend enough time in combat duty and you learn the importance of having someone you can trust watching your back while you sleep. Makes all the difference."

She wanted to stay awake, to talk to him more about his time in the Army, but heaviness pulled at her eyes again.

"Sleep, sweetheart. We've got all the time in the world to talk later."

As she fell back asleep, she realized his hand was still linked with hers.

# CHAPTER 23

THIRTY-SIX HOURS after arriving in the hospital, Zac was helping Annie check out. They'd wanted her to stay another night, but she'd insisted she knew enough about herself and her injuries to know that wasn't necessary.

Not to mention, she hadn't been able to get a minute's rest because of all the visitors. Her hospital room had resembled some sort of mix between a circus and tropical rainforest with all the balloons and flowers she'd received.

But Zac could tell she liked it, even though it made her uncomfortable. She was so used to being invisible that the focus on her still caught her off guard. If it weren't for her being a doctor, she wouldn't have known how to handle attention at all.

She argued with the hospital staff that she didn't need to be wheeled out. Only when Nurse Lusher arrived, complete with arms crossed over her chest and eyebrow raised, did Annie get into it.

He lifted her gently into his truck, wincing as she did at the pain in her midsection. "Rib injuries are a bitch."

"Have you had them before?" she asked.

"Yes." There was no way he was telling her this story. "On a top-secret military mission." Or because he'd been a young idiot fooling around with Finn.

"Oh. I guess you'd have to kill me if you told me."

Or just be humiliated. "Something like that." He closed the door and jogged to his side.

"Thank you for being my chauffeur. Do you think we could go by the grocery store? I need to stock up on a few easy-to-fix items. I'm not sure how mobile I'll be."

If she thought she was going home and taking care of herself alone, she was nuts. Not only was he not going to leave her alone and in pain, but until he had a chance to talk to Sheriff Nelson and find out more about this rapist, it just wasn't happening. There was no chance he was going to leave Annie unprotected. But he had to convince her. Be reasonable. Logical. Use Annie-speak.

"Look, I'm not sure you staying alone is the best idea."

She shrugged gingerly. "Except for the ribs and getting to a standing position and back down, I probably look much worse than I feel. There's no medical reason I can't stay by myself."

"Annie—"

"I was thinking about it this afternoon. Coming up with a plan. I have an armband I use when I go jogging to hold my phone. I'll just wear that all the time. That way, if something happens and I need help, I'll have my phone in easy reach."

"Woman, you are nothing if not practical."

She tilted her head to the side. "Of course." Her tone left no doubt of her certainty in the statement.

He started the truck. "Okay, so no medical reason. What about emotionally?"

Bleakness passed through her eyes before she turned away. "I have to be alone sometime."

"And you will, but it doesn't have to be today. You'll be ready soon enough. But for right now, it's perfectly fine to want to be around people."

She nodded but didn't look up. "I guess you're right. I could get a room at The Mayor's Inn. There's always people around there."

They both flinched at mention of the hotel. "Why don't you come stay with me?" he asked softly.

She let out a sigh. "That's probably not a good idea, Zac. I know we've been...hanging out a lot for the past week—"

He could feel his eyebrow finding a new spot in his hairline. *Hanging out?* "I'm assuming you're referring to all the mind-blowing sex, not to mention a lot of great conversation, and just general fun being together."

She continued as if he hadn't spoken. "But we've both worked a lot of hours during that time, and I'm not sure you're ready for me to be in your home on a full-time basis."

He took a breath. *Be reasonable. Use Annie-speak.* "I'm not talking about you moving in permanently." Although, honestly, the idea scared him much less than it probably should. "Just about you staying with me for a couple days until you're healed. Or if not with me, with Riley or Wavy, although until we figure out more about who did this, I don't think that's a good idea."

"You think he might come back?" Her voice was tight.

He smothered a curse. He wasn't trying to scare her. "Not necessarily. I'm just not willing to take any chances with your safety. At least at my place, you're on Linear property, and the guys and I are around all the time. More of a home-field advantage."

She stared at him for a long minute before giving a small nod. "I'll need some clothes."

"Okay, let's go by your house."

They made the drive in relative silence. The farther they got from the hospital, the more pinched her features became. She hadn't wanted to stay longer, but neither was she ready for regular life. It would all take time. The shadows would creep up on her without warning.

Zac couldn't prevent that. She had an awareness now of her own frailty that she hadn't before. An awareness of what could be done to her without her consent, despite her desperate fight not to let it happen.

As a doctor she'd known these things, of course. She'd seen it when she'd treated Kimmy and Veronica. But even then, she'd witnessed the brutality from a distance.

Now every ache and pain would remind her of her inability to control a situation in which her own safety had been involved. He'd known that sort of helplessness during the twenty-six and a half hours he'd spent in a Taliban prison before his men had gotten him out.

It was scary as shit to have no control over what happened to you, and he planned to help her through it in whatever way he could.

They pulled up to her house. Riley had grabbed a pair of scrubs from Annie's office for her to wear home, but she needed other stuff. Zac pointed to the couch once she told him where he could find her suitcase, but she refused to sit.

"I'll pack for myself." She set her lips in a mutinous line.

"How exactly are you going to do that? You can't bend because of your ribs and your hands are bandaged."

He shook his head as she followed him into her bedroom, wisely keeping his smile to himself as she turned an adorable shade of pink when he picked items out of her underwear drawer. When he grabbed the matching red set from last week, she actually growled from the doorway.

"What?" No, he couldn't keep his smile to himself.

"Move it along, Mackay."

He reached into her other drawers, grabbing more of her favorite scrubs as well as some pants and shirts.

"That's way more than I'll need for a couple days."

Zac just shrugged. There was no way he was letting her come back in a day or two. "We'll pack it all, and if you feel up to coming home tomorrow or the next day, we'll bring it back. No problem."

Maybe she would feel up to it tomorrow, not that he wouldn't try to talk her out of it. Maybe she'd feel like the worst was past, and she was ready to face everything on her own. But looking at her now—exhaustion and pain pulling at her more and more—he doubted it.

He got her to his place and made soup and some grilled cheese sandwiches. Zac was actually a very good cook, but the culinary arts were going to be lost on someone with a bruised jaw like Annie. Soft foods would be key for a day or two. And there was something to be said for a grilled cheese.

He set out her medicine, but she didn't want to take it. "It's going to make me sleepy."

"Why wouldn't you want to sleep? Won't that help your body heal?"

"Yeah, but I don't like just lying around." The sullen pout in her voice made him want to kiss her. "I'll help with the dishes."

He rolled his eyes at her. "How about we watch a movie? I'll even be a gentleman and let you decide which one. But first, I've got a surprise for you. Go sit on the couch."

"I don't like surprises." God, he loved her skeptical, pouty little voice, so different than how she normally spoke.

"You'll like this one."

She glared at him. "What is it?"

He shook his head. "Couch. Now."

He left the dishes in the sink. If he sat with her, she would relax. Otherwise she'd try to be up helping him with whatever he was working on. She grumbled but shuffled into the living room. He rushed back to the laundry room, easing the door open and grabbing the big surprise. "Just for a couple minutes, okay?" She didn't protest, so he hurried back out, shutting the door behind him.

Her face settled into a grumpy, guarded mask as she sat on the couch. Pain bracketed the corner of her mouth, but hopefully the meds she'd finally agreed to take would ease that soon.

He kept the surprise behind his back.

"What is it?" She eyed him suspiciously.

As he brought it out her face lit up.

"Oh my gosh, Duchess had her puppies? She's so beautiful, so tiny," she said of the puppy he held in his hands. "Can I hold her?"

"It's a he, but yes." He placed the small, sleeping bundle of fur in her lap. "But only for a few minutes. Duchess will get worried. She had a litter of three."

"When were they born? The last time I saw her she looked ready to burst."

He raised an eyebrow. "You mean the morning you snuck out on me? They were born that afternoon. She and the pups are here now, but Finn and Ethan have had them at their house."

She rubbed her cheek against the pup. "What's his name?"

"I thought maybe you could name him. He's going to be mine once he's old enough. So, you're going to be around him a lot too."

"Is that so?"

He wasn't sure if she meant him trusting her to name the pup or having her around a lot. The answer to both was the same, so it didn't matter. "That's so."

"What if I want to call him Cuddles or something?" She snuggled him into her arms.

He winced. "Well, maybe he won't get bullied too bad."

She smiled. "There's really only one acceptable name for this little guy, particularly since his mama's antics with you are what got him here."

"Oh yeah, what's that?"

"Harley."

He reached over and kissed her smiling face. "You're right. That's perfect. Harley it is."

A few minutes later, he returned Harley to his mom. He turned on the action movie she'd picked out, sat down on one end of the couch, and grabbed a pillow. Annie eased herself down next to him, then slowly lowered her head until it was in his lap. Zac relaxed for what felt like the first time since he'd found out about her attack. She was here with him. Safe. Maybe not perfectly whole, but not shattered.

Whatever pieces needed to be rebuilt, they would do it together.

# CHAPTER 24

HIS BUZZING PHONE on the end table woke Zac up. Annie's head was still in his lap. She'd fallen asleep before he had, and the movie was half over. He looked at the text from Aiden.

*Got time to talk? Sheriff is here.*

He tucked a stray strand of hair off Annie's face and shook her shoulder gently. She was out cold.

*Let me get Anne moved to the bed then you guys come over here.*

He wasn't leaving her alone. He doubted she would wake up until morning, she was a sound sleeper even without her meds, but he wasn't taking any chances. She stirred a little, face pinched, as he eased her off his lap, then reached back down to pick her up and carry her to bed, leaving her in her beloved scrubs. He turned on the bathroom light and left the door cracked.

Sheriff Nelson was sitting at his kitchen table, looking over some notes, face drawn. Finn and Aiden were grabbing beers from his fridge, Dorian—God bless that man—

was loading the leftover dinner dishes into the dishwasher.

"How's the doc holding up?" Finn asked, sliding a beer across the table toward him.

"Sleeping now, meds knocked her out. I convinced her to stay here until she's feeling ready to deal with everything."

Aiden sat down across from the sheriff. "She'll be ready physically before she is emotionally."

The other guys nodded. Sometimes it took the mind a lot longer to heal from wounds than the body. Dorian was a prime example of that.

Zac grabbed his beer and leaned against the counter. "She can stay here as long as she wants. What did you guys find out?"

Sheriff Nelson leaned back in his seat, rubbing his hands across his face. "We definitely think it was the same guy."

Zac took a sip of his beer. The news didn't surprise him. "Why?"

"While Dorian was combing the scene, trying to find anything he could, I decided to look in to why Anne was walking in the first place," Aiden said. "Why hadn't she parked in the hospital lot? Turns out her car was parked at the Frontier. She'd gone in to grab some breakfast on her way to work."

"Yeah, that's not unusual for her."

"I tried her car, Zac. It wouldn't start. When I cracked the hood, I saw the problem immediately: some spark plug leads had been disconnected."

"Shit." Maybe that would've been understandable if he hadn't just had her car completely serviced.

"Baby wouldn't have missed that," Finn said about his

brother. "Not under any circumstances, but *especially* when you asked him to check out her car for the express purpose of her safety. Spark plugs would've been one of the first things Baby looked for."

"So, like the other women, the rapist was targeting Annie specifically." Zac put his beer down and looked at Dorian. "Did you see anything? The guy's calling card?"

"No." Dorian turned from the sink. "When Anne left the hospital, she would've had two routes to get to her car. So, he would've had to watch her from somewhere to see which she took. I expected to find some sign of him in the southwest corner of the parking lot, since it doesn't get much light. But there were none of his little stacks of rocks anywhere."

"Do you think he deliberately didn't leave one this time?"

Dorian folded the towel in a perfect half and hung it on the rack. "I'm no criminal profiler, but I think he wants credit for each attack. That's why he leaves them in the first place."

"So, not bored while watching for his victim to arrive like we first thought?"

Dorian shrugged. "Maybe it started that way, but now he likes being able to brag."

"Rubbing it in law enforcement's face?" the sheriff asked.

"Yes. I think he probably wants to announce it to everyone but can't, so he likes that law enforcement knows at least." Dorian looked at Zac, then inclined his head toward the kitchen doorway. A few seconds later Annie walked through.

Zac had long since stopped being in awe of Dorian's

almost supernaturally developed senses, but damn, he was spooky sometimes. Zac hadn't heard Annie at all.

He walked over and put an arm around her. "Hey, sweetheart. I thought your meds would keep you out for the whole night."

She stared down at her bare feet. "I didn't take them. It was ibuprofen instead. I was hoping that would be enough."

And now she was paying for it. Zac shook his head. "You're a much better doctor than patient, you know that? I'm going to have to watch you closer."

Finn grinned at her. "You're as bad as Ethan not wanting to take his vitamins."

"I'll take the meds now." She smiled up at Zac, but it didn't reach her eyes. She'd been afraid upstairs. He hadn't been there to help her.

He trailed a finger down her cheek. "Let's get what you need, then I'll come get in bed with you, okay?"

"I feel like a ninny."

"You would be the first person to say that taking prescribed medications does not make a person a ninny. Neither does wanting to have someone nearby." He kissed her forehead. "Now, using the word *ninny* might make you one."

She gave the tiniest breath of a laugh, then went to the counter that had her medicine and got out a pill. Annie tucked a strand of hair behind her ear. "Are there any updates?" she asked the sheriff.

The older man looked over at Zac, who just held out his hand toward Annie. "Don't look at me for permission. She can handle it." Annie wasn't someone who needed protected from reality. She would function best knowing all the details.

The sheriff cleared his throat and turned back to her. "Sorry, Anne. I just don't want to upset you."

"I'm okay. I would rather know."

Dorian handed Zac a glass of water, and he walked back to her, keeping one eyebrow raised as he watched her take her medicine for real this time. She gave him a sheepish smile.

"Trey didn't see anything when he got to the alley," Sheriff Nelson said. "With two ways in and out, it was a smart choice for the perp. Well thought out."

She took another gulp of her water and nodded, her grip tight on the glass.

"Anne," Dorian asked, "can you tell me why you chose to walk through town?"

"My c-car was broken. It wouldn't start that morning, so I left it at the Frontier."

Zac reached up and took the shaking glass from her. "We don't have to talk about this right now. It can wait. I know you can handle it, but you don't have to this minute."

Everyone in the room vocalized their agreement.

"No. I'm okay. It's just..." She shrugged, fading off.

"It feels really close right now," Zac finished for her, wrapping an arm around her shoulders and pulling her gently against him, mindful of her wounds. "Every single person in this room understands that sentiment."

"I feel his breath on my ear. The heat of it," she whispered. "That's what woke me up."

God, he wanted nothing more than to wrap her in his arms and never let anything or anyone ever hurt her again. "Let's go to bed. I'll be right there beside you."

"Yeah, Annie," Finn said. "We'll even take turns down

here on the couch if it will make you feel better. Nothing will get to you."

She hid her face against Zac's chest and took in a breath before looking up at him. There were tears in her eyes. She turned to the guys. "Thank you, Finn. I know that I am more than amply safe here. But it means the world that you would make the offer."

Finn winked at her. "Are you kidding? Purely selfish reasons on my part. Ethan's staying with Aunt Wavy, and have you slept on Zac's couch? It's like the most comfortable place on the planet."

She leaned on Zac's chest, and his hand automatically wrapped around her hips, keeping her against him. "I have, in fact, and can't say I blame you for that feeling."

"Let's go up to my room, and I'll show you how comfortable my bed can be."

Finn rolled his eyes and stood. "That's my cue to leave before I say something that causes Mackay to punch me, and the sheriff to arrest him."

"Wouldn't arrest him," the sheriff muttered.

Aiden just snickered.

"You didn't finish, Dorian," Annie said, stopping the banter. "It's okay to ask it."

"I think Dorian asked his question, sweetheart."

Dorian shook his head. "No, she's right. I actually did have another ultimate question. Why did you choose to walk through town rather than cut through the park?"

He felt her tense against him. "I noticed the lights in the park were out. Situational awareness. I thought I was being smart, doing what we talked about, keeping myself safe. But it didn't make any difference."

He met Dorian's eyes over Anne's head. It had been a

setup from the beginning, the perp getting Anne to go exactly where he'd, wanted her to.

"That actually tells me why I didn't find his calling card in front of the hospital. We were looking in the wrong place," Dorian said. He grabbed his jacket off the chair. "I'll be back."

"We'll come too," Aiden said. "You'll need as many eyes as you can get."

They were all gone a few moments later.

"I don't understand." She turned in his arms. "Where are they going?"

"The rapist always leaves a little pyramid he makes out of rocks or whatever is around while he waits for the woman he's hunting. A calling card of sorts. We found one near both Kimmy and Veronica's crime scenes."

"But you didn't at mine?"

"Dorian wasn't looking in the right place. He thought the rapist would have to watch you leave the hospital and see if you chose the park or the town."

"But he'd already taken the park out of the equation, so he knew which way I would go."

Zac nodded. "He waited for you, but not where we thought."

And it meant this guy had been planning his attack much longer than they'd assumed. Zac tucked her against him again. He didn't like how any of this was playing out.

"Let's go to bed. This time I'm not letting you out of my sight."

# CHAPTER 25

THREE DAYS LATER, Anne could finally take a deep breath without wincing. The abrasions on her palms had healed enough that she could open her own medication to take when she needed it, which wasn't as often. She looked in the mirror now. Her contusions were turning from a deep, fresh purple into a sickly brown. They were healing.

But God, they were ugly.

She'd never be able to look at minor bruising so clinically again. Pain was more than just physical, it also took an emotional toll.

And it seemed like no matter how lucky she told herself she was—especially compared to what Kimmy and Veronica and perhaps multiple other women had been through—she couldn't seem to put it behind her.

It wasn't the memory of the pain of her face crashing again cement, or even the fear of drowning in two inches of water that woke her in a cold sweat late at night. It was of the attacker's hot breath on her cheek, his voice in her ear that haunted her.

It would wrap around her so insidiously, so unexpectedly. In the steam of the shower, or when she opened the dryer door. The heat sent panic bubbling up from her gut to choke her.

*I always catch what I hunt.*

She heard that voice everywhere. She tried to block it out, to pretend like nothing was wrong, but it was always there inside her mind. It was so damn frustrating. She'd suffered so little compared to the other women, but she couldn't seem to get over it.

She tried to push it from her mind now as she dried her hands on the towel next to the sink, then joined Zac in the kitchen. Today she'd managed a home-cooked dinner without thinking of that voice once. Until now.

Being at Linear helped. Being around the guys did too. Linear was so much more than a *shooting and fighting free-for-all*, as she'd once described it. And the guys had just accepted her presence without question.

Finn had winced in sympathy as she'd cradled her ribs after turning too suddenly as she stood in their office yesterday. They'd all been sympathetic.

Aiden and Dorian had taken great delight in telling her about the *top-secret* event that had led to both Zac's and Finn's rib injuries. Yes, they'd been repelling down a wall, but they'd been racing each other.

Aiden described some kamikaze flying leap Zac had taken to try to pass Finn. Their ropes had tangled, and they'd fallen on each other.

All four men were laughing by the time the story was finished, Finn and Zac both swearing it was the other man's fault. Aiden and Dorian had congratulated themselves on having the good sense not to get involved.

These men were brothers, she realized. In every way but blood. It didn't have to be said. It was just accepted.

Anne also enjoyed watching them work. They had groups who came in for different types of training. Most were self-defense lessons or firearm safety. They also did a concealed-carry certification class that would allow graduates to apply for their permit.

Three older men came in to work on their target skills one morning. And a kid had a paintball birthday party during an afternoon.

Anne had been fascinated to watch it all. Like the ER, day-to-day action at Linear Tactical was never the same, rarely routine. A lot of it was training, helping people know how to properly use weapons or protect themselves. And most of that was done outside, in the barn, or in the warehouse at the back of the property.

But beyond that, they'd also had a meeting with a couple important-looking people in suits one afternoon in the office's conference room. She hadn't been invited to that one.

When she'd brought it up to Zac that night, he'd just told her that he and the guys sometimes did consulting work with organizations who had employees working in dangerous situations outside the US. K and R consulting, Zac had called it.

"What's K and R?" she'd asked as they'd sat down to dinner.

"Kidnap and ransom. We offer advice on different situations, both domestic and international." He'd shrugged. "Sometimes outside, unattached people like us can see things people closer to the situation can't."

"Are you ever part of the rescue teams?"

"Not often, but sometimes."

Evidently the guys hadn't left danger completely behind with their special ops missions.

After lunch, she'd watched as Zac and Aiden had taught a self-defense course to four women: a pair of mothers and their teenage daughters. At first, she'd been up on the swing, but soon the moves the guys were teaching had interested her. She'd walked over so she could watch more closely.

What to do if someone grabbed their wrist. Or from behind. Had them on the ground.

This was the sort of stuff she could've used. Zac had mentioned self-defense when they'd looked over Veronica's crime scene, but neither had acted on it. Her eyes met his from across the mat they'd put out on the grass to teach, and he gave her a nod, obviously thinking the same thing she was.

She wanted to know how to protect herself. There was no one better than Zac and the guys to teach her. She'd watched, trying to memorize as many of the movements as she could even if she couldn't physically do them right now.

But she needed more than just self-defense moves. She needed her life back. The best way to do that was to get on the horse again. Right now.

She glanced over at Zac, who was obviously enjoying the baked ziti she'd made.

Maybe not a horse, but definitely a ride.

She knew he wanted her; that much had been very obvious when she'd woken up with him pressed against her the past three mornings. He hadn't acted on it, neither then nor any other time, although she wished he had. She wasn't afraid of Zac. He would never hurt her. Her brain had no trouble distinguishing between him and her attacker. But Zac had always initiated the lovemaking in their relationship, which was more than fine with her. She liked to feel desired, to watch him pursue her, then lose a little of that infamous Cyclone control once they got close.

Now he was giving her space, which she appreciated. He didn't want to do anything to scare her.

"I've been holding out on you," he said after taking his last bite of the ziti and groaning. "But after that meal, I realize it's completely unfair of me to do that."

"Oh yeah, what about?"

"The best feature of my house."

She gave him a once-over, eyebrow raised. "I thought I was already intimately familiar with that."

"Yeah. Nope." He shook his head, grinning. "You're probably going to be pretty mad about this." He led her back through his bedroom to the bathroom. She'd already seen this, of course, but he pulled up the blinds on the back window, then slid it all the way open.

"Something wrong with your door?" she asked.

"No doors leading to this. I keep meaning to change this out to one but haven't gotten around to it yet." He took her hand and helped her through the window. A couple days ago she wouldn't have been able to make it through with her sore ribs.

It led to a secret back screened-in porch. Complete with a small hot tub.

It wasn't as big as a regular tub. It was really just meant for one person, like an oversized bathtub.

"It's connected to the water flowing to the house, so I can fill it up with fresh water and no chlorine is necessary, but it has heaters and jets, so you can stay in as long as you want. Reinforcing the barn to be able to hold it was a huge pain in the ass when I built this place four years ago, but I love it."

She stared at the tub, then at him. "This is amazing."

"Enjoy. You're the only one besides me to ever use it." He gave her a half smile. "Actually, that's not true."

Yeah, she couldn't imagine Mia not pouncing on this. "Let me guess, Mia?"

She had to laugh at his scrunched-up face. "No, I never brought Mia here. No women at all, except you." He grabbed a piece of her hair and slid it through his fingers. "Ethan used to love to play in it all the time when he was younger. When Finn first got custody of him, that little guy wasn't in great shape. But he loved the water. Even though it was the middle of winter, he would play in that tub for hours."

"Well, I would love to play in your tub too." She took a step closer, gathering her courage, wanting to ask if they could both fit.

But before she could get the words out, he gave her a friendly smile, scooped an arm around her shoulder, and led her back into the bathroom. "Here's a towel. I'll go clean up the dishes. You enjoy the tub for as long as your heart desires. Keep the door cracked so I can hear if you need me."

He was gone without another word.

Anne took her time removing her clothes, using the bathroom, pinning up her hair as best she could. She looked over her face and ribs once again in the mirror. Decidedly not sexy.

But she wasn't going to wait any longer. She could do this. She wasn't going to let her would-be rapist retain any more power over her.

Wrapping herself in a towel, she called out for Zac. He was in the bathroom just a few seconds later.

"Hey," she said.

"Everything okay?" He had a dishtowel over his shoulder. "Problem with the tub?"

"Um. Well, I was wondering if you thought it could hold both of us?"

He took the towel off his shoulder and began folding it in perfect squares. "I do, in fact, think we both could fit." His eyes caught and held hers.

She didn't know if she was ready. She didn't know if she would freak out if Zac touched her in a sexual manner, and she didn't want to ruin what was between them, but she so very much wanted to move forward.

She could do this. Just start it, then Zac would take over. All she had to do was drop the towel.

She looked down, shifting her weight, then looked back up at him, her fingers evidently incapable of loosening their grip on the cloth. "I had a big seduction planned. Call you back, get naked, invite you into the bath for hot and heavy sex. But I can't seem to let go of the towel."

He took a step closer and hooked his hand where she held the cloth. "Although every single one of those elements sound like the makings of a great plan, you know there's no hurry."

"I know, but..." She had no idea how to explain this.

"It just sounds a little bit less like you want sex and more as if you want to prove to yourself that you're capable of muscling through it."

She sighed. "Maybe a little. But I do want to have sex with you. Despite the massive bruising, which has to be a turn off."

He pulled her a little closer with his hold on the towel. "Those just prove you were strong enough to fight. To survive."

Her head tilted forward until it rested against his chin. "I don't feel strong. I feel like I might never be again."

"You are, and you'll get stronger every day. And you'll take it one day at a time. One minute at a time if you have to."

His hands eased their way up to her shoulders and just held her, turning his head slightly so her forehead was against his cheek. They stood that way for long minutes.

"I want to have sex with you," she whispered. "I don't want to let him win."

He put his hands on her cheeks, easing her gaze up to his. "And we will. And you won't let him. But right now, we'll just get in the tub. Okay?"

She nodded. "Okay. Thank you."

"We've got all the time in the world."

# CHAPTER 26

HOLDING Annie's naked form against him in the tub was more than Zac thought he would ever get again, and definitely much more than he deserved.

"I don't know how you ever get out of this." She sighed, her back resting up against his chest, her long legs tangling with his. The heater and jets were both on, and they were up to their shoulders in lovely warm water—and in the strawberry bubble bath she'd dumped in generously, courtesy of Ethan's last tub visit.

"Yeah, I don't get in here as often as I should. I would've shown it to you last week, but I was really enjoying showing you the second-best part of my house."

"I love tubs. Always have."

"Actually, I remember that. Or how Becky never understood it." He laughed at the memory. "She always said baths were just lying around in your own germs and dirt."

"She wasn't wrong, you know. Showers are much more sanitary." He swallowed a groan as she snuggled down further into the water, her hips wiggling against him as she did. "But not nearly as luxurious."

This—Annie in his arms, driving him crazy—was exactly how he'd envisioned using this little hot tub when he'd gone through all the trouble of hooking the water to the house and reinforcing the deck to hold the weight. Maybe not Annie herself, but... actually, hell yes, maybe Annie was who his subconscious had been thinking of the whole time.

Regardless, he was glad it was here for her now. And he planned to use it with her every chance he had. Sex, no sex, he didn't care. He just wanted to be here with her.

He rubbed his fingers up and down her arms under the bubbles.

"I think I always liked them because my parents never bothered me in the bath. If they saw me with a book just sitting around the living room, they couldn't quite grasp it. But lying around in a tub...that was acceptable. I didn't care. I loved it. Loved to relax."

"Becky said you always studied in the tub. She didn't know how you didn't drown."

She laughed. "All through med school too. I always had a chair with books sitting against the tub. I've always had a tub except..."

"When?" he prompted when she didn't continue. The jets shut down, leaving it quiet between them, but they didn't turn them back on.

"Baths aren't as popular in Florida as they are here. Too hot. And after I separated from my ex-husband, my place didn't have a tub at all. Just a shower stall."

"Why did you guys split up?"

She blew out a stream of air onto the bubbles. "You know how some men go through a midlife crisis and trade their wife in for a newer, shinier model?"

"Yeah. They're generally known as assholes."

"Well, Darren realized much earlier that he wanted someone shiner and fancier than me. He wants to go into hospital administration—that has a lot of politics involved. I may be a damn fine doctor, but I'm not much when it comes to social graces. You know that."

"Like you said, you're a damn fine doctor. I've seen you in critical situations, keeping a cool head, doing what needs to be done. I'll take that over a social butterfly any day."

She shrugged one shoulder up and rubbed her cheek against it. "I know I stutter when I get nervous. I know a lot of that is psychological. Darren thought it was something I could get over with enough work. And when I tried, I did get much better."

Those brief sentences told Zac a lot, that she had tried to conquer her speech impediment for her husband. That he'd pressured her to do so. That it hadn't been enough.

"Anyway, he found Christina, a pediatric nurse. Blonde, bubbly, and witty. The perfect person to have by your side if you're trying to wine and dine a hospital board or pharmacy rep. He decided she was a better fit."

"I hope you cleaned him out during the divorce."

"Neither of us had any money. We were buried under student loans, his higher than mine because of the lifestyle he tried to live while in school. We'd been making big payments on his to try to get out from under it. But during the divorce, the judge decided that we should both just take our own debt."

"So, you'd paid a bunch of his and then still had all yours."

She shrugged. "I'm not great with conflict. I should've gotten a better lawyer. Besides, that wasn't nearly as bad as working with them after the divorce. Not that Darren was mean or anything, it was just that everybody *knew* we'd been married, that he'd tossed me aside. His bubbly little wife got pregnant like two months after they got married."

He wanted to kiss her and tell her how ridiculous her jackass of an ex-husband was.

"The worst part? I never really loved him. I knew that from the beginning. I never should have married him. I had pretty much sworn off men when I moved to Florida. But he admired how focused I was, how professional. So, he kept asking me out, and I gave in. Same thing about marrying him. I just gave in."

"Why did you swear off men?" He already knew the answer and hated himself for it. But he had to hear it from her.

"Zac, it doesn't matter."

"You mean after what happened with us. I hurt you enough that you left the only home you'd ever known and jumped into the arms of an asshole because he showed you attention. Annie, what happened that night…"

She grabbed his knees. "What happened that night happened. We don't have to let it choke us anymore."

He wrapped his arms around her chest, crossing them so his hands cupped her shoulders, molding her to him. "I'll never talk about it again if you don't want me to, but I want to make sure you know one thing. The things I said that night—"

"You were drunk. I know you weren't trying to be cruel."

"Once I remembered more…" Damn it. He didn't know how to explain this. "Becky was the only woman I'd ever been with, and then being with you… I wanted you, Annie, so damn much. You were a virgin and it caught me off guard."

"I know. I'm sor—"

He put a finger up to her lips. "Don't you dare apologize. All I'm trying to say is that it was *me* I was so angry and upset with that night. In my drunken state, I knew I had to get you out of the room, but it was *myself* I hated." He stroked his hands up and down her arms as she tensed. "I said those things to you, but they were really directed at me. I promise. I'm not just saying that now to try to make up for them or erase them—which can never be done anyway. I was drunk and didn't handle the situation well. Hell, I probably wouldn't have sober. But—"

She slid to the side, so she could reach up and cover his lips with her finger. "It's okay. I appreciate what you're telling me, and I accept it. I even thank you for trying to make me understand it further." She removed her finger and kissed his chest. "The thing about the *now* Zac knowing the *now* Anne is that our *nows* are a product of those *thens*. If that night hadn't happened the way it did, who knows how things might have turned out. Maybe I would've never moved away. Maybe you would've never moved back. Or maybe we would've both lived in Oak Creek for the rest of our lives, but never actually found each other again."

"Because we'd missed our moment."

"Yes. Exactly. Because sometimes it's heartbreak that ties people together. And maybe pain is the tightest bond of all."

This woman. God, he was the luckiest bastard in the world to have a second chance with her. "I still wish I had never hurt you. I wish I had never driven you from this place you love. Even understanding that it might've changed everything, I would go back and fix that night, make you understand what my drunk mind thought it was clearly explaining. I'd make love to you the way you deserved for your first time."

"We're here now. That's enough. More than, actually. We can't fix the past, but we can start again from here and see where it takes us."

Sitting with Zac in this tub, with the Wyoming sky she'd missed so much spread out in all its majesty overhead, and the ridiculous strawberry bubbles floating around them, everything truly felt like it was going to be okay.

She didn't need his apologies, but she appreciated the heartfelt nature of them.

"I want to keep you in here and protect you from ever being hurt again, Annie. By me or anyone else. Emotionally. Physically." He trailed wet fingers down her cheek. "In whatever way you need."

"Being out here, where I can see the stars and smell the air, it's healing. Being with you helps too." She didn't want to talk about the past anymore, or pain. She ran her fingers from his knee to the top of his thigh. He tightened behind her. "I'm not going to let that bastard beat me."

"Anne." She ran her fingers toward the inside of his thigh and his voice deepened. "We don't have to do this tonight. There's no hurry. Nothing you need to prove."

"You're wrong. I do need to prove something. To myself." But she didn't want to put pressure on him if he didn't want to take on that responsibility. She turned further so she could see him. "But if you're not up for it, I totally understand. I really do."

One of his perfect eyebrows raised and he gently thrust his hips against her in the water. There was no doubt he was up for it. "Believe me, *you* naked in this tub? I've *been up* for whatever you want all night. But I want it to be what you want."

"You are what I want."

She pulled his mouth down to hers, smiling inwardly as he yielded to her demands. Good. She wanted this.

"Only one rule," he said against her lips. "Anything makes you nervous, brings back bad memories—you tell me right away. You don't try to power through anything or worry about me and if I'll be upset about stopping. I won't be."

"Okay."

He took control of the kiss then but kept it gentle because of the bruising at her mouth. She tilted her head back against one of his arms, so he had access to her throat and breasts. His hand slid up her hip, along her waist to the breast that was popping out of the water.

She moaned as his fingers found her nipple with the firm touch that did so much for her.

"I love the sounds you make when I touch you. It's so honest. So damn sexy."

He tugged harder at her nipple as his lips found her neck and nipped there. It was as if he had a direct line to the hottest, most feminine part of her. She moaned again, her head falling further back on his arm.

This. She hadn't let herself think of Zac much over the past six years because it was too hard. But *this* was what her fantasies had given her when her subconscious mind had taken over.

Zac. Wanting her. Driving her crazy.

His hand trailed down from her breast to her core, his fingers deftly working the bundle of nerves there. Anne gasped, instinctively closing her thighs together.

"Open your legs as wide as the tub will allow," he said in her ear before biting the lobe. "Put them on top of mine."

Her heart fluttered in her chest as she did what he asked. All she knew was she wanted whatever Zac was giving. His fingers slipped inside her, first one, then two. From this angle, he hit the spot that set off detonations up and down her spine. His thumb kept constant pressure on her clit.

"I'm never going to be able smell strawberries again without thinking of you. Of this." His voice was deep, rough in her ear. His hot breath sexy and wild, not frightening in the least.

Zac bent his knees, raising her legs atop his to rise with them, bringing her hips down a little farther. Her head flew back against his shoulder as he worked his fingers more quickly, more firmly.

Allowing the pleasure to eclipse any lingering pain in her body from the attack was how she won. By giving Zac the control, knowing she was completely safe—mind and body—she beat the hold the attacker had on her.

She started flying apart as his fingers thrust one last time and his thumb gave her the firm pressure she needed. His teeth gently biting her neck ensured her fall.

There was no fear. Just the dizzying pleasure only Zac could provide.

# CHAPTER 27

"I'VE EXPANDED my search to all the surrounding counties. Landon Rogers or I have personally called each sheriff of every county in Wyoming, Colorado, and Utah. There have been some rapes reported, but we've got no evidence to prove those are the same guy. Just like we can't be one hundred percent sure the guy who attacked Anne is."

Sheriff Nelson was sitting at the head of the Linear Tactical conference table. They didn't use this room a lot, generally only when they were taking dangerous outside cases rather than anything instructional onsite.

Zac was looking through one of the files the sheriff had brought. One of dozens. Finn and Aiden were looking through the others.

"These are all sexual assault cases?"

"Yep. For the past eighteen months," the sheriff said. "For any surrounding counties. Some can be eliminated outright because the perp was caught, or the circumstances are completely wrong."

"But some could be our guy," Aiden finished for him.

The sheriff nodded. "I think this guy has been attacking women for much longer than we've known about it."

"Have there been any reported cases since Annie's attack?" Finn looked up from a file.

"Not from any of the counties we're in contact with."

Zac leaned back in his chair and rubbed a hand over his face. "Annie's returning to work soon. She hasn't said anything, but I know it's coming. As much as I'd like to keep her here on Linear property for...basically ever, I know I can't."

He wanted to try. He wanted to keep her here with him where he knew for certain she was safe. But she had to go back to the hospital and the profession so critical to her own identity and confidence.

The day after the hot tub, she'd found him sparring with Finn and had climbed into the ring. "I've been watching what you do here. You train them to be more than what they are. You make people into warriors. I want you to do that for me. Make me a warrior."

She was so beautiful, so strong, so determined, he could only answer with the truth. "You already are one."

Getting Annie in touch with her inner warrior hadn't been hard. She might be quiet, but she wasn't weak. She chose to fight for good, but that didn't mean she wasn't a fighter.

As she'd healed, they'd spent hours training and strengthening muscles that weren't necessarily important in her daily life, but might be critical in a fight.

He didn't teach her how to fight fair. If she wanted to learn that later, he'd be glad to teach her. But for now, he taught her how to fight to *win*. Gouging eyes. Breaking noses. Incapacitating knees.

Some of the moves ran afoul of her physician's pledge to

do no harm. She knew firsthand the damage the moves would inflict. But she'd learned them. He wasn't surprised to find she was a natural at it. Annie was good at damn near everything she set her mind to.

He'd made love to her every single night since the hot tub—and the morning and any other time he could talk her into it. Or she could talk him into it. He liked the new I'm-going-to-embrace-life-and-take-what-I-want Annie.

Especially since what she wanted happened to be *him*.

"We'll escort her," Aiden said. "A Linear employee, or some townsfolk. The women will walk together or grab a guy to walk with them. This isn't something that just falls on one group of people. I haven't lived in Oak Creek as long as you guys, but one thing I know about this town: it bands together."

Finn nodded. "Aiden's right. We all need to look out for one another. In the meantime, we do what we can to help Sheriff Nelson find this guy, make sure he doesn't hurt anyone else."

They were right. It was a poor strategic plan to want to try to protect Annie all on his own. He'd always been good at utilizing all resources available in a battle. This was definitely a battle, and the people of Oak Creek were a resource.

But when he saw Annie a few hours later putting on her scrubs in his bedroom, he knew he'd been right. She was ready to return to the real world, her real life. But somehow the urge to keep her close swallowed all logic. He needed to keep her safe, even if that meant keeping her locked away.

He stood in the doorway. "What's going on?"

He cursed himself when she yelped and spun around. Damn it, he knew better than to sneak up on her, even now. Their training had taught them to move as silently as possible, but he and the guys had gone out of their way to make sure Annie always knew when they were coming close to her.

She took a breath after a moment and then let it out. "I'm going back to work. It's time, Zac. They need me in the ER, plus—"

"You're ready."

She looked relieved that he understood. "Yes. I may not be one hundred percent the way that I was, but I'll never be that again anyway."

He walked over to her and pulled her into his arms. "I know. But you've established your new baseline. I understand how important that is, I really do."

She snuggled into him. "Thank you. I didn't want you to think I'm not grateful for everything you've done for me. Puppies, babysitting, letting me sit around and watch everything, all of it."

"But now you want to start easing back."

She nodded against his chest. "I can't hide here forever. I don't want to."

"One of the guys or I will escort you for a while, to and from work. The sheriff is going to spread the word about traveling in groups—everyone, day or night, until this guy is caught."

"I promise not to be one of those too-stupid-to-live chicks in a horror movie who goes out to check on the loud noise by herself when a known serial killer is on the loose."

He smiled but kept her against him. "The sheriff is going to catch this guy, and we're going to give whatever he needs to help him do it. I'm not going to let anything happen to you, little warrior."

"I just don't want it to happen to anyone else either.

Maybe he's moved on to somewhere far away. But that doesn't mean he's not hurting other women."

He brought his fingers under her braid at her scalp, rubbing gently, loving how she burrowed into him. "It's hard only being able to fight one section of the war, but that's all we can do. I want to catch this bastard, make him pay for what he's done. But first and foremost, I want you to be safe." He forced her head back with his fingers, kissing her softly. "Stay with me."

She groaned. "I can't. I told them I'd come into work."

"I mean after. Once you're done tonight, come here. Hell, every day when you finish, come here."

Those big brown eyes, now behind her glasses, blinked up at him. "Are you sure that's what you want? My schedule is crazy. I never know when an eight-hour shift is going to turn into eighteen."

"I understand crazy schedules. We'll work around it. I want you here where I know you're safe." He pulled her in closer. "But mostly, I just want you here with me for as many hours of a day as I can get you. Definitely until this guy is caught, but after that too. Plus, you need to come check on Harley."

She smiled. "And on you too?"

"Yes. Although I can pretty much promise I will be lying naked in bed waiting for you whenever you get off work at some crazy hour."

"That's a good enough of a reason for me."

# CHAPTER 28

THE FIRST WEEK after returning to work, Anne felt eyes on her everywhere. At the hospital. At her house—although she was rarely there alone. At Linear.

By the second week, she felt the same way but just learned to live with it. God knew there were enough on her all the time anyway, people watching to see if she would have a breakdown, to see if she and Zac were still together. Maybe she would always feel like a bit of an outsider in Oak Creek. Most of the town still held her at arm's length and reserved and isolated would always be more of her nature anyway.

Mia didn't keep her at arm's length. Dirty looks flew from her all the time. But instead of making Anne nervous or uncomfortable, they had the exact opposite effect of what Mia intended. They made Anne realize that Zac was truly hers. He showed her that with his body every chance he got, but it took dirty looks from a drop-dead gorgeous woman to push the point home.

Zac didn't want Mia. He wanted Anne.

And she wanted him. She loved that they could talk freely now about Becky and Carol and how much both women had meant to them. She'd even shared the quiet words Becky had once whispered to her about how she would've given Zac to Anne if she could.

He'd yanked her on top of him in the bed, wrapping his arms and legs around her, burying his face in her neck, and just held her, both secure in the knowledge they had Becky's blessing. She'd shared her family with Anne in life and then again in death.

And the guys at Linear were becoming family too. Every day she was around them, the more this place felt like home. Finn teased her about her relationship with Zac. Aiden taught her more self-defense moves. Dorian, she found out, loved to read as much as she did, and they were constantly talking about books of all kinds.

When she stuttered around them, as she still sometimes did, they didn't try to finish her sentences for her. They just waited patiently until she got the words out.

She was watching now from the monitor room as they trained a group of law enforcement guys who'd driven from Sweetwater—Wyoming's largest county, a few hours away—specifically for this. They didn't have the resources to keep training facilities as current as possible in SWAT practices, so they sent their teams to use the facilities here twice a year.

The respect between the Sweetwater SWAT team and Zac and the Linear guys was obvious. The team was excited to use the large warehouse training facility, which could simulate different situations: robbery, hostage-taking, and forceful entry.

Dressed in full SWAT gear, the men went through their exercises using some sort of paintball-type bullets to shoot bad guys. Zac and Finn were with them, pointing out tactical advantages, errors, strengths, and weaknesses for the way the team handled each crisis.

Zac was obviously the teacher. He had a gift for it. He was able to engage the other men, get them to see their mistakes without having to point them out. They all responded. And Zac obviously loved the action of it all.

The last hour of the day was spent in a good old-fashioned paintball competition between Linear and the SWAT team.

Sweetwater's team was good, but they didn't have a chance.

Of course, Zac and the boys had the home-field advantage. It was their facility and they knew all its ins and outs. But more than that, the Linear men had years of training and operations with each other. From her vantage point at the monitors, she could see how they practically read one another's mind.

They moved in a formation that spoke of years of experience, communicating with just the barest of signals or taps on each other's shoulders. It wasn't long before they'd taken out the entire SWAT team.

The good-natured ribbing between the guys stalled when Sheriff Nelson entered the facility. His tense face had her running out of the room and down to the main level. Everyone was silent. Zac slipped an arm around her.

"Curtis, what is it?"

"Another rape. Same M.O. New Mexico this time. We only got word about it by accident. So, it looks like our guy is moving farther away."

None of them looked happy about that. She wasn't either. As long as that guy was loose—it didn't matter what state he was in—she was always going to be looking over her shoulder. Always feeling his hot breath against her cheek.

*I always catch what I hunt.*

She shuddered, and Zac pulled her closer.

"But I came here for you." The sheriff turned to Dorian. "We have three inexperienced hikers who haven't reported in for two days. They were out in the area near Mt. Bannon, which was hit hard by storms last night. The National Forest Service guys are already up to their eyeballs with other issues and asked if my office could help. We can but—"

"Lindstrom would be a hell of a lot quicker," one of the SWAT guys finished for him.

"I know you think Dorian is your book buddy," Zac whispered in her ear, "but you should see him in the wilderness. It's uncanny."

Looking at the large, quiet man, she didn't doubt it. He read to escape. Being alone in the wilderness was not much different.

Dorian nodded. "I'll get changed and be ready in fifteen minutes, Sheriff."

"Need assistance. Everyone and sheriff. Dragon Strike." Then the coordinates repeated over and over.

Zac, Finn, and Aiden were all frowning the next morning at the electronic message they'd just received from Dorian's HC-12 transceiver.

It wasn't unusual that he'd sent one via the radio transmitter—cell signal out in the middle of the forest area surrounding Mt. Bannon was sketchy at best. But the message itself was more than odd. "Dragon Strike" was the code name of an operation they'd been a part of in Afghanistan. There wasn't a whole lot particularly memorable about that op except that they'd all had to work together to move stolen missiles they'd reacquired down the mountain. One soldier's ankle had been broken in the middle of the operation, but he'd kept going.

"Why the hell is he talking about Dragon Strike?" Aiden asked.

If one of the lost hikers needed medical assistance, Dorian would've said that rather than referring to a relatively obscure piece of their military history.

Finn shook his head. "I used that as an example when he and I were teaching Frank Jenkins's group a couple weeks ago. But that had to do with how the body could sometimes be pushed more than you thought. Mind over matter stuff. I have no idea why Dorian would mention it now."

"Who cares why. He wouldn't be asking for us if he didn't need us." Aiden pointed to his computer screen. "Look at this location. Hell, we can drive almost all of it. Then it should just be about an hour hike."

Zac nodded. "Something has to be pretty damn wrong if Dorian stopped there rather than getting those hikers the rest of the way out. It should've been easy at that point."

Finn was already heading out the door. "I'll notify the sheriff and get paramedics rolling in that direction. Meet you there."

Ten minutes later, dressed in fatigues and boots, Aiden and Zac were storing their Remington 700s in the truck, sidearms at their waists.

Something about this didn't feel right.

Zac called Anne as they sped toward the coordinates. It

wouldn't be long before they lost cell coverage completely. She answered after the first ring.

"Hey." He could hear the smile in her voice. He couldn't stop the one that covered his face in return.

"Hey. Listen, we got a message from Dorian. He needs assistance with the hikers, so Finn, Aiden, and I are heading out to help."

"Okay. I'm done here in a few minutes."

"Do me a favor and go straight to my place, okay? I know it looks like the attacker has moved on, but I don't want you alone at your house. Ethan misses Duchess and the pups, and Wavy will be bringing him over to the office."

"Okay. I'll get someone to walk me to my car and go straight there, promise. And you be careful."

"Promise." The signal cut out before he could say any more.

"Signal already gone?" Aiden asked.

"Yeah, this is kind of a fifty-mile dead spot. Cell companies have been saying for years they're going to do something, but I guess since there aren't any houses and not much traffic, it's not a big priority."

They drove as far as they could on the road toward the coordinates, then went off-road for a while. When the trees became too tight to drive through, they slid the rifle straps over their shoulders, spun them around so they were on their back, and took off at a jog.

As they came up on Dorian's coordinates, they slowed, bringing their rifles around in case there was trouble. But at the location Dorian had sent them were three men sitting around a fire. Zac approached while Aiden stayed behind to cover them if there was danger.

"Hello, camp!" Zac called out, not wanting to get shot by inexperienced people who might be jumpy.

"Hello?" one called out. "Thank goodness. We have an injured man down here, and we're pretty much lost."

Zac kept his rifle in a position that wasn't directly threatening, but would be easy for him to use if needed.

"Who's wounded?" he asked as he approached.

"The guy who found us. Named Dorian Lindstrom."

What the hell? *Dorian* was wounded? "Where is he?"

One of the guys pointed to a small overhang. "We laid him right over there after he passed out."

Dorian had been tortured to within an inch of his life, and the man hadn't passed out.

Zac placed his rifle back over his shoulder but kept his hand near the Glock at his hip as he moved quickly to Dorian's unconscious form. "What happened to him?"

He took Dorian's pulse. Strong, which was good. But he was out cold, not sleeping. Dorian would never sleep through this anyway.

"He found us yesterday afternoon. I think we were about eight or ten miles away. He led us here, but then it got dark, and it was raining, so he said we would stay here for the night and walk out the rest of the way in the morning."

"Okay." That sounded about right. "Did he get hit with something? Attacked by something or someone?" Zac felt Dorian's head for any bumps that would signal the cause for his unconsciousness.

All three men started talking at once. Zac held out his hand and pointed at one. "You. What's your name?"

"Mario."

"Tell me what happened."

"Jeff," he pointed a thumb at the guy next to him, "wanted to know more about Dorian's communicator. He's a tech geek. Dorian was showing him how it worked and said it was used mostly for military purposes, but that he happened to have one. He said we didn't need it because he knew the way back to town."

"Okay. Skip to the part where Dorian is unconscious."

Mario shrugged. "That's just it, man. None of us knows what happened. We were stoked to see him because, like I said, we were lost. He led us here, and we all went to sleep. When we woke up this morning, Dorian wouldn't."

"So, which one of you sent the message this morning?" Zac asked.

Mario looked around at the other two guys. Jeff shook his head no as did the other one. "Someone sent you a message? I don't think any of us did it."

Zac pointed at Jeff. "You were most interested in the transponder. You didn't send the message asking for help?"

"No. I would've liked to mess with it, but I was afraid Dorian would kick my ass or leave me out here. He's a little scary."

"Maybe the other guy sent it," Mario said.

Goddamn it. *"What other guy?"* Zac asked through clenched teeth. These men were morons.

"There was another guy we met up with this morning," Mario said quickly. "We were happy to see him because we didn't know what to do when we couldn't get Dorian to wake up. I saw him fiddling with the radio, but then he said he was heading out and would send help."

"And then he left?" Zac looked around at all three, who were nodding their heads.

Aiden walked into the campsite. "All's clear out there, Zac," he said, startling the other three men. "Nobody is around." Aiden's presence didn't make the younger men less nervous.

"Dorian's out cold. I'm pretty sure he's been drugged. Doesn't have any wounds as far as I can tell."

"None of these guys could get the drop on D anyway." Aiden glanced at them dismissively before kneeling beside their unconscious friend.

Zac agreed. He didn't think they meant anyone any harm. Even if they did, they wouldn't have been able to get a hit in on Dorian. But drugging his food or water? "One of them is missing. Took off without a word."

"Said he was a big game hunter and was after the one who got away," Mario told them. "I don't know what that means, and honestly, I'm glad he's gone because he was a little weird."

"How so?"

Mario shrugged. "Talked about hunting all the time. Said he'd picked up some new ways lately. All over Wyoming and Colorado."

Zac's eyes narrowed. "What sort?"

Mario, Jeff, and their other friend looked at each other nervously.

Jeff finally answered. "The guy said he liked to trap his prey."

"Which was fine," Mario continued. "It is still done in some places. But then Frank started talking about how he liked trapping his prey in alleys."

*"Frank?"* Both he and Aiden's faces flew up.

"Yeah. Guy said that his prey was best when they were nice and bloody." Jeff's face was a little green. "That he liked to get them scared. Then said he wanted to stay and make sure Dorian was all right, but he had to go hunting for the one that got away."

Zac's stomach dropped. He stood, looking at Aiden. "Oh, dear God." He got out his phone with a picture that Frank had sent him last week after the third Linear class he and his posse had taken, thankful now he hadn't erased it.

Frank was in the middle, right under the Linear Tactical sign, one arm around Zac, the other Finn, his buddies on either side. He was grinning from ear to ear.

They'd been led out here. Lured where there was no cell phone coverage for miles and Annie—*the one who'd gotten away*—had been left alone. And someone she knew, even though she may not like him, was the one who had been attacking women.

He spun the phone to Jeff. "This. Is this Frank?"

# CHAPTER 29

EVEN THOUGH IT wasn't even noon, and the sun was shining high in the sky, Anne still refused to walk alone to her car at the back of the parking lot. Not because she was afraid, but because she had promised.

She barely refrained from rolling her eyes when she saw Mia was also getting ready to leave. They could both call for one of the pedestrian escorts the hospital was now providing, or just bite the bullet, save some time, and go together.

Mia sighed when she saw Anne. "Shall we?"

All the way across the parking lot, Anne waited for some sort of insult or another threat disguised as a heartfelt warning. But nothing.

"What?" Mia asked as they neared the back of the parking lot. "You're looking at me like you expect *me* to attack you any second."

"No. Just waiting for the warn-off about Zac."

Mia shook her head. "Don't worry. I'm done with that."

"No longer afraid I'll get my heart broken?"

"I've seen how the guys look at you. You've got everyone's attention now. So yeah, I'm a little concerned you might decide you like it, and Zac will suffer. You're a late bloomer. No one would blame you for wanting to bask in the attention you didn't get back in the day."

"Nobody else is giving me any, Mia."

The blonde shook her head. "Oh, they are. You just don't notice. You never did."

"I'm not looking for anyone's but Zac's."

She shrugged. "You feel that way now, but you might not always."

Anne watched as Mia got into her car, then walked the few spaces to her own. Well, things had certainly come full circle if Mia was now afraid *Anne* was going to break *Zac's* heart. No doubt she planned to be there with open arms if Anne did. That much hadn't changed.

Who could blame a girl for holding out hope for Zac? Anne had certainly done it most of her life.

She drove directly to Linear as promised, the place seeming empty with no classes or people running around with guns. She parked in front of the office, so she could let Duchess out and see Harley and the other pups.

And yeah, she may still be there playing with them when Zac got home. She couldn't resist those little bundles of fur.

She'd been sitting on the ground with them for a few minutes, Harley scooped against her chest, when she saw it.

A small pyramid of rocks stacked on the arm of the couch.

She blanched, fear cutting off her oxygen. What was that doing here?

Her phone ringing in her pocket caused her to let out a little scream. She looked down at the display. Wavy.

"W-Wavy?"

"Hey girl, you doing okay?"

"I-I-I..." She forced her lips shut, trying to get in air so she could talk. She needed to Calm. Down.

Wavy evidently didn't even notice. "Listen, I just wanted to let you know that Ethan and I came by there a little while ago and let Duchess out."

Anne took another breath. "You-you-you were here?"

"Yeah, but we had to go. Ethan's teacher has a special project she wanted him to work on and needed to go over it with him."

Ethan had been here. Ethan was always building things. "C-can you ask Ethan if he built a tiny pyramid out of some flat stones? On the arm of the couch in the office?"

She heard Wavy ask her nephew.

"He said yes. He saw the design somewhere and thought it was interesting."

Relief rushed through her. Not the rapist. Just Ethan. "Can you ask where he saw it?"

Had the attacker been waiting somewhere else? God forbid, near the school? Or maybe Ethan had heard Finn, Zac, and the guys talking about it. Maybe he'd seen a picture.

"He doesn't remember. Typical seven-year-old. He can recall the date, time, and second if you promise to take him out for ice cream. Everything else, especially if he's looking at a video game? Forget it. Is it important?"

Maybe Ethan had seen something and didn't even know it. She would talk to Finn when he got home. "No, it's fine, don't worry about it."

"All right. This is just a thirty-minute session, so we'll come hang out afterward, okay?"

"Sounds great. See you then." It would be nice having

someone else around. Anne usually liked time alone, but she was a little spooked now.

Puppy cuddles made her feel better. They were getting older now, moving around more, even though they didn't wander too far from their mama. She cuddled all three in her lap, watching to see if it bothered Duchess. But the dog was like most mothers of toddlers, whether of the canine or infant variety: exhausted.

She looked over a few minutes later at her phone's chirp to find a text from Wavy.

*Ethan remembered where he saw the pyramid pattern. On the fire escape in the training warehouse the night the power blew. Hope that helps.*

Anne set the puppies off her lap. One of the attacker's calling cards had been left *here on the day she was attacked*.

The rapist had been on Linear property. Had been here —had probably created the electrical damage that had only finally been fixed a few days ago—just before attacking her.

He'd been making sure Zac was otherwise occupied, that he wouldn't do anything like come pick Annie up for a romantic dinner or even just give her a ride home.

Whoever had attacked her was someone who'd known she and Zac were already a couple, maybe someone Anne had come in personal contact with before.

At the slamming knock on the office door, a short yelp of fear fell from her lips. Her phone was in her hand, Zac's number already dialed—he wouldn't care if it was the UPS man at the door and she was an idiot—but it went straight to his voicemail. What could he do anyway?

She stayed frozen, hoping the person would leave. But the pounding came again. Then a voice. A familiar one.

"Zac? Finn? Is anybody here?"

She watched, frozen, as the knob turned, and the door

opened. Frank Jenkins walked in. More like *stormed* in, actually.

Frank knew enough about the Linear property to damage the training facility and make sure Zac was away from her that night. Also, about what Zac had taught her to predict she would notice the broken lights at the park and turn toward town.

She took a step back, her hands coming out in front of her in an instinctive gesture to protect herself.

"Dr. Griffin. Hey, um, is Zac here? Or Finn? Or any of the guys?"

Frank was breathing hard, like he'd been running. She couldn't let him know that she was alone. That all the guys were out somewhere in the wilderness.

That no one was here but her and Frank, who was looking at her with wildness in his eyes.

"I've really got to talk to them right now," he continued before she could say anything.

"Y-yeah." She finally found her words. "They're all here somewhere. Somewhere close. Let me get Zac for you. Why don't you sit down on the c-couch?"

He took a step forward, farther inside, and she took one back.

*Lesson one.* Zac's voice floated through her mind. *You win one hundred percent of fights you don't get in. If you can get away, always try that first.*

She had to get out of here.

"Okay, yeah." Frank nodded frantically. "If you could get him—any of them—that would be great. I need to tell them something."

He sat down and ran a weary hand across his face. Had he come here to confess all his crimes? What he'd done to her and those other women? Bile rose in her throat. She had to get out. Keeping her eyes trained on him, sure that he would jump any minute to grab her, she backed toward the door.

She was almost there, her hand finding the knob behind her and opening it, when Frank turned to her, arm outstretched.

"Anne, I'm so sorry. I never dreamed—"

She watched the blood drain from his face.

A voice, *that* voice, whispered in her ear. Hot breath burned her the way it had in the alley. "I think what Frank is trying to say is that he's sorry he brought me into your life."

She looked over her shoulder. Frank's buddy, Shawn. The *friendly* one.

He wrapped a hand around her throat and pulled her against him. Frank lunged for them, but Shawn just stepped aside, then pulled out a gun and shot Frank in the chest.

# CHAPTER 30

"NO, MAN. FRANK WAS THIS GUY." Jeff pointed to one of the men at the side of the picture Frank had sent him. Shawn.

The friendly one. The one he and Finn had agreed was much more useful and bearable to have around than Frank. The one who had come early to every class, asking relevant, insightful questions, even though he'd sometimes seemed to already know the answers.

He hadn't been there to learn. He'd been there to *infiltrate*. Maybe his attacks on the other women hadn't been more than a hunt, but he'd chosen Annie specifically and deliberately.

And he'd gotten them all out here—out of reach—and Annie was alone.

Zac turned and began running. He could hear Aiden saying something to the men and knew his friend would be right behind him. Finn was bringing paramedics who could help Dorian. They had to get to Anne, or at least out of this cellular dead spot, so he could call someone—Baby, someone from the hospital, hell, the damn milkman—and get them to Annie.

Zac ran faster than he ever had in his life. He could not lose Annie. He'd survived losing everything once, but wouldn't survive losing her. He ignored the burning in his lungs and muscles and pushed forward. His body would recover. He knew from years of experience how far he could push himself before he couldn't go any farther.

And if needed, this time, he would go past that point.

He would do whatever he had to, to make it to Annie in time.

The only thing stronger than her fear of that hot breath on her neck, and that voice from her nightmares, was her medical training. She pushed away from Shawn's hand at her throat, trying to get to Frank and stop his bleeding. He'd been shot in the chest but could still be saved.

"No." Shawn yanked her back. "Leave him. His death plays into my bigger overall plan. I've already put seeds in place that he's the one who's been hunting the women. Police will find even more evidence when they get to his apartment."

Which meant he had no plans to keep her alive either.

She could hear Duchess barking and the puppies whining behind the room Shawn had locked them in as he dragged her outside, keeping one hand at her throat, his gun pointed at her head. "I wanted us to do this right, but Frank ruined my timetable by showing up here. I wanted us to be in the woods where we could have a full chase. I could be a true hunter, and you a true prey. But we don't have that kind of time, so we're going to do a miniature version."

Fear pressed at her thickly, making his words difficult to understand. Miniature version of what? Why wasn't he trying to rape her now? Or throwing her down to the ground?

He forced her through the yard toward the warehouse, and she began to understand. He wanted a *chase*, a hunt, but somewhere she wouldn't have an opportunity to get away.

No.

She twisted, bringing her elbow back hard against his abdomen, reaching to scratch at his face with her nails. Now he did push her down to the ground, facedown, covering her with his weight, and bringing his gun back up to her temple.

"C'mon now, Anne. I know Zac taught you the most important rule. You can't ever forget that one."

*Survive.*

That was the key point Zac had drilled home, not only with her, but in every class he taught. It was what Linear Tactical was all about; what Zac and his brothers-in-arms had learned in their years as soldiers and now passed to others. To survive.

"So, you either come with me, we do our hunt, and you have a chance, or I kill you right now. Plan B isn't pleasing for either of us."

Plan A wasn't some big party either. But she nodded, trying to gather her wits. He snatched her up by her hair and marched her over to the door of the warehouse, yanking the heavy door open.

"I was blown away by this place when I got the tour."

"Was it you who did all that wiring damage?"

"Yes. I had to make sure Zac didn't leave while you were walking to your car." He ran a finger down her cheek, and she shuddered. "It's because you were such a good study that I knew you would notice the lights being out in the park. I was watching you and Zac outside the veterinarian's office, saw him show you the light I'd shot out. He probably gave you the same situational-awareness spiel he gives in all his classes."

He said it all so calmly, as if he wasn't a violent rapist. "You're a damn sicko."

"Tsk, tsk, Dr. Griffin. I would expect such a highly respected doctor to be a little more clinical in her terms."

"How about psychopath with homicidal tendencies and a proclivity for sociopathy and delusions?" She threw the words at him with a boldness she didn't feel.

His smile grew wider. "So basically, a damn sicko." He pushed her farther inside the building. "I knew you had to be my next hunt. You getting away...that was frustrating, but then perfect. I came here. Got to be close to you and all these soldiers who really know so much."

She wanted to plug her hands over her ears and yell, so she couldn't hear his words. All this time he'd been so close, and she'd never known. Should she attack him? He still had the gun. But in some way, she'd prefer that to whatever sick game he had planned.

What would delaying do? She didn't want Wavy and Ethan walking in on Shawn's psychotic games. He wouldn't hesitate to kill them too.

"We need to get started," he said as if he could read her mind. "We don't want the game cut short. Now here are the rules. One." He took a zip tie out and slid it through the two handles of the double door, tying it shut. "The door is closed. Not impossible to open, but it will take a couple minutes, won't it? So, if you want to get out, you'll have to go through me.

"Two," he continued, putting his gun in a waist holster. "I won't use this. Where's the fun in that?" He reached down and pulled a nasty-looking knife with an eight-inch blade out of a holster at his calf. "But I will have this. I look forward to using this on you, Annie. To hearing you cry again. Do you remember how scared you were when I pushed you down into the ground, my body over yours? How much stronger I was?"

He was trying to scare her.

It was working.

She was breathing heavily, her feet backing her up of their own accord. "N-n-no."

"There it is." He licked his lips. "That's the look I've been waiting for."

She was giving him exactly what he wanted, but she couldn't help herself. Couldn't remember one single thing Zac had taught her.

"Nobody's going to hear you scream in here, Doc. I made sure to check the plans on this building. Sound-proofing was something the town required before giving them permission to build it. To make sure it was insulated and isolated enough that no one would be disturbed by any ruckus." His voice became deeper. "Ready for some ruckus?"

Chills racked her body even though the temperature was comfortable. Her teeth began to chatter.

He walked behind her, his breath blowing hot on her neck once more. "Come on now, Anne. Don't make it too easy for me. I'll give you a two-minute head start. Then the hunt is on."

She stood staring at him, a roaring in her ears. She couldn't make herself move; it was taking every ounce of strength she had just to stay upright. That voice. That hot breath. The fear drowning her.

"One minute fifty seconds. Run, Anne."

*Survive.*

*Make me a warrior, Zac.*

*You already are one.*

Something snapped in her brain, like a rubber band that had been stretched to the very edge of its breaking point, then released. She hissed out loud at the burn in her psyche, but the roaring in her ears stopped, and everything came into focus.

*Survive.*

She ran.

The fear was behind her, much closer than Shawn and his knife. She had to avoid both, because the fear would drop her just as fast as the knife if she let it.

"No one's coming to save you this time, Annie," he said in a singsong voice. "Not someone taking out the trash, not your precious soldier. He's not coming to your rescue."

She didn't respond, just kept moving. She didn't need Zac to rescue her. He'd respected her enough to teach her how to do it herself.

*Use your strengths and figure out your enemy's weaknesses.*

She wasn't as strong or fast as Shawn. She didn't have a weapon or his training.

But she damn well knew where the emergency exit was in this building. She ran for it in the back corner, unwilling to wait and see if he was going to keep his word and give her however many seconds she had left before he started his chase.

She pushed herself, running at the door full force. And was promptly flung back onto the floor when it wouldn't open at all. She groaned, her barely healed ribs screaming in agony.

"Sorry, Annie, I forgot to mention I blockaded the outside. Good thinking though!"

Was he closer than he'd been before? It was hard to tell over the sound of her breathing.

What should she do? Run? Hide?

*Movement is life. Staying where you are almost always means death.*

She heard Zac's voice in her head, his coaching from the past few weeks. She had to keep on the move while she came up with a plan. Shawn would expect her to hide.

She scurried under a wooden deck used by fighters to hide behind while training here. Her natural inclination was to stay there, hidden, but she rolled until she was out the other side, then crawled and scooted around a corner. Not moments later, Shawn's voice was right where she had been under the deck.

"I sort of expected you to hide, little Annie. Isn't that in your nature? To stutter, stammer, and make yourself invisible?"

It was in her nature, he was right.

She darted away from the corner, hiding behind another barrier before scurrying to a different one. Where was Shawn? His silence was much more frightening than his monologue.

*Think about your strengths, your enemy's weaknesses.*

Damn it, what were her strengths? Somehow, she didn't think organization and memorization—the two that had helped her most in med school and her years as a doctor— were going to help her now.

She ran and hid behind a car covered in paint from all the battles held here, the same one Zac had used when he and Finn had finished off the Sweetwater County SWAT team a few days ago. She'd watched it all from the control room.

For the first time, the smallest seed of hope bloomed in her chest. That was her strength. She'd studied this place, watching Zac and the guys. She knew it. Knew where the different barriers and hiding places were located. Maybe Shawn did too.

But would he know them in the dark?

Because that was her only strength in this situation, her spatial awareness and ability to memorize. If she could cut the power, she would still be able to find her way around easily if she visualized the facility. Shawn wouldn't.

She hoped.

She quickly made her way toward the back, zigzagging behind various objects and walls, keeping herself low. She didn't think Shawn would expect her to move in this direction. It was a dead end. If he caught her here, she'd be trapped.

She reached the electrical closet, opened the door as silently as she could, and quickly found the master power switch. This was it. As soon as she hit this, the facility would go dark, only the faintest glow from the emergency lights in the corners offering any sort of illumination at all. Definitely not enough to see very well.

And once she did it, he would know exactly where she was.

She would have to make a break for the door, but he would be expecting that, and she couldn't be able to get the zip ties off anyway.

She needed his knife. That meant taking him by surprise.

Becoming the hunter, rather than the prey. She'd been

making herself invisible her whole life. Now it was going to serve her well.

*Use your strengths.*

She flipped off the master power, then ran.

Across the building, close to the door, Shawn muttered a curse. She'd been right, he hadn't expected her to go for the lights.

Sticking to the shadows, visualizing the layout in her mind, she slipped toward the door. She could hear Shawn stumbling around, fumbling to find his way in the dark.

"I'm not playing with you anymore, bitch. It's time for you to start screaming."

She climbed as silently as she could on top of a stack of crates, fighting terror with every step. An emergency light several feet away let her see just enough without casting a shadow that would give her away. She would only get one shot at this. Shawn was still wandering in the dark, looking for her in the low hiding places, exactly where she would've been before Zac had taught her. She waited until he was barely past her, took a breath, then jumped.

They both crashed to the floor as she landed on top of him. Immediately she rolled, using her elbow, muscle memory now after hours of practice with Zac, to slam into Shawn's face. The doctor in her knew exactly what that sickening crunch signified and totally didn't care.

She swung her leg around hard to connect with his arm, sending the knife sliding across the floor. She scrambled for it, but he grabbed her ankle, yanking her back.

He roared as he grabbed hold of her by her hair and dragged her to her feet. She had no way to avoid the fist that crashed into her face, throwing her to the side. As she came back up she tried to jab at his throat, but he caught her hand with one of his as the other slammed into her abdomen. She doubled over, gasping for breath, as the pain exploded.

He pulled her up again by her hair, and despite the blood from his broken nose streaming down his jaw, he still grinned at her. He liked it. Liked her struggle. Liked what he had planned for her next.

She neither stopped, nor hesitated. She swung her knee as hard as she could straight into his groin, then slammed it down on the top of his foot. He let go of her and fell to the floor. Anne turned and ran, sweeping up the knife from the ground on the way.

Her breath wheezed in and out and she used the deadly blade to cut through the zip tie. She could hear Shawn getting to his feet, knew he still had the gun. Even if she sprinted out the door, she wouldn't make it to the tree line before he shot her.

But she was damn well going to try. Because she'd discovered her enemy's biggest weakness: he had underestimated her and how much she wanted to *live*.

She flung the door open, the bright Wyoming spring sun blinding what she could see from the eye that wasn't swelling shut. She stumbled forward a few steps, as he roared behind her and shuffled out of the training building. "I always catch what I hunt, you bitch!"

The sound of a single bullet blasted loudly in the sunshine. She waited for pain. None came, so she kept moving forward.

"Next shot isn't going to hit you in a nonvital organ, asshole. My daddy taught me how to shoot when I was eleven, and I'm a Wyoming girl, so you can bet I haven't forgotten how."

*Mia?*

The blast of a second shot rang out from her other side. Behind her, Shawn cried out.

"The lady said she had no problem shooting you. But I wanted to get in on the fun too." A man's voice, also familiar, but she couldn't see very well out of her swollen eye on that side.

"That's right," a third voice yelled at Shawn. "Stay down and keep your hand far away from that weapon. Because you damn well better believe my shotgun will finish the job that Trey and Mia started."

"Mayor?" Anne turned around, realizing Shawn had well and truly been subdued. Three guns were pointed at him. Mia with some sort of tiny Smith & Wesson, Trey to her left holding his own handgun, and Mayor Dimont had a shotgun hiked to her thin shoulder.

And cars were squealing into the Linear driveway, more townspeople running toward them with weapons ranging from high-powered rifles to baseball bats. Susan Lusher. Riley. Finn's brother, Baby.

Mia was the one who rushed over to Anne and helped ease her to the ground.

"What?" she asked the other woman. "I don't understand. How did you know to come here? Why?" She couldn't even figure out the words, just held out her arm to the crowd that was growing larger by the minute. "How?"

Mia wrapped an arm around her. "This is what happens when Oak Creek gets word that one of our own is in trouble. We come running."

# CHAPTER 31

BY THE TIME ZAC ARRIVED, except for the ambulances, Linear looked like it had last summer, when they'd had a Fourth of July party and had invited the whole town, minus the pies. Everybody was there and talking.

The thirty-eight minutes and fifty-two seconds it had taken for Zac to make it to cell phone coverage had been the longest of his life. He'd run faster than he ever had before. Aiden had jumped into the truck next to him as he'd torn off down the path, a sideview mirror and probably half of his truck's suspension left behind in the wilderness surrounding Mt. Bannon.

Annie's phone had gone straight to voicemail. Aiden had kept trying while Zac had called the person who'd always had Oak Creek on speed dial, and would know exactly how to get people to where they were needed the quickest.

Mia.

It had taken her about four seconds to realize that something was wrong, and to her credit, she hadn't taken even a moment to play the woman spurned, something for which Zac would owe her for the rest his life. She had listened and then cut him off midsentence when she understood the gravity of the situation. She'd promised she would get Annie the help she needed.

He'd never dreamed it would be Mia herself.

And evidently the rest of the town.

Five different people had already called to tell him what had happened. How Annie had burst out of the warehouse with a knife, and how Mia had shot Shawn as he'd come after Annie, about to shoot her in the back.

They were fifteen minutes out when Baby had sent a picture of the wounded Shawn, in cuffs, being placed in an ambulance. In his next shot, Annie, Mia, and Riley were sitting on the ground, close together, whispering like old friends. Annie was even leaning into Mia.

*Scary, huh?*

Zac hadn't known if Baby meant the bruise on Annie's face, her being chummy with a woman he had dated, or the fact that Shawn had had them all so totally fooled and had set up such an elaborate trap. He'd even tried to kill Frank Jenkins. The man had been alive, barely, when help had arrived and rushed him to the hospital.

Zac had just needed to get to Annie. To wrap her in his arms and never let her go.

Fifteen minutes later, he was doing just that.

Everyone was still milling around when he parked and jumped out of the truck, his eyes seeking out Anne, but unable to find her. He moved around people, barely able to answer their questions or listen to their version of what happened.

He needed Annie.

"She got overwhelmed," Riley said. "She was okay, but

all the people on top of what happened... She went to your place."

"Thanks, Riley."

Riley waved her arm out at all the people. "They all came for her, Zac. Every single one dropped what they were doing and rushed out here when they heard Doc needed help. You make sure she knows that, as overwhelming as it might be. She'll never be invisible in Oak Creek again."

Zac nodded and marched off toward his apartment, avoiding talking to anyone even when they tried to get his attention. Annie needed him.

He saw Mia and knew he should at least say thanks, but she waved him away. "Another time, Mackay. You and Anne can buy me a drink. Or ten. Besides, she did all the hard work."

He walked over to her and squeezed her shoulder. "Thank you, Mia." The words were so inadequate, but they were all he had.

She smiled. "Go get your girl, Zac. She needs you. Almost as much as you need her right now."

He turned and ran the rest of the way to his apartment.

"Annie?" He slowed down his motions, not wanting to frighten her. Not knowing what sort of emotional state she'd be in.

No answer.

He took the stairs two at a time to the second floor, calling for her again. Then he heard it. The sound of the jets running in the hot tub. Of course.

He stepped onto the porch. She was already in the water, her brown hair hanging out the back.

"Hey, sweet Annie," he crooned, the words as soft as he could make them.

"Zac?" Her voice was hoarse, his name muddled from the swelling in her jaw.

He rushed to the side of the tub, heart breaking at the sight. Except for kicking off her shoes, she'd gotten in fully dressed. "Hi, sweetheart. Mind if I join you?" He reached out and touched her face where she'd taken a blow. "Did someone check that for you? Looks pretty bad."

"Yeah, nothing broken. I should put a cold compress on it, but I was already too cold. I just wanted to get in the tub."

"I think you'll be more comfortable if we get your clothes off."

She actually smiled. "Don't worry. I'm not having a nervous breakdown. I just don't have a bathing suit here, and I was afraid someone was going to come looking for me. And then my brain wasn't working enough to come up with another solution."

Some of the pressure eased off his chest. She wasn't broken. She'd just wanted her damn bathtub. He helped peel off her clothes, then stepped out of his own.

"We should probably go down there and talk to everyone," she said.

He slid in behind her and wrapped his legs and arms around her. He would pull her into his very skin if he could. He breathed in her hair for long minutes, trying to convince his mind and heart that she was well and truly safe.

"When I figured out what Shawn had done—the lengths he'd gone to, to get you alone..."

"He was going to kill me," she whispered. "And Frank. He came to warn us. Oh God." She lost her words on a sob.

"He's still in surgery," he whispered. "Don't give up hope."

She nodded. Then they sat in silence for long minutes, just holding each other.

"I'm so sorry I left you alone, let myself become complacent. You're mine to protect and I didn't. I failed you." He would never forgive himself. She moved, and he opened his arms, so she could go if that's what she wanted.

But she turned around, arching her back so she could be face-to-face with him, crawling into his lap. "The only reason I'm here right now—not broken, raped, and probably dead—is because of you. Because of what you taught me. What you convinced me I could do. And I believed it, Zac. I was a warrior, and I beat him because he was expecting a coward."

He cupped her face as gently as possible. "You amaze me. Your strength, your courage, your intelligence. Every single day. You've never been a coward. And there's a whole town's worth of people ready to stand by your side and fight if you need it."

He kissed her, much softer than he wanted to, mindful of her injuries. Never again. That bastard would never hurt her again.

She eased back, keeping herself trapped across his lap, lowering her head to his shoulder. "I guess we should go talk to everybody. I know the sheriff is going to want a statement."

"In a minute. Right now, it's just you, me, and the Wyoming sky."

# CHAPTER 32

*TWO WEEKS Later*

The Eagle's Nest was crowded once again. The whole damn town seemed to be here, celebrating Frank's release from the hospital. The younger man was here, sitting in a front booth in a position of honor, talking to everyone.

Three days after surgery from the bullet that had punctured his lung and almost ended his life, Frank had woken up a hero. Mostly because Anne had told everyone how he'd tried so bravely to stop Shawn. If Zac didn't know better, he would've said Frank seemed a little surprised by that version of events, but who was he to judge?

Frank definitely didn't have anything bad to say about Annie anymore. And he was probably going to use his newfound hero status to try to get a job at Linear.

Hell, maybe he'd even get one.

Today had been interesting. He'd gone before Jordan Reiss's parole board to testify about the person who'd fallen asleep behind the wheel and killed Becky and Micah. He had told the board in no uncertain terms that Jordan should be released from prison. She should've been a long time ago. If her family's last name wasn't Reiss, she probably would've been.

So today, thirteen years to the day after he'd asked Becky to marry him, he'd told a judicial board the person who'd killed his wife and son should be set free.

Becky would've approved. Hell, Becky would've been pissed that he hadn't done it long before now.

Zac looked over to where Annie was standing at the bar with Wavy, Riley, and Mia, buying drinks. She winked at him over her shoulder, and it was all he could do not to drag her back home and not let her out of his bed for the rest of the night.

Oddly enough, he knew Becky would've approved of that too. And of the fact that he never planned to let Annie go ever again.

"Oh, dear Lord," Aiden muttered from next to him in the booth. "Do you see the color of those drinks? It cannot be good for you to drink something that neon. Dorian had the right idea staying home tonight."

Dorian was doing fine but would use any excuse he could not to be part of a crowd. Even a friendly one.

"Yeah, Dorian's the smart one," Zac said. "But I'm pretty sure Finn has drunk stuff that color before, and he's relatively normal."

Finn didn't respond, staring across the room.

"Or maybe not," Aiden said.

Zac looked for what had drawn Finn's attention. Not what. *Who.*

Charlotte Devereux.

She was standing alone near the corner of the bar. She

probably hadn't expected it to be this full on a Wednesday night. Riley saw her and waved her over. After the women hugged, Charlotte slipped off her jacket, obviously ready to join them. But when Riley pointed back to their booth, Charlotte froze when she saw Finn. Just stared at him.

The way he was staring at her.

Charlotte whispered something to Riley, then slipped her jacket back on. She finally broke eye contact with Finn and bolted for the door.

Finn stood so fast he knocked into the table.

"Damn, man, did you get a wasp down your pants? Be careful." Aiden began grabbing napkins to wipe up his spilled beer.

"I…" Finn trailed off, shrugging, then looking back at the table from where his eyes had been following Charlotte.

Zac just nodded at his friend, storms brewing in his dark eyes. "We'll catch you later."

Finn was out the door in seconds.

"What the hell just happened?" Aiden asked.

"A long, long story."

The ladies made it back over to them, each carrying handfuls of shot glasses with the bright blue liquid in them.

"Holy hell," Aiden said. "What are those?"

"Electric Smurfs!" Mia yelled over the music. "Annie picked them out."

Zac looked up at Annie, who was absolutely glowing and starting to dance around with the other girls. He'd lose her to the dance floor soon. At least for a song or two, until he followed her out there.

He pulled her down into his lap as everyone started to clink their glasses and drink the scary liquid. She had two shots left in her hands.

"Is one of those for me?"

Her eyes got serious. "If you want. I know you don't drink. But I promise if you'd like to have a couple, I'm more than happy to make sure nothing gets out of hand."

He trailed a finger down her cheek. She would always be willing to give up her own fun to look out for the people she cared about. "You would really take care of me like that?"

She kissed him, grinning against his lips. "Of course. I may take advantage of you back home once you're drunk, but I would certainly make sure you got home all right first."

He grinned too, pulling back from her. "And give me all your loving?"

Her eyes turned serious once again. "Every bit I have is yours. It always has been."

"I love you too, Annie. There's so much to love about you." He kissed her again.

Aiden cleared his throat from across the table. Zac rolled his eyes at him. "Go dance with a girl."

"I think I just might." He stood. "But after a couple more of these, I won't be able to walk straight anyway." He grinned and headed toward the bar.

Zac kept Annie in his lap and took the shot from her hand. "So, if I drink this you'll take care of me as long as I need it?"

"Promise." That smile. God, he would never get tired of seeing her quiet, gentle smile.

He threw back the sweet liquid, then gave her a kiss. "I hope you're a woman of your word. And I hear this Electric Smurf stuff stays in your system for about fifty years. So, I'll need you around at least that long."

He kissed her once more and felt her sweet smile against his lips. "Then I guess that's how long I'll have to stay."

# OTHER BOOKS BY JANIE CROUCH

All books by Janie Crouch

LINEAR TACTICAL SERIES
   Cyclone
   Eagle
   Shamrock
   Angel (2019)
   Ghost (2019)
   Echo (2019)

INSTINCT SERIES
   Primal Instinct
   Critical Instinct
   Survival Instinct

OMEGA SECTOR SERIES

Infiltration
Countermeasures
Untraceable
Leverage

OMEGA SECTOR: CRITICAL RESPONSE
Special Forces Savior
Fully Committed
Armored Attraction
Man of Action
Overwhelming Force
Battle Tested

OMEGA SECTOR: UNDER SIEGE
Daddy Defender
Protector's Instinct
Cease Fire
Major Crimes
Armed Response
In the Lawman's Protection

# ACKNOWLEDGEMENTS

The Linear Tactical books have been wandering inside my head for a long time. Deciding to take a chance on a big-effort indie series was not made lightly. As I write this, I still don't know how it's going to go... but I'm going to try.

*Sometimes we have to stop being scared and just go for it. Either it will work or it won't. That's life.*

First and foremost, I want to thank my husband of over twenty years who has never once said to me *maybe you should be more cautious* even when I probably should have been. He may never have read a single book of mine, but he doesn't have to. I talk about these characters enough for him to know them almost as well as I do.

And to my four kids. For every time you had to say something to me twice (or seven times) because I was trying to finish a chapter. For every time I texted you some random sentence because you were the first up on my phone and I didn't want to forget something I'd worded perfectly in my mind while I was stopped at a red light. Thank you for learning how to feed yourselves so you don't starve. To you guys and Dad: YOU ARE MY GREATEST ADVENTURE.

To my mom and Aunt Terri, for exploring Wyoming with me (where are the mountains???) and helping me realize what needed to happen. Thank you for your encouragement and love and willingness to travel crazy place.

For my tribe: Marci, Girl Tyler, Anu, Stephanie, Regan, Nichole, Julie, Beth, Lissanne, Elizabeth. THANK YOU. For the emails and FB posts where I have rambled endlessly trying to work out stories. For your encouragement, smiles and occasional tough love. I am so grateful to call you mine. (And Lissanne, sorry my moments and minutes are still so long)

To my editors and alpha readers: Elizabeth Nover, Jennifer at Mistress Editing, Marci Mathers, Elizabeth Neal, Stephanie Scott, and Aly Birkl, for crying out loud, women: THANK YOU. You took a hot mess of a manuscript and made CYCLONE into a book I love and am so proud of. Thank you for your feedback and attention to detail. To Marci, in particular, who probably knows these characters better than I do, and is still mad that I didn't change the Afghanistan Zac/Shane line.

To Kim, Tanja, and the other wonderful folk at Deranged Doctor Designs, makers of my gorgeous covers: you are truly artists and such a pleasure to work with! Thank you.

And to Lauren at Sly Fox Designs. Woman, I feel like if I got married right now you'd have to be in my wedding because we've spent so much time together. Thank you for the gorgeous banners, ads, and graphics that helped launch the Linear Tactical series. You're amazing and so wonderful to work with. You have kept me sane these last few months.

And finally to readers, both new and those who have been with me for a while: thank you. When I think of how exceptionally blessed I am to make a living as an author, I am humbled and honored. Your support means everything to me. I promise I will always endeavor to write the stories that keep you enthralled from page one. Life's too short for boring books!

With love and appreciation,

Janie Crouch

# ABOUT JANIE

"Passion that leaps right off the page." - Romantic Times
Book Reviews

USA TODAY bestselling author Janie Crouch writes
what she loves to read: passionate romantic suspense. She is
a winner and/or finalist of multiple romance literary awards
including the Golden Quill Award for Best Romantic
Suspense, the National Reader's Choice Award, and the
coveted RITA© Award by the Romance Writers of
America.

Janie recently relocated with her husband and their
four teenagers to Germany (due to her husband's job as
support for the U.S. Military), after living in Virginia for
nearly 20 years. When she's not listening to the voices in
her head—and even when she is—she enjoys engaging in all
sorts of crazy adventures (200-mile relay races; Ironman
Triathlons, treks to Mt. Everest Base Camp) traveling, and
movies of all kinds.

Her favorite quote: "Life is a daring adventure or nothing."
~ Helen Keller.

facebook.com/janiecrouch

twitter.com/janiecrouch

instagram.com/janiecrouch

CPSIA information can be obtained
at www.ICGtesting.com
Printed in the USA
BVHW080824090523
663836BV00006B/239

9 780998 881522